To Alicia,

Thank you for
taking a chance
on an aspiring
Author.

Rise of November

By Mario E. Perez

For my Mother and Father,
Dick, Lynette, and all those that listened.

Day 1

8:00 a.m. and the sound of my alarm rings impatiently as I stagger out of bed. It's a Monday, and I have to be at work in an hour. May not seem early to others, but for someone like me, it's early if the clock still reads "a.m."

After taking a shower I stop to comb my hair, and realize the stillness in the air. My parents have always left for work before me, but today it seems as though the house has been vacant for years.

The weather outside appears cold while looking out through my bedroom window. Such that I put on my black leather jacket over my navy blue scrub top while heading out the door.

Thin purple clouds stretch across the sky like fingers as I approach my blue Hyundai. Their arrival brings about a sense of gloom to the already brooding day. I soon notice that my parents' cars are parked at the house. I stop to wonder if they're still at home, but quickly realize that it's now twenty till nine and I'm running late.

While hauling ass to work, I thank God that traffic is good to me today, as there are no cars to be found up ahead. Granted, the back roads to my job are through a few vineyards, which have always proven peaceful with little traffic. But today, the drive seems desolate.

While breaking the sound barrier at about ten miles over the speed limit, I suddenly come to the only stop sign on the two-way road. My abrupt stop causes my body to slightly pull forward. Its subtle jolt forces me to catch my breath as I light my first cigarette of the day.

Before driving off, I take notice to a white broken-down truck off to the right side of my lane. Smoke steadily steams from underneath its cracked hood as my gaze becomes drawn towards movement. From the bed of the truck, an elderly man slowly climbs out and approaches. His right foot drags across the dirt while pacing towards me, the blank expression on his face making it unclear who he's addressing.

It is now five till nine, and I have no time to help this poor bastard, so I make haste and speed past him. He quickly grows smaller and smaller in the distance. His body sways and fades through my rearview mirror as I drive away.

While still feeling lucky that traffic was good to me today, I pull into my regular parking spot and finally arrive at work. "Animal Care Clinic" is lit up in big blue letters that reflect off my mirrors.

The sign's very image causes me to cringe, yet I find comfort in seeing that its doors remain locked.

9:06 a.m. and I'm relieved to see that I'm the first person to show up to work, an unusual development given the current circumstances. As I step out of my car, I take a deep breath and quickly make my way inside, thinking of how well the day has gone so far.

The air feels stagnant within the clinic. Like it did in my house earlier today, a feeling of desertion now surrounds me. Its aura comes at me in waves and feels more sterile than usual; a sensation I've grown used to, yet suddenly find unsettling. While making my rounds, I turn on the lights and proceed towards our treatment area. Its section resides past a small lobby and adjacent exam rooms.

I keep myself busy as I now prepare for the day, bringing in the lab box, clearing out the rooms, booting up the computers, and running calibrations on our in-house lab equipment. All while staying efficient to things that should have already been done. A routine I've grown accustomed to as I finally open the door towards treatment.

A sudden smash of metal is heard as Presley, an eleven-year-old Australian shepherd with pancreatitis, growls and barks at me through his cage. Startled, I stagger back and take a hard look at the dog, shocked by its recent aggressive behavior.

He came from a good family, loving and caring. They always brought him in for routine vaccines and checkups, along with the occasional ear infection. He was a very friendly dog... almost too friendly, who loved to play and was a pain in the ass to hold still while drawing blood.

As he continues to snarl, I realize that taking him out for a walk is out of the question. My limits, however few, have never subjected me to stupidity. After finally remembering to clock into work, I slowly begin to pull his IV line through his cage.

All while trying not to get bitten.

9:20 a.m. and no one has yet to arrive at work, oddly enough the phones haven't rung either.

As I begin to draw up some Cimetidine to administer through Presley's IV, I stop and glance at Snowball, a white, six-month-old cat that was spayed and declawed two days ago. While growling and hissing, she stands in the corner of her cage, her eyes cautiously fixed to my every move.

Ten minutes now pass and I'm still alone at the clinic. I can't help but question if we have the day off, as I head towards the lobby and pass the doctor's office. Dr. Creswal Kibbs is my boss and the owner of the practice. He's always late, yet his absence is also unsettling.

Before I can even reach for the door, Presley begins to freak out again while trembling and foaming at the mouth. At first, I assume that he is having another one of his seizures, yet at the same time the damn dog is staring me down while frantically trying to escape. This isn't normal. Even though he seems to be convulsing, I can tell by his eyes that he retains focus and will attack at the first chance he gets.

I rush to a nearby phone and give Dr. Kibbs a call, but there's no answer.

Three minutes pass and I repeatedly try to reach him while keeping a close eye on Presley, but there's still no answer. The ruckus the dog makes has become an extreme annoyance and now puts the cat on edge. In the middle of Presley's cries and Snowball's growls, I suddenly stop to hear the subtle ringing of Dr. Kibbs's cell phone within his office.

Relieved that I'm not alone, I shout for the doctor. My anticipation, although built, does not mask my nerves from the sight of his door left slightly open.

Vomit rushes and fills the top of my throat at what lies before me. Unable to swallow it all down, I regurgitate its lingering remains onto the floor. Panic hits me in more ways than one as I stand in horror at the sight of Dr. Kibbs's dead body, his cell phone alerting him of missed calls on the floor. His corpse lies slouched upon his chair, and by the looks and smell of him, it seems as though he has been dead for a while.

I close my eyes and open them in hopes that I'm dreaming, yet he's still there. Each time revealing the man I once knew in his expired and decrepit state. Yet there are no wounds present, a mysterious cause of death as he merely lies there, as if sleeping. I now start to question what might have happened here, of what might have gone wrong.

Ten minutes pass and there is still no sign of any other staff members. I begin to wonder if they are responsible for the doctor's demise. While still shaking at the sight of the body, I frantically pick up the phone and call 911 again, but the line keeps ringing.

My mind can't comprehend the dilemma I'm in, but I have to do something. Death is one thing that I've grown accustomed to during my years of working with Dr. Kibbs. I've seen many creatures die expectedly and unexpectedly, willing and unwillingly, yet this is different.

I wasn't properly trained for this.

I become frustrated and angry after repeated attempts to call 911. Their lack of cooperation prepares me to transport the body myself.

Then I see it.

Presley now stands calmly in his cage, no longer barking or trying to escape, but waiting patiently. Thick strings of blood drip down from his mouth and form a puddle near his paws, congealing with the strands of hair and shards of teeth from his recent struggle. A mixture of blood, urine, and diarrhea now cover the poor dog and his cage. I take notice to his blood-shot eyes and realize that he is no longer paying attention to me, but to something behind me.

My body swiftly turns as I come face-to-face with Dr. Kibbs, and I suddenly become paralyzed. The brief ten seconds that pass seems to last minutes as he now stands upright and stares directly at me. His eyes are blood-shot as well and replace all trace of color. A rotten smell of dead flesh and blood creeps from his mouth and begins to make my eyes water.

All the terror I now feel becomes unimaginable as he suddenly reaches out for me. Such force he uses to grab a hold that it causes me to fall back on the floor. I frantically slip my way backwards, inch by inch upon the slick tile floor while pulling myself up.

He follows me closely with each sluggish step, real clumsy like, as though he's been drinking. His white lab coat is smeared with blood and hair, and slowly sways with each step he takes. His now gray complexion develops blotches of brown around the rotting portions of his face. Although he has no obvious wounds that I can see, he seems to be decaying from the inside.

While desperately backing away, I try to reason with him but my cries are ignored. Unaware of what's overcome him, I now fear for own my safety. As I keep backing away, a sudden crash of metal is heard as Presley breaks out of his cage. Now frightened, I watch both the dog and Dr. Kibbs rush towards me.

My body reacts as I quickly turn; shutting the door that now separates them from the front office. I desperately brace myself up against it as Dr. Kibbs tries to breakthrough, forced to endure the sound of Presley's nails scratching at the door. I press hard up against the wooden barrier, feeling every bang that the doctor makes with his fists upon the door.

A minute goes by and the shaking eventually stops, yet the sound of Dr. Kibbs's breathing is still heard. Then I hear it, the screams. The doctor's cries are so frightening and piercing that it causes me let up on the door.

I'm now forced to make my move, running as fast as I can out of the clinic and towards my car. While out of breath, I lock myself inside and start up the engine. The low rumble and tremors of the four cylinder engine are minimal compared to how bad my body shakes. Its influence helps clear my mind of my remaining paralysis.

Within moments I rest my head on the top of the steering wheel, but become startled yet again by the sight of Presley.

The rabid dog is relentless and continuously rams his face into the window to my left. Blood splatters upon impact and grows larger with each ferocious attempt, eventually cracking the glass while letting blood seep through.

I quickly put my car in reverse and back up over Presley's leg, detached by fear as I instantly hit the vehicle behind me. For a moment I stop to look back at the black SUV I ran into, dreading the repercussions of a hit and run, yet unwilling to linger any longer.

Without warning Presley jumps onto the hood of my car. His right front leg slowly tears from his shoulder as he now attempts to breakthrough my windshield. The amount of blood before me is immense, obscuring my vision as the glass slowly begins to give way. I drive from the parking lot before anymore damage is done, forcing the dog off the hood of my car as I speed past him.

As I leave the clinic behind, I pull up to a stop light and use my windshield wipers to wash the blood away. While still obeying the rules of the road, I wait for the light to turn green. My conscience for whatever reason gets the best of me, as I look through my rearview mirror and spot Presley yet again.

The son of a bitch runs towards me and seems unfazed, his sprint at full speed with now only three legs. Ticket or not there is no fucking way I'm sitting through this light. My actions speak louder than words, guided by fear as I make haste and drive back home.

10:04 a.m. and while driving back home and pushing speeds beyond legal limits, I think of my encounter with Presley. I begin to wonder what exactly happened to him, and why he became so ravenous. Let alone be able to run after just losing a limb.

I didn't mean to run over his leg and I kind of feel bad about it. But then again, I had to come to work on my day off to take care of that little bastard so fuck him. However I can't believe that Dr. Kibbs tried to attack me. His eyes glared with intent to kill and his movements were without hesitation.

I can't imagine what he would have done if he had got a hold of me. I start to question if he was really sick or on drugs, for he sure as hell wasn't dead. His aroma and appearance told me different though. His skin, although unscathed, smelled and resembled that of decay.

I don't know what's going on or let alone where everyone's at, but I have to make sure that my parents are alright.

While still trembling, I pull a cigarette from my almost empty pack and fumble to light it. After some effort, I finally exhale the recent rush of panic that overwhelms me. I slowly begin to calm down, relaxing at the same pace that the smoke exits my lungs. Steady as I may seem, my heart continues to race as I pull up to the only stop sign on the road yet again.

I look to my left and recognize the broken down truck off to the side of the road. While leaving the car running, I put it in park and take a moment to look around. There is no sign of the old man I saw earlier. My surroundings remain calm and quiet, as I get out and walk towards the truck.

The sky is still overcast and lets off a cool breeze which sends a shiver up my spine. As cold as it is, it is nothing compared to the chill I feel inside. The ongoing fear of the madness I just endured.

I slowly take ten paces towards the white truck and it suddenly hits me. The old man, his demeanor and posture was all fucked up like Dr. Kibbs. I instantly feel sick to my stomach as I turn to face my car, the cigarette in-between my lips now trembling with fear. All the signs I overlooked could not prepare me for this. The reality of it all is unreal, as I come to find the old man sitting in the passenger's seat of my car.

With the door wide open he now waits patiently within, his eyes dripping and stained with tears of blood. I try gesturing to him from where I stand but receive nothing in response. His silence, although unnerving, becomes suddenly broken as he starts to twitch. Soon his head begins to shake from side to side, so rapidly that his face is no longer visible. Only the thick strings of blood escaping from his eyes and nose are seen as they spread throughout my car.

A shock of panic immobilizes me as it did with Dr. Kibbs. Its sensation keeps me planted as if anchored to the ground. I can't help but stare as the old man convulses and abruptly stops. I can feel his gaze upon me, his eyes although dark and distant, still manage to strike fear into very soul. After close to a minute passes, I finally get a grip of myself and realize that I need to lure him out.

Without a clue in the world as to what I'll do next, I slowly step towards my car. My entire body now shivers with fear, which I unwillingly make apparent with each drastic step. The old man's eyes follow my every move as his chest rises with each labored breath. Its frequency increases with my approach at about one hundred breaths per minute.

A deathly grin stretches across his blood streaked face as I now draw near. While clearing my throat, I try to wave at him through the driver's side window, but the son of a bitch won't move.

The stench of rotting flesh hits me again after getting dangerously close. Its smell is familiar and that of a dead dog left baking out in the hot sun. I'm forced to step away as I keep my eyes fixed on the old man, his gaze ever vigilant and without blinking.

While backing away, I nearly trip over a rock the size of a tennis ball. Thinking that I now might be able to draw him out, I pick it up and grip it firmly in my right hand. I try to stop myself from trembling with fear. My uncertainty takes hold as I take a deep breath, wind up, and throw.

The stone quickly connects with the old man and manages to pass through the window, ultimately hitting him in the shoulder. In response he becomes agitated, and immediately tries to come at me through the driver's side window. Then I hear the screams. They plague me like nails on a chalkboard while spewing from the old man.

I watch in terror as he frantically worms his way out of my car, forcing himself to collapse onto the road. My paralysis fades as I run to the right side of the broken down truck in an attempt to outfox him. Although he manages to pull himself up rather quickly, he begins to walk slowly away from my car.

His momentum now builds as he rapidly drags himself towards me. With only the truck standing between us, I try to keep a safe distance while making my way around towards my car. He growls and screams while staring directly at me, all the while he abruptly slams his fist upon the bed of the truck.

I now end up playing pickle with the old man, bobbing from side to side while attempting to throw him off. Eventually my strategy fails as he ends up flanking me.

I have no choice but to make a run for it as he tries to cut me off. His outreached arms graze the back of my leather jacket as I remain too frightened to scream. I approach my car only to be suddenly caught within his grasp. I now panic, and in my state of fright I twist and force myself loose.

Once inside I instantly feel his hand grip around my neck. His cold and slimy fingers press against my skin as I reach for my car's transmission. The rotting smell of his breath is similar to that of Dr. Kibbs. Its aroma intensifies as he opens his mouth and leans in close. While struggling, I pull away and take off in my car, relieving the tension I feel as the old man is forced to let go.

He continues to chase after me as I drive. His speed is something to be admired, as I now slowly lose him in the distance.

10:14 a.m. and I arrive at my house in record time to find that my parents' cars are still at home. I remain in shock from my recent attack. My body quivers with the imprint around my neck, as I exit my car and stumble my way inside. The dead silence lingers within my home as I now begin my search; its emptiness surrounds me with every door I lock. My concern builds with each disappointment as I desperately try to find my parents.

Ten minutes fly by and still no sign of my mother or father. I've searched everywhere with the exception of my backyard, which I will not even bother, considering that my dog Mountain is out there. Best not to take the chance seeing as how my luck with animals hasn't been very good today.

After finally sealing every entrance, I head towards my bedroom at the far end of the house. My door remains locked like always which is a good sign, and as I make my way inside I catch a glance at myself in the mirror.

My body still trembles as my neck and scrub top remain stained with blood, along with my jeans which is probably due to the crazed old man or Dr. Kibbs. I strip down to my blue pinstriped boxers and turn on my television and laptop, using the inside of my scrubs to now smear the blood off my body.

The television displays nothing but static and rainbow colored bars that bring about a painful pitch in my ears. My laptop however, continues to boot up as I stare at my reflection in the mirror.

I look frightened. My eyes widely opened to their fullest reveal the blue that makes up my irises. My black hair remains well kept with the occasional strand that sticks up, in contrast to my clean shaven face. The blood wiped from my neck now turns my light skin slightly darker, while a few spots still lie beneath the hair on my chest.

My breathing remains shallow as I log into my laptop, and to my disappointment the wireless internet refuses to respond. I try many attempts to find a connection but end up failing. I can only assume that the servers must be down, and it isn't until then that I notice that my cell phone no longer has reception.

I am completely cut off.

The filth crusting on my body is now unbearable as I grab a towel and head to my bathroom. While letting hot water runoff my shower, I attempt to call 911 from the house phone. Like before, I'm forced to endure a continuous ring without any response.

Steam slowly begins to fill the bathroom and fog the mirror as I ease into the shower. Its warmth, along with the water running down my back gets me to relax, as if I'm put in some sort of trance by the shower. I waste no time as I douse myself with soap and begin to vigorously scrub. While washing away all the left over blood off my body, I watch it smear like oil mixing with water.

The intense heat eventually begins to increase my blood flow, as I now become overwhelmed with warmth. It's as if I could slowly feel my blood boil within me.

I start to wonder where my parents are at, and if they are alright? It's not like them to up and disappear like this, but then again, nothing today has been the same. I can't help but fear the worst for them as I pull my face up towards the shower to wash the pain away.

Suddenly, a loud crash is heard as the bathroom door breaks open. My trance soon disrupted by the arrival of a new threat. I remain startled with my back against the wall of the shower, as I unwillingly face the dark figure ahead, forced to stare at a pair bloody handprints pound and smear on the sliding glass door to my left.

The horror from my vulnerability now brings an unsought paralysis. My eyes then shut as glass sprays before me followed by an outreached arm, covering me yet again in blood. Its fingers bleed and remain punctured as it desperately tries to reach me, causing me to now look ahead.

Soon the sight of the blurred figure behind the glass begins to throw its head back, forcing me to step as far as I can towards the sliding glass door to my right. My will, although broken still provides me with the nerve to move.

Within moments, more glass shatters as a head smashes through the door to my left. The terror I feel holds no bounds as I recognize my father's face, his expression maddening as he smiles. His face is covered in blood and sheds the same crazed look that I've encountered twice today.

I now scream as I watch his neck rub against the broken glass. Its edges dig deep into his flesh as he struggles to breakthrough. I take a leap of faith as I grab the glass door to my right and slide it open, causing my father to get trapped in-between the two doors. I quickly jump out of the shower to get around him as he screams and breaks free, leaving trails blood and fragments of flesh stuck upon the glass.

For fear of my life I run down the hall and into our kitchen, dripping wet and completely nude, followed closely by the echoing screams. The sound of which is beginning to feel all too familiar.

In a state of panic, I pull out two large kitchen knives from a nearby drawer to arm myself with. The cold air within the house brushing against my damp and naked body finally catches up with me, as I stand with a knife in each hand and wait for my father's next move.

With my teeth chattering I begin to feel my eyes flood with tears, as I know all too well what is going to happen next. Then I see him, madly running down the hall while heading straight towards me, his screams now mixed with laughter.

I yell and beg for him to stop as he draws near, only to find myself stabbing him with both knives as he tackles me to the floor.

While on my back I come face to face with my father, the two knives impaling him are all that stand between us. Blood and saliva drips from his mouth and onto my neck and chin as he grabs a hold of my head. I quickly recognize the smell, which is that of rotting flesh and blood that seeps as he pulls my head back.

My father is a big man, and although not very tall, he makes up for it in mass.

He overpowers me easily.

As I struggle to break free, my leg carelessly slips which causes his knee to smash my groin against the tile floor. The sharp and unbearable pain instantly rushes and fills my body with rage.

Now furious, I twist the knives within my father's stomach so that they don't move, and push him off. The excruciating pain still lingers as I pull myself up and grab my crotch in hopes to numb the pain. All the while my father gets back on his feet and lunges at me once more. With only the extreme pain fueling me, I reach for the knives embedded in his gut and throw him aside, causing him to fall back onto the floor.

A memory flashes before me of a time I borrowed my father's gun while camping with some friends. The thought of which gives me purpose, as I now storm into my parents' room and lock the doors behind me.

I frantically open my old man's sock drawer and scramble through everything inside to reveal the Colt Python .357 Magnum. It lies before me waiting, beckoning my name while followed closely by the screams.

As I pull it out, I get a feel for its weight and get reacquainted. Its intimidating shine helps soothe my fear as my father suddenly breaks through, forcing me to take aim. While hoping to God that it's loaded, I tremble to hold it up as I open fire.

I instantly take him down with two shots to his right leg while feeling the unexpected recoil. Still in shock, my body overwhelms me with hesitation as I tremble with fear.

I slowly step back as he continues to drag himself towards me, his right hand constantly clutching at the wind. Still hell bent on killing me, the knives embedded in his gut pull their way further down and begin tearing him open. I hold the magnum with both hands to keep it steady, yet it still trembles, and with my eyes flooded with tears, I aim for my father's face.

My hesitation builds with each passing second, creating fear and doubt as I now close my eyes, think of a better place, and squeeze the trigger.

I open my eyes to see what remains of my father lying before me, his body surrounded by blood and fragments of his skull.

He lies there... lifeless, his blood absorbed by the white carpet around him. His face is no longer recognizable by the .357 round that completely disfigured him. I drop to my knees and begin to sob, trying to hold back the tears in front of my father even though he's dead. As I sit there, now wet and streaked with blood, sobbing while still naked, I make an attempt to pull myself together.

After awhile I have no more tears to spare as I pull myself up. I can't help but wonder how someone could still be moving after getting stabbed in the stomach twice, let alone getting shot in the leg. I come to realize that the only thing that stopped him was a bullet to the head.

The pain from my crotch has greatly subsided as I'm relieved to see that no serious damage is done. The fear of it all begs me to move, as I come to find only three more bullets left in the sock drawer, which I take for my own.

I now walk to my room again, leaving a trail of bloody foot prints behind while replacing the three missing rounds in my magnum. My sadness overwhelms my current pain as I feel the sudden craving for a cigarette. Once inside, I close the door to my room and toss the gun on my bed, using another towel to smear the blood off me yet again.

I can't help but think about what has happened and what I've done. I just killed a man. I killed my father. I question if there was anything different I could have done, although all scenarios point to the same conclusion. His attack was rabid and fierce, his intent made clear by his mere gaze. My imagination runs wild with the possibilities of what it all means. It all happened so fast that I'm surprised it turned out the way it did.

A quick and dreadful end to what should have been an everlasting bond.

I no longer feel safe at my house and plan to find somewhere to lay low. The severity of it all seems unreal and only encourages my denial. I now very slowly slide on a pair of blue jeans along with a black undershirt, preparing my leave as I grab my camping bag from the closet. I make sure pack the essentials within my bag, a few extra pairs of pants, two white and black undershirts, thermals, socks, boxers, tooth paste, tooth brush, soap, and my leather jacket.

As I walk into my garage I see my father's red V8 Silverado waiting quietly in the darkness. Not a second passes as I decide to ditch my shitty compact and claim the truck as my own. I then open its door to find its keys laying for me inside. Relieved that I won't have to visit my father's corpse again, I begin loading my camping bag in the truck along with a case of bottled waters.

While back in my room, I pick up my father's gun and take a moment to examine it. My black hair now hangs low off my head as I hold back the demise of my father. His untimely end at my hands makes me not want to think about my mother. The thought of her becoming crazed and trying to kill me is unimaginable, for I don't think I would have it in me to fight her off. Which begs the question as to why this is happening? How my old man could attack me with such rage?

Two cigarettes are now left in my pack as I spark one up and sit on my bed, wondering as to what to do next. The buzz of nicotine rushes up my head as I stand and wedge the magnum in-between my belt. I prepare my leave like I would any other day in an attempt to maintain my sanity. I grab my wallet, apply some deodorant, put on my black wrist watch, and take my phone.

While back in my father's truck, I start up its engine and open the garage door. Its unlubricated track screeches as its steel frame slowly lifts and sheds light to the darkness around me.

12:05 p.m. and as I back out of my driveway, I endure the sound of rock in Español from the stereo. I think of how irritating this will eventually become, and as I put the truck in park, I remember that my MP3 player is still in my car.

While leaving its engine running, I hop out and walk into the garage and back towards my room again. Once inside, I put out my cigarette and grab the car keys that remain on my bed. While taking a moment to look through my bedroom window, I stop in horror at what lies await.

My eyes deceive me as I reluctantly stare at Jimmy, the six year old boy that lives next door, now sluggishly walking towards my truck. Just like the old man, the boy walks off balance, only this time he drags a large red fire axe behind him. In hopes that the little bastard doesn't go after my tires, I rush out of my room and back into the garage.

Without giving a second thought, I draw his attention as the door slams shut behind me. I don't know what I fear most, the child or what might transpire. The vivid imagery of what I've witnessed now takes its toll as he slowly walks towards me.

Slight twitches force his head to jerk to the left as he continues to drag the axe behind him. The boy's pace quickens as I call his name, the sound of the axe dragging now intensifying. His face is completely covered with dry blood, which abruptly chips away as his head randomly twitches.

With my right hand, I hold on to the magnum wedged in my belt, unwillingly bracing myself as the boy approaches the garage door.

My body freezes again.

Unable to force myself to shoot the boy, I continue to shout for him to put the axe down. His black eyes with surrounding redness begin to bring back bad memories, visions of the hell I've encountered so far. While now five feet away he screams and grabs the axe behind him, holding it with both hands as he maintains eye contact, and swings.

My reflexes kick in as I lean back and feel the clean swipe of the air getting sliced inches from my face. His upward swing leaves him vulnerable as I quickly kick him to the ground. Now screaming, he continues to struggle and grab at my leg while I have him pinned to the floor, his eyes never seeming to leave my sight.

Within his efforts, I slowly reach down and pick up the axe with my right hand while keeping him at bay. His resemblance is no longer that of the kid who played soccer in front of my house. Hate and fury are all that is expressed as I raise the axe high over my head.

The boy's screams are now cut short. He falls silent by the heel of the axe that I brought down upon his face, eliminating all sense of consciousness in the boy. Whatever madness has befallen the world seems to have sunken low enough to effect children, an atrocity to the fact that Jimmy was so young and innocent.

While almost forgetting why I'm outside, I quickly unlock my car and grab my MP3 player from the center console.

I question if I should lock him up somewhere, as I take a moment to observe the boy. Looking far less threatening now that he is unconscious, I can't help but feel remorse for him. I think about doing the humane thing and putting him out of his misery. Similar to my old job where we would put an old dog or cat to sleep that no longer has the will to live. Nevertheless, I can't and won't bring myself to kill the boy, for his parents might still be out there.

After placing my newly acquired axe in the passenger seat of my father's truck, I continue to back out of the driveway. While coasting through my neighborhood, I drive in hopes to find someone who hasn't gone insane, desperately looking for answers, yet realizing that I'm dangerously low on gas.

The streets remain empty as I slowly drive towards the gas station near my house, in hopes that my presence goes unnoticed. Within three miles I arrive, only to find myself feeling more alone than ever.

Evidence of chaos and unforeseen panic litters the streets along with the gas station I pull into. A vast wreckage covers the entire parking lot of the plaza ahead. A sea of cars smashed against one another remain abandoned with a few of their doors left ajar.

I pull up to pump number seven and slide my credit card through its automated cashier. While pumping gas, I can't help but stare at the large convenience store beyond the sea of wrecked cars ahead. Its ruins, although near, failed to reach the gas station as its distance lies across the plaza. The cluster of vehicles creates a sort of maze that reveals only a few openings within the parking lot. Beyond the metallic labyrinth lies John's Club, a large fortress like store which towers over the cars below.

The odds of running into another crazed person are much higher in a store like that, such that I begin to make my way towards the gas station. While leaving the truck to fill up with fuel, I stare up at the cloudy purple sky which glooms above. Their longing for sunlight now matches my despair.

As I approach the entrance, a pair of automated glass doors calmly slide open to reveal a trail of blood. My heart races at the sight that leads towards the cashier's desk to my right. I tread lightly once I enter the store and steady my breathing, pulling out my magnum while now following the blood. Shredded magazines and broken potato chips litter the floor as I carefully scan my surroundings. The randomness of the destruction around me is without purpose, for if it had one, it was to merely make a mess of things.

As I reach the cashier's counter, I make my way around and become stunned at what lies on the floor.

Nausea hits me again as I come to find a pair of legs torn from its occupant's body. The grotesque sight fills me with terror. I take a closer look to see that it is the waist and bottom half of a woman, for its torso and upper body are nowhere to be found. Red velvet high heels are all that occupies the naked limbs as they lie sprawled out before me. The sight, although revolting, seems less threatening as I slowly step towards them and lower my aim.

The floor remains covered in blood which has clotted and formed a gelatin that gets dragged along my shoes. While trying my hardest not to pay attention to what lies below, I start to grab cartons of cigarettes and set them on the counter behind me. With a plastic bag

I begin to place my supplies inside, as I now stand with the corpse's limbs spread across my feet. I gather about twenty lighters and a lot of gum and place them in my bag, and take a moment to look out the window to see that my truck is still waiting outside.

Blood slowly smears down my pants as I feel something wet and warm rub up against me. My jaw suddenly locks and I begin trembling again, as I now fear what I'm feeling. I look down and become stricken with horror to find the severed legs and hips grinding up and down my left leg. It movements are slow yet vigorous as its hips gain momentum. Its blood splattered thighs begin to squeeze and hug on my leg, its desire slowly causing its calf to wrap around mine. The moisture I feel is warm as well as cool, its skin hot from the friction while its excrements remain cold.

Unable to bear it any longer, I vomit on the naked limbs and kick them aside, causing them to slide across the floor near the wall a few feet away. The woman's torn waist struggles to get up as I watch its legs spread and lift in the air. The sight and pigmentation of its ulcerated thighs and vulva causes me to vomit again.

With a loud clank it plants its high heels on the bloody floor and attempts to raise its hips at me, unable to maintain as it slips uncontrollably. While wiping the vomit off my chin, I grab my bag and run over to the refrigerators to get some water. Unable to stop from dry heaving, I now wash away the accumulating vomit in my mouth.

I finally get a grip of myself and realize that I need to get the fuck out of here.

The sound of the naked limbs struggling is heard as I make my escape and head out the door. While setting my bag of supplies in my truck, I quickly replace the gas pump and start up its engine. I begin breathing heavily as my widened eyes reflect off the rearview mirror. My stomach feels scrambled as the thought of being molested again by half a woman runs through my mind.

It doesn't take a genius to know what I'm up against. I've seen plenty of horror films and if these people aren't the living dead, then I've completely lost my mind.

But why is this happening and since when are the undead real?

Most importantly, why am I still alive? Is it possible that I could have slept through all the chaos that was happening Sunday night? I'm stuck with questions without answers, and now forced to admit that my family is truly dead.

12:45 p.m. and I still have close to six hours until it gets dark. I think about everyone I know and care about and hope that they're alright. For whatever started all of this seemed to have rid my home of any existence. Then it hits me, that maybe it's just this town that is infested with the undead. It's a long shot, and an unlikely one, but I'm no longer left with many options.

With my mind still in denial with what I just saw, I shift my truck to drive and head towards the freeway. The streets are a mess with shattered glass and wrecked cars as I make my way down Fragile Road. Ignoring the rules of the road, I make a fifteen minute drive in about half the time, using all lanes to avoid broken down cars and numerous corpses lying about. The ruins of the city and its desertion distract me from the road as I'm suddenly forced to stop.

I exit my truck at the arrival of the freeway heading south. The smell of burnt rubber and oil flows from the sight of the on-ramp, which is completely blocked. Piles upon piles of cars remain stacked atop one another. Their numbers somewhere in the twenties, reveal an impenetrable wall of rust which delays my escape.

I pull out the last cigarette from my pack and light it as I examine the wreckage. From the looks of the damage, it seems that everyone rushed into the on-ramp at the same time in a state of panic, causing a chain reaction that totaled every car entering the freeway.

While taking notice to all the luggage and corpses that occupy them, I start to wonder how the hell I could have slept through it all. I can't even remember what I did yesterday. Other than tending to Presley in the morning, everything else seems a blur.

Unable to bear the sight of burnt women and children, I take off in my truck and head towards the next on-ramp which heads north. The northbound exit is not nearly as blocked as the one going south, so much that I'm able to squeeze through the rubble in my truck.

I'm now finally able breathe as I accelerate on the freeway heading north. Its obstacles are few as I make my way around forgotten vehicles and tattered limbs. My only problem is that I need to be heading south.

I drive for about ten minutes until the freeway runs along its opposite side. It doesn't take long before I find opening, and drive across a patch of grass that separates both roads. I now head south and can only hope that the road ahead remains clear.

1:32 p.m. as I pull out another smoke and light it. My cravings for cigarettes have doubled in the past few hours than they have since I was a teenager. I slowly exhale the sweet, sweet, smoke from my nose and think about my bad habit, which now seems bleak. For in reality, I would much rather die from cigarettes as opposed to being eaten alive.

The day is still overcast with the same purple clouds that stretch across the sky while heading south. The freeway, although less cluttered, remains splattered with corpses ripped apart and tossed throughout the road.

I need to go somewhere safe and familiar, for my poor father is dead and I can only assume that my mother shared his fate. I plan to visit the only family I have left, which is my older brother Eric. His house lies an hour south of my parent's home in the city of Santee. He made the choice to sell drugs out of his house, which was always a very secure place for his lifestyle.

I love my big brother, and if anyone could survive this nightmare it would be him. My excitement for seeing him blinds me from the fact that he might not be alive anymore. Regardless of what happens when I arrive, it's the only place I have left to go. The constant surveillance of his house will help me sleep at night, not to mention the weapons he has. If I'm lucky enough, I might be able to find an arms dealer or a sporting goods store; somewhere to get more rounds for my magnum and maybe a few more guns.

Nature eventually calls as I pull to a stop in the middle of the road so that I can take a piss. While walking to the edge of the freeway, which is now suspended by a bridge, I begin to see fires brewing throughout the city before me. Black smoke creeps up and paints the sky dark as the town below me lies in ruins.

As I urinate off the edge of the freeway, I watch the flames consume a nearby shopping plaza, my attention now drawn to the vast number of people walking the streets below. Over a hundred of them continue to wander the city's ruins, each of them stumbling while tripping over themselves. Grown men, women, and children roam freely while bearing the mark of the undead. Most of them feast on corpses lying about, while the rest walk aimlessly while carrying their meals.

As I finish relieving myself I take a moment to observe, in hopes of finding someone who hasn't turned undead. My chest caves in and the air grows thin as I soon realize that my brother is probably gone, if not one of these monsters already.

I light up another cigarette and continue to watch the undead.

Hunger seems to be what drives these monsters. A sick need to feed causes some of them to eat their own limbs and flesh. They also seem to feel no pain, for every other one I look at suffers terrible injuries. Some go about their business with an arm torn off or missing a hand or part of their stomach, along with the occasional few that drag themselves with their legs missing. Apparently their limbs can also remain animated as I've learned earlier today.

While taking the last few drags of my smoke, I think of how the whole world must be affected by this plague. The thought of which is something I cannot bear, as I now flick my cigarette down below with the rest of the monsters, and take off.

2:45 p.m. as I approach the exit that leads to Eric's house. Lucky for me the off-ramp isn't blocked at all, as I slowly make my way through the industrial part of town. The city of Santee lies in ruins as well. Bad memories loom in the air while passing the destruction around me. Debris floods the streets along with a few wandering figures in the distance.

Within a few blocks from my destination I try to give my brother a call, but still no signal. My attention then drawn to the sight of three women feasting on a corpse in the intersection ahead.

Fear consumes me once again, yet as I hesitate, I unwillingly press on the gas and drive faster.

I don't know why I'm doing this or what's come over me. Any and all second thoughts are now gone as I reach the point of no return.

The V8 engine roars with its acceleration as I close in on the undead. Suddenly one of the women looks up at my truck, blood dripping from her nose and chin while the other two are face first in the corpse's stomach. They seem frantic with their food, constantly nudging one another away from their meal.

I quickly brace myself by holding tight on the steering wheel. My mind suddenly consumed by guilt and the impending repercussions as I plow through the undead.

Blood instantly covers my windshield and blinds me while now forced to pull to a screeching stop. I exit my truck in a state of shock and paranoia. Its sensation causes me to pause and look around before grabbing the axe I acquired earlier. While using its reach, I cringe as I pull the severed torso of one of the women off the hood of my truck. Its corpse falls onto the street and lays lifeless as I move on to the remaining two.

The woman who looked up at me before the impact is now dead. Her body lies with her head completely removed after my truck's grill tore her apart. Only one survives as she now struggles to pull herself up. The screeching sound of her screams draws needless attention as I approach and wind my axe back.

My body tells me to swing but my conscience says otherwise, the thought of what I just did still corrupting my mind. Our eyes connect and I see the smooth portions of chewed up organs that hang from her teeth and hair. The horror I feel from the grotesque sight and screams, suddenly fills my body with grief as I'm forced to swing.

Silence now surrounds me as my axe lies embedded halfway through the woman's neck. My hands still tremble with fear as blood continues to spray after having to pry it out. Once free, the woman begins to scream while her head hangs low like a PEZ dispenser. Her cries, now deafening, cause me to wince along with her gaze that pushes me away. With one deep breath I overcome my terror, putting an end to her suffering with one final swing of my axe.

My body still trembles as I hyperventilate. The time I take to think, along with the cigarettes in between, finally gets me to calm down and come to terms with what just happened. After cleaning my windshield with a bottle of water, I waste no time to get back on the road again.

The nicotine swirling in my lungs helps me cope as I think about what I just did. I've now killed again. Only this time it was three women. The feeling is such that I cannot bear its vivid imagery, for the sound of their screams still haunts me. I don't know if I have it in me to do it again, let alone face whatever lies await. For all I know this could all just be a dream, an epic nightmare to which I'll wait to awake from.

3:02 p.m. as I arrive at Eric's house and approach his front door. I've always had a key to his place in case I needed somewhere to stay, which works wells on his first lock. The second, however, is a digital combination. The pass code proves no problem as it has always been my date of birth, which I supposed helped Eric remember my birthday.

As I open his front door I recognize the camera posted near the keypad. My brother is a pretty paranoid guy, but I suppose years of being strung out on drugs will do that to you. Considering that he sold mostly weed nowadays, he promised my parents and I that he'd been clean and stopped using hard drugs. Although by the looks of security, it seems that old habits die hard.

After setting my bag of supplies on the floor, I take a moment to scan my surroundings. I think to myself that Eric's folly is my advantage, as I lock myself inside, ready my magnum, and begin to search for my brother.

The air within is thick and humid as I slowly pace myself through the living room. Its feeling is such that it causes me to sweat. The house itself is a complete mess with various signs of struggle. Its evidence lies among the numerous holes in the walls and trash lying about.

Suddenly, the sound of music is heard and begins to echo around me. I follow its call as it now leads me towards Eric's bedroom.

While holding on tight to my magnum, I walk down a narrow hall and stumble upon some powder. The white dust lies in a small pile and makes a trail that leads towards my brother's room. The door itself is closed and smeared with bloody hand prints and strands of hair. For whatever reason, I bend down to scoop a small portion of the powder and give it a taste.

It's cocaine.

The familiar flavor of its bitter sweet richness is reminiscent of a time long since past. I continue to rub some more on my gums and begin to feel my mouth grow numb. Its taste, along with its sense of enlightenment, makes me now realize what might have happened here.

The rotten smell of death hits me in waves as I open the door to find my brother's corpse lying before me. His body is still and stiff, resting comfortably on his bed with massive amounts of cocaine covering his lips and nose. All the while his eyes remain fixed towards the ceiling.

A black rubber tube used as a tourniquet is tied around his left arm, along with a depleted three milliliter syringe that sticks out his vein. I now feel out of breath again, stricken by the sight of Eric's overdose. I didn't know what to expect once I'd arrive here, but certainly not this.

After a while of staring at his blank expression, I begin to get the gist of what happened. Although I force a smile, I do feel happy for my brother as I remove the syringe and tourniquet from his arm. I'm glad that he did not meet his end like my poor parents did; that he chose to end his life the way he wanted to, and not at the hands of the undead.

The haunting sound of "Nutshell" by Alice In Chains now ends and changes to one of Eric's favorite glam rock tracks. Its drastic transition proves unnecessary towards the current mood and state of affairs. For the best thing about Eric was given his rough exterior, he had little regard for his questionable taste in music and style.

I pull a pillow over his face and press the barrel of my gun upon it. I don't want to disgrace my brother's death, but at the same time I can't take any chances. The cocaine, however, helps with my emotions, balancing my sadness and loneliness with a strong sense of euphoria. Its numbing sensation causes a string of saliva to drip from my mouth as I pull the trigger.

Small pieces of cotton now flutter around me as the gunshot becomes muffled by the pillow. Its noise, although concealed, still brings about an aching pain in my chest. With the overwhelming feeling of guilt and shame, I reluctantly cover his body with his white bed sheet.

The smell of my brother's corpse no longer bothers me as I lie next to him and have a smoke. My mouth still numb makes this cigarette all the more sweeter.

4:12 p.m. and after being lost in my thoughts, I roll out of Eric's bed and head towards the bathroom down the hall. While exiting his room, I make sure to gum some more coke along on the way.

The bathroom is ransacked as expected, its mirror broken with spots of blood where its impact occurred. Everything lies thrown across the floor and counter: deodorant, hair products, toothpaste, toilet paper, and a broken bong. So much has happened here that I don't know where to begin.

I lift up the toilet lid and stand in awe to find a piece of paper taped to its bottom. It rests folded neatly against the lid while written from front and back in what looks to be Eric's handwriting. I anxiously pull out the paper and unravel it to find an old photo of my brother and I. The picture is of us sitting on some stairs while smoking, trying to look hard as Eric has his arm around my shoulder. I smile and think about how much I loved this photo and the good times I had with him. My infinite sadness never ends; it only becomes numb as the drugs course through my body.

While putting the photo in my back pocket, I pull down my jeans and sit upon the cold porcelain and try to get comfortable. The door to the bathroom remains open so that I can see and hear everything that goes on in the house, such that I retain a clear view of Eric's body lying under his sheet.

As I now straighten the paper in front of me, I see that it is in fact written by my brother. My excitement fills me with enthusiasm, as I light up a smoke and frantically read the final words of my brother's life.

To whom this may concern,

My name is Eric Cunningham and I am an addict. The time is now 11:00 p.m. Sunday November the 6th, and I'm glad to say that will be the last time I'll have to introduce myself like that. The world is ending around me and I'm surrounded by the constant screams and sounds of monsters trying to break into my house.

To answer the obvious question, yes I am high on drugs, and no I am not hallucinating the creatures outside. They have been at it for hours, growing in numbers and somehow able stare directly at me as I watch them through my surveillance. Regardless of the drugs I'm on or the amount I will soon be taking, the monsters that have consumed all human life are very real, and are trying their damnedest to kill me.

It all started at around 7:00 p.m., when the television put out emergency broadcasts of numerous "terrorist" attacks that swept the world. The attacks seemed rapid as from what I gathered from the news anchor. Canada was the first to report riots breakout throughout the country. Ten minutes later it showed Europe up in flames, which was said to be caused by arsonists. Ten more minutes rolled by and the United States was in chaos, the reports claimed that "terrorists" have launched bio-chemical attacks throughout the States. Shortly after, the entire continent of Asia was destroyed with no communication left to the outside world. So much for terrorism.

At around 8:00 p.m., all broadcasts both televised and radio were shut off. Half an hour later all internet servers went down as well as cell phone reception. I've become completely cut off. Whatever happened seemed to have turned our way of life back a few centuries within an hour. Everyone was evacuating, to where I have no idea, and it wasn't long until the "terrorists" were at my front door.

Dennis was a regular customer and acquaintance of mine, and I was expecting his arrival as I made the mistake of letting him inside. Unfortunately for Dennis I had to kill him, the crazed son of a bitch attacked me throughout my house and was trying to kill me. I had to empty an entire clip from my nine millimeter in order to bring the fucker down.

These things, they're like zombies, flooding the streets around my house in large numbers and able to take a whole lot of hurt. Dennis was only the first, and as soon as I stowed him away, dozens of them began to show up at my door. I'm surrounded by these monsters, hopeless and alone. I'm unable to reach my parents or my little brother. I hope they're alright, I hope to God that these monsters haven't reached them yet.

Whoever is reading this I can only hope that you now understand what you're dealing with. These things are ruthless and fast. Why they are here I do not know, or how they arrived is still unseen. My nine millimeter is hidden underneath the pillow I'm lying on, I pray you can make better use of it than I could. I now realize that the world is coming to an end, and I'll be damned if I meet my fate to these creatures. I hope whoever you are that you've found a way out of this nightmare, and find the truth behind all of this. My life has been a complete disappointment, and maybe this last ditch effort to redeem myself will take me to a better place after I die.

The screams… the terrible screams of death are unbearable. I can't take it anymore. I can't stay trapped in this house forever. I love you mom and I love you dad, and I'm sorry for letting you down all my life. Take care of them little brother and I will see you all very soon.

Tears drop from my eyes and onto the letter as I finish reading Eric's last words. The large tail of ash that developed from my neglected cigarette now hangs low as I flick it aside. His note slides easily into my left rear pocket as I wash my hands after using the bathroom.

While heading towards my brother's room again, I take a moment to stop and rub a little more cocaine on my gums. My mouth begins to feel as though it is full of clouds as I stand over Eric's dead body. The spot of blood seeping through the white bed sheet slowly spreads above the wound on his forehead.

I gently lift his head along with the pillow he rests on to reveal the Ruger nine millimeter handgun, along with an extra clip lying next to it. As I hold the gun with my right hand and the extra clip with my left, I remember the times when Eric and I would go shooting. I was a decent shot but nothing compared to him. His accuracy would stay sharp even while firing with one hand.

While leaving Eric's bedroom I arrive at the living room and fall on his couch. Now feeling a little hungry, I unpack the bag of supplies I got from the gas station earlier. The television my brother has is similar to the one I once owned, a 42 inch LCD flat screen which lies ahead of me. In-between is an amber colored table that he made in wood shop during the eighth grade. Its wood and structure however, have seen better days.

With my magnum and Eric's nine millimeter now on the table, I begin to open a bag of chips that I forgot I grabbed while leaving the gas station earlier. After fumbling with the remote control, I change the television's input so that it shows the surveillance from all four cameras surrounding the house. Lucky for me my brother and I had some similar tastes, enough to make me smile as I grab one of my favorite beers from his fridge.

Slowly but surely, one beer turns into three, and soon five empty bottles are left on the table before me, along with an empty bag of chips.

6:33 p.m. and darkness has crept over the sky as I now focus on the one night vision camera on the television. Before me lies a small pile of cocaine, along with a few grams of weed. My means of escaping reality, although poor, prove efficient as I gum some more coke and open my sixth beer.

The booze and drugs that dwell within me help mask my fear, and I can only hope that eventually my mind will allow me to sleep. I keep thinking and assuming that when I wake up it'll all be over, that this is all just a dream; that I will wake up back home, in my bed, and probably late for work again. Unfortunately the thought of this is anything but reassuring.

While sitting I watch a few undead walk aimlessly through the surveillance, as I'm now pretty drunk. The haze I feel guides my hand as I light another cigarette and fill my mouth with both clouds and smoke.

The undead I watch don't seem to be very coordinated. Their comings and goings are few and far between, but as they arrive I observe intensely. My mind still can't get over what I've witnessed today as I become lost in reality. Everything that mattered to me in life has been taken away in a single day. I've done things that I never thought I'd be capable of within the past few hours. I've now succumbed to my sense of denial, hoping that everything will go back to normal once I finally rest.

8:00 p.m. as I finish reading Eric's letter for the fifth time. With my mind scrambled, I begin to realize that this nightmare might not end. The thought of this only hinders the buzz I feel. As I lay on Eric's couch my eyes begin to drift in and out of consciousness. It brings about a void of darkness that eventually causes me to give in, and fall asleep.

I suddenly awake to the sound of the front door on the verge of breaking.

Out of breath and in a state of paralysis, I gasp at the sight of the house now surrounded by the undead. For every slam I hear now brings the door closer to breaking off its hinges.

I panic and push the couch up against the door in order to buy me some time. The sound of its wood breaking is relentless, causing me to back away and shiver with each crack. The crowd surrounding the house is massive, so thick that I'm unable to see past the bodies on the surveillance. There is no escape.

I now know that I will surely die today, and that this will be my last stand. With both guns in hand, I face the front door with my axe resting at my feet. With only six rounds in my magnum and ten shots left in my nine, I think of how short this fight will be. My body begins to sweat as the fear consumes me, forcing my breathing to become shallow. I ready my aim high in order to get in some head shots. My lack of concentration proving fatal as the door suddenly breaks open.

Death has many faces although non like the little girl that rushes in. The child must be no older than six years old, her pigtails sharpened to points while held together by dry blood. Her eyes are fixed upon me along with a sinister grin across her blood splattered face.

I desperately lower my aim but its too late, for the little girl now has her teeth embedded in my leg.

She was too quick. The little bitch hurdled over the couch like nothing and quickly latched onto me.

The pain I feel is unbearable as she shakes her head vigorously and tears my calf apart. My anguish guides my magnum over her head as I open fire, causing her to release her grip and collapse to the floor.

I immediately look up to find myself accompanied by the endless undead that swarm through the house. I run as fast as I can, limping my way towards Eric's room while followed closely by the monsters' wrath.

Once inside, I lock myself within and stand facing the door.

The pain from my leg now causes half of my body to go numb. A large trail of blood stains my path and follows me as my eyesight grows dim, and I soon begin to get lightheaded.

Within moments the wound causes my leg to spasm and burn. Its sensation slowly works its way up my body while forcing me to drop my magnum. Eventually the sound of the door breaking becomes muffled as I slip into a haze of blood loss.

I no longer feel any pain, only a sensation of suffocation all over me. It's as though my entire body is being choked. My heart races as my skin begins to leak profusely, my temperature rising to an all time high. I become weak and fall to my knees, now desperate and frail as I find myself surrounded by the undead.

They stand there watching me...waiting.

Unable to breathe, I manage to keep myself from collapsing and remain kneeling.

They seem to be waiting for me to change.

I can feel it now, my life slowly slipping away from me; that very same feeling I'd get when I'd have my blood drawn, only so much more.

The nine millimeter in my left hand feels as though it weighs forty pounds as I struggle to lift it up. All the strength I have left can only bring its barrel underneath my chin, as I muscle the will to pull back its hammer.

I take a moment to stare into the eyes of every undead in the room. Their excitement remains emphasized in their expressions, to which I clench my teeth and pull the trigger.

I now watch my death through a pair of unseen eyes as the bullet travels up my jaw and out the top of my head, sending a splash of blood across the ceiling. My body instantly falls to the ground as blood continues to pour out the back of my head. Smoke slowly seeps from my mouth as my limbs continue to twitch while lying on my side. I no longer gasp for air as I finish convulsing, its end bringing the undead in the room to move in closer.

I now watch them all tear through my body. Two of them begin to pull and rip my arms from their sockets as another grabs onto my head. The undead that stands over me plunges its filthy hand into my hanging jaw and grabs the roof of my mouth. It pulls and pulls until my neck begins to crease open.

The others continue to feast on my legs, tearing through my jeans and ripping out portions of my thighs. My neck soon begins to tear as blood sprays over the undead, its volume increasing as my head rips from my body. The one responsible dances and proceeds to smash it against the walls and a nearby desk. Its rabid tantrum disfigures my face until it's no longer recognizable.

The two that have my arms now sit on the floor and begin eating. Starting with my fingers, they bite off each digit while spitting out fragments of bone and nail. The rest continue to rip through my stomach, pulling out organs and running off with their meal. Eventually they remove my intestines and begin to hit each other with them, as if playing with their food while indulging in my flesh.

One by one they come and quickly pick me apart, blood constantly spraying from their ferocious appetite.

All the blood... all my blood, then everything goes dark.

Day 2

8:00 a.m. and the sound of my alarm rings impatiently as I awake. Now startled I abruptly sit up on Eric's couch, dripping with sweat and out of breath from my nightmare.

I quickly glance at the television which still shows the house's surveillance, and am relieved to see that no undead linger outside. All hope of waking up to a normal life is instantly diminished once I realize where I'm at. Anger and depression hit me in more ways than one as I try to come to terms with my new reality. I press my hands on my head and shut my eyes while counting to ten, in hopes that I will wake up back home.

To my disappointment I open them, only to find the guns and drugs lying on the table before me.

There is no escape, this is really happening.

My hangover finally catches up with me after standing. Its effects make my head feel heavy while my stomach churns with the remnants of the beers I drank. The light within the house causes me to squint as I stumble my way towards the bathroom. After relieving myself, I brush my teeth in hopes to eliminate the rancid taste in my mouth.

Shocking is the cold sting of water as I begin to wash my face, its morning chill forcing me to snap out of my buzz.

I stop for a moment to look at my reflection. I see myself before me as I take notice to my facial features. My skin is a lighter flesh tone which is a few shades away from becoming pale. My complexion stands out from my black hair and eyebrows, which now hang low from my ongoing distress. It seems as though I've aged a little in the past day which I can't understand, but for whatever reason, I seem different than before.

Today I begin my new life as I prepare to leave, but before I go I must give Eric a proper burial. His death was a natural one, natural in the sense that he didn't fall victim to the undead, and for that he should be put to rest.

My stomach feels as though it's eating itself alive, as I haven't had any real food to eat since Sunday. While searching the kitchen, I proceed to light my first smoke of the day. Only something like the world coming to an end would cause me to eat this early in the morning. Sustenance as oppose to coffee and cigarettes cause me to grab some eggs which have yet to spoil, along with some bacon. Eric must have recently gotten groceries for he still has a full carton of orange juice left.

I begin to set my ingredients aside as I prepare my meal, the thought of which now intensifies my hunger. I cringe as I'm forced to scrub away the dry blood and flesh along the stove and dining table. All the while I puff on my cigarette, which now gives me the displeasing taste of menthol from just brushing my teeth.

8:34 a.m. as I sit alone and eat breakfast. My culinary skills, although lacking, still provide me with a decent meal, which consists of two scrambled eggs, five slices of bacon, and a clean glass of orange juice. I stop to think of how many more meals like this I'll be having in the future. I suppose it's best to embrace the little things in life while I still have the chance.

My mind and body begin to feel better while eating, as my hangover now slowly dissolves. At the moment some coffee would be ideal, but I don't seem to have that luxury, for Eric's coffee pot lies smashed upon the corner of the floor.

I make a few attempts to catch a signal on my cell phone with no success, along with the radio which seems to only broadcast static. I've come to terms with the fact that I cannot stay cooped up in this house. My nightmare was a foreshadowing of things to come. They would eventually find me here and I would be trapped, forced to endure the pain of being eaten alive. I can only hope that if it boiled down to it that I would have the strength to end my own life, like Eric did.

The thought of my vivid dream and the pain I felt dampens my appetite if not removes it, yet I keep eating. I can't help but wonder if there's anywhere left to hide, somewhere to lay low and wait for this all to blow over. My initial thought that the undead only roamed my home town has completely changed, a fact proven yesterday once I saw the city off the freeway in ruins.

These questions flooding my mind seem to only heighten my ongoing distress, as I desperately attempt to block them out. Yet I can't help but dwell on my sudden loss and misfortune.

9:05 a.m. as I continue to search the house for a shovel, its interior remains a complete mess, which makes finding anything near impossible. I almost resort to using my axe to dig, until I notice the closet at the far end of the hall leading towards the bedroom.

I stand in shock as I carelessly open it and become revolted by what lies inside. Unable to differentiate where the rotting smell was coming from, I assumed it coursed from Eric's corpse. I was wrong. For the body of an undead is stuffed tightly within the small closet before me. Its blank expression stares at me as its body seems broken and contorted to fit inside. Various tools clutter around its body, one of which is a four foot tall black shovel.

Still startled, I stand back and unwillingly wait, half expecting the corpse to come alive and attack me. I soon realize that this must be the undead that Eric mentioned in his letter, this is Dennis. I calm myself down as I take notice to the several bullet wounds that disfigure his face, their numbers now offering me reassurance.

As I reluctantly reach for the shovel, I quickly become engulfed with the rancid smell of death that consumes each of these monsters. The stench is so severe that I begin to gag. The eggs in my stomach briefly stop digesting as I quickly grab the shovel and slam the door shut.

While walking towards the front yard, I try to picture Dennis's demise from the damage done throughout the house. The attack must have started right when Eric opened his front door, which lead to a scuffle and imminent chase. From the looks of the house, it must have taken awhile before my brother plugged him full of rounds.

As I arrive outside I instantly spot my truck in the driveway. It remains untouched while now painted and stained with blood. I plunge the shovel into my brother's front lawn and pause for a moment. I think of how shitty it would be to be buried in the front of somebody's house, for the scenery just doesn't fit the mood. Unfortunately for Eric, my options are limited.

My eyes become narrow from the brightness of the sky as I bask in the warmth of the sun. Its beauty drawn from the gloom of yesterday, now mocks me for what I'm about to do.

10:22 a.m. as I stand overlooking an empty grave. The black shovel stands embedded in the grass as I sit alongside its edge and have another smoke.

I've been taking my time to dig the grave, a sad attempt to prolong the act of putting my brother to rest. I now sink further into myself, trying to find the will to live on, but only seeing myself die like in my nightmare.

Smoke slowly escapes from my nostrils as I stare into the bright sun. I would almost prefer a gloomy day over the beauty that shines above me, for the weather is in contrast with my current mood.

My anger consumes whatever grief I have for my losses.

I hate these monsters. I hate them for killing my family, and I hate them for leaving me alone in the world. I no longer have anything to live for, no purpose in life.

Survival is all that drives me, but to what end? If I am to stay alive I must be smarter, faster, and stronger. I must learn from my experiences and let my anger pave the way towards my survival. In order to do that I must leave Eric's house and learn to adapt. More importantly, I need to find more guns.

10:41 a.m. and I'm back in Eric's bedroom standing over his corpse. Unable to look at his face, I use his bed sheet to wrap and form a cocoon around his body. His limbs, now rigid, make the task that much easier to accomplish.

While slowly pacing myself, I carry him in both arms back towards the front yard, each step now more difficult than the last. His wrapped up corpse is as stiff as a board, yet his head hangs from lack of support.

Once outside, I gently ease my brother into the grave and begin to shovel soil upon him. Each load of dirt grows heavier and heavier as I cringe at what I'm forced to do. No words can explain what I'm now feeling. My jaw is tightly locked and presses against my teeth as I shovel the last few piles onto his grave.

Then I hear the screams.

I don't bother looking as my head rests on the pole of the shovel. I now recognize the screams of death, and by the sounds of it, there must be a few of them up ahead.

My hand curls tightly around the shovel as I look up to see the three undead down the street. Their pace is slow at first, yet heightened as I acknowledge their presence. Within moments they advance to a full on sprint, their distance now providing me the advantage.

Sweat trickles down my spine as I think of how I will kill these monsters, and as they draw near, I pull out Eric's nine millimeter and take aim. The gun trembles within my hands yet I manage to maintain focus. I aim at the undead closest to me, roughly fifty yards away and squeeze the trigger.

The shot instantly connects with its left shoulder which now seems to piss them all off. I take a moment to calm my nerves, their approach delaying the process as I take a deep breath, steady my aim, and fire.

The wounded undead gets sent backwards as another round tears through its head. It lands on its back twitching while the remaining two tumble over its corpse. With their bodies lying fifteen yards away, I grab the shovel with my left hand and walk towards them.

I keep the gun aimed with my right hand as I march on, blinded by my own sense of fear and madness.

By the time I draw near, the undead to my right is back on its feet, but ends up crippled as I tag both its legs with two rounds. While no longer a threat it remains face down on the street. It screams violently as it struggles to pull itself towards me.

My eyes immediately glance to my left as the remaining undead is now up and approaches a few feet away. Without a moment to spare, I grip the shovel tightly and throw a back handed swing to my left, causing it to smash across the monster's face and stagger back. I find my opening and within seconds, I pull back the shovel and forcefully plunge it into its stomach.

I stand with the outreached shovel in-between the undead and I, its length now the only thing keeping it at bay. Its arms desperately reach out for me and begin to grab onto the metal pole. Blood seeps around the head of the shovel as it digs its way further into its abdomen from its struggles.

I suddenly feel a hand grab onto my right leg.

Its touch is startling, as I see that the undead I crippled moments ago has finally dragged its way to me.

I abruptly kick it away and send it lying on its back, and quickly turn while pointing my nine millimeter at the undead embedded in my shovel. Its eyes pierce through me as I stare and watch it grin. Its teeth are stained orange with blood while its lips slice open from smiling.

Unable to bear its gaze any longer, I squeeze the trigger and embrace the flash which sends the undead flying back. The impact from the gunshot causes its body to pull from my shovel and fall onto the street. Although still smiling, it remains lifeless, resting quietly on its back with trickles of blood running down its head.

My attention is now drawn to the undead I left crippled. It slowly drags its way towards me again, moaning and reaching out for me with its deathly intent.

I holster my nine millimeter against my belt and begin walking towards it with the shovel in hand. I kick the undead onto its back while pinning it down firmly with my right foot. Its desperate attempt to tear through my jeans is futile, yet without purpose. It somehow stands inferior to my fear, as I slowly press the tip of the bloody shovel upon its throat.

Its black metal edge rests comfortably above its Adam's apple, a perfect fit to a perfect end. Like the last one I killed, it never ceases to stare and smile. Only this time, it begins to stick out its tongue and lap at the air, constantly trying to reach me one way or another. After awhile I stop stalling and immediately stomp on the right peg of the shovel, causing its edge to tear through the undead's neck.

It now lies still.

Blood rushes along both sides of the blade and forms a puddle behind its head. I listen to the sound of metal being scraped against pavement as I begin moving the pole. I twist and turn the shovel repeatedly until the bone gives way and the undead is left with its head hanging off its body.

Without feeling the least bit exhausted, I drop the shovel and stare at the corpses around me. My mind now distracted from my brother's death, brings about an uncomfortable sense of calm as I bask and light myself another smoke.

11:04 a.m. as I put out my cigarette and leave the three undead to bake in the hot sun. Although the nicotine helps calm my storm,

I can't help but refrain from shaking, for I've killed again, this time without mercy.

The act of burying my brother might have fueled my rage, but I can't see it getting any easier. Regardless of how I feel, I know that only more death lies await for me. So much blood for such a small time spent.

Once inside the house, I begin gathering my supplies as I get ready to leave. After loading up my truck, I almost take off, yet remember one last thing.

My brother's drugs now rest before me on the table in front of his couch.

The way I see it, I might not ever come across such a fine assortment of recreation, so I might as well indulge. I keep my eyes focused on the surveillance as I roll a few joints from what is left of Eric's weed.

It's the little things in life that keep us sane.

It's the trivial things that matter most.

11:35 a.m. and my thumbs are green and sticky from the weed that has embedded itself in my fingerprints. The five joints I managed to roll rest comfortably within my current pack of cigarettes. It doesn't take long until I move on to the cocaine.

I use my credit card to start cutting a line that I intend to do before I leave. I've smoked weed every now and again, but I never frequently got into cocaine or any other hard drugs at that, although I think I can make an exception today.

The line of cocaine I cut is roughly four inches in length, with a thickness of that of a pencil or close to it.

I figure if I'm going to do it I might as well do it right.

Before I indulge I get ready to leave. I light up another cigarette, put on my leather jacket, and place my nine millimeter and extra clip in my inside pockets. I then finish by holstering my magnum in-between my belt and pants once again.

I roll up a one dollar bill and hold it tightly in my right hand near the cocaine. Air steadily fills my lungs as I take a deep breath, exhale, and snort my line.

I take in half of the rail with my right nostril and finish off the rest with my left. Its burn is quickly felt as it travels up my nasal passage and curves down the back of my throat. I can feel and taste the remnants that linger behind, slowly becoming dissolved by my mucus membranes.

I quickly stand and become kicked in the face by the overwhelming rush of the high. My movements, now fluid, remain slightly animated as I sway back and forth.

Moments later I rub the excess coke with my finger and brush my teeth with it. I take in one of the best drags of a cigarette I've ever had, and slowly exhale its smoke. My body feels amplified, indestructible, and I feel like running.

I am now ready to leave.

11:52 a.m. as I take off in my truck. The shooting range that I've been to is roughly forty minutes away. It lies along the boardwalk of a nearby beach, which I'll search in hopes of finding any survivors, if not ammunition.

This would be the first time I've gone there without Eric.

To my surprise, I reach the on-ramp to the freeway without any signs of the undead. My current mood leaves me disappointed as I head east on the freeway. Its emptiness provides me with the speed I need as I accelerate my way forth.

12:19 p.m. and I now arrive near the beach. Its calming view of the ocean stretches far beyond the freeway ahead. Its image is such that I can almost smell the rocks on the shore being kissed by the waves, as I now take in the aroma that I've missed so much. The sight of the beautiful horizon and the sea brings a feeling of tranquility that soothes the adrenaline coursing through my veins. My trance, although peaceful, is suddenly interrupted as I pull forward while making an abrasive stop.

Not even the most beautiful ocean in the world can restrain my blood from now boiling. The shimmering sun and bright blue sky are in contrast with the crowd of undead blocking my path ahead. The freeway I'm on has only two lanes, yet is blocked from one end to another by the undead.

While waiting patiently, I stop to observe the crowd, their numbers limited as they remain spaced apart.

I have no choice but to force my way through.

My foot and thumbs tap anxiously as I watch the undead walk in unison. Roughly twenty of them gradually approach, all gaining speed and eager to die.

Suddenly, my body becomes overwhelmed with panic and excitement. The very same feeling I got before I had sex for the first time, incredibly anxious yet unsure of what's going on.

I take one last long drag of my smoke and immediately punch the gas and race towards the undead. Remembering the impact from when I ran over the three women yesterday, I brace myself again by clenching tight on the steering wheel.

It feels as though my heart is racing faster than my truck. My anticipation builds, as I turn on my windshield wipers to clear the blood that is about to spray upon me.

Within seconds of my approach the crowd gets split as my truck plows through them. My windshield wipers act quickly and remove the bloody fragments of flesh along with a severed head from my view. All the blood thickened with hair now forces my hand as I pull to a sudden stop.

I watch the undead through my rearview mirror as I put my truck in reverse, and see that the crowd has now split into two smaller groups. While accelerating, I steer backwards to take out one of the smaller groups to my left. Its numbers, somewhat few, bring about a confidence that stands no match for my truck.

I find myself feeling as though I'm bowling, trying to recover from a two-way split. As I break through the undead, I become blind from the blood that covers my rear window. Taking caution to not drive off the road, I quickly come to a screeching halt.

Although redundant, my strategy proves safe and effective as I switch the transmission to drive, and take off towards the remaining undead. My face tilts down as I increase in speed, ignoring the sound of what I believe to be an undead that jumped onto the bed of my truck.

With the last group consisting of only a few, I begin to hear the monster riding along now trying to break through. Its cries, although distant, are left unheard as I drive into the lingering crowd ahead.

The impact from clearing out the remaining undead is minimal, so insignificant that I retain focus and immediately stomp on the breaks.

My abrasive stop forces the undead hitching a ride to fly forward. Its head clips against the roof of my truck as its body drags and lands ten feet ahead.

With my axe in hand, I step out of my truck and walk towards the undead. Now struggling it lies on its back, its left shoulder dislocated as it slowly attempts to stand. I keep it grounded as I immediately raise my axe high and plunge it down on its leg, slightly above its right knee.

The small sparks from the impact are that of a lighter being flicked.

It continues to smile as it now screams, slowly sliding its way backwards while tearing itself from its impaled leg. My clean cut must have sliced through its joint, for its leg still fidgets on the road with its tendons protruding.

While now crippled, I make my way back and begin pouring water on my truck to wash the blood away. Through the monster's screams which I ignore, I use my axe to pick off large pieces of flesh and bone from my truck's grill.

Within moments I light up another cigarette and take a sip of what's left of my water. Its chill quenches my thirst and dissolves the lingering cocaine. Although distracted, I soon come to hear that the echoing screams have stopped.

I turn and become revolted at the sight of the undead eating its severed leg. Its hand curls around its ankle as if it's a turkey leg, and continues to chew off portions of its calf. It lies on its back while feasting, no longer interested in my presence as I grab some rope from my camping bag.

Its short attention span refocuses with my approach.

As I get in close, I'm forced to keep it at bay with my axe while it attempts to reach me. After a bit of struggling it stops to throw its severed leg at me, causing it to bounce off my left shoulder. Now feeling disgusted and slightly insulted, I vigorously begin to tie the rope tightly around its remaining leg.

While dragging the undead away, I look back to watch it struggle. Eight thin lines of blood perfectly parallel to each other trail from its fingertips, which are now worn to the bone.

Such hate I feel seems alien to me while fueled by the lingering drugs. The likes of which no longer bear any meaning, as I tie the end of the rope to the back of my truck.

I quickly start up its engine and drive, muting my MP3 player to ensure the sound of screams. The smoke from my tires clears within moments of accelerating, as I now watch the undead get dragged along the asphalt through my rearview mirror.

12:46 p.m. and the cocaine that filled my body is long gone, but I don't mind much. I find amusement in watching the undead behind me, skimming over the road like a rock skipping on water.

I'm not far from the shooting range as I near my exit and decrease my speed. Sea Breeze Blvd is the road that leads to the boardwalk, which lies empty as I approach. The smell of the ocean remains crisp in the air, which I now relish while making my way towards the beach.

12:54 p.m. as I pull into the parking lot of Gods and Ammo, the shooting range that lies at the far end of the boardwalk. As I shut off the truck's engine I take notice to the broken locks on the front door. Its grim sight is a bad omen and now leaves a pit in my stomach.

Once outside, I begin untying the rope attached to the lifeless undead. Its body remains torn and skinned, to which I drag to the middle of the street. While taking my time, I bask in the bright sun and ocean breeze as I slowly make my way towards Gods and Ammo. The sound of the waves crashing is hypnotic and puts me at ease, a feeling suddenly interrupted by the caw of seagulls.

They now circle high above me, their white feathers representing purity and the only sign of life that I've seen. I stop to stare and marvel while lighting another smoke, watching and envying the birds. Their sense of freedom is emphasized while soaring overhead, almost taunting me, which begs the question as to why they'd linger.

As I watch I wish that my life was as carefree as theirs, up until one of the god damn birds has the audacity to shit on my truck. With the moment lost I turn to face the entrance to Gods and Ammo, and with my nine millimeter in hand, I slowly make my way inside.

The windows surrounding shed beams of daylight throughout the store, as particles of dust now swirl and fill the air. To my disappointment I find the shop completely ransacked. I'm not surprised however, in the event that the world's gone to hell, why wouldn't anybody arm themselves to the teeth?

Broken glass and empty shells litter the concrete floor and pave the way towards some collapsed countertops. I sigh and exhale the drag from my current smoke and press on, hoping to find more ammunition.

A baby blue gym bag rests idly in the distance atop a smashed counter; its contents remain empty which once held handguns. After claiming it for my own, I make my way around the display cases while shuffling through empty shells. To my excitement and after frantically searching, I stumble across some ammunition.

I find an abundance of refilled nine millimeter rounds which I now place within my blue gym bag. Each package consists of twenty rounds of which I acquire thirty. I also manage to find nineteen bags of forty-five millimeter rounds, as well as the only box of ammo left for my magnum.

Bullets of a different caliber are stowed away, which I ignore as not to overburden myself, yet I take a few twelve gauge slugs just in case. I then set my nine millimeter on the counter and continue my search for more guns.

My eyes now widen at the most beautiful sight, hollow point rounds. Its small blue box falls as my hands desperately reach for it, causing a few bullets to scatter on the floor. The excitement of it all makes me anxious, impairing my movements as my heart suddenly stops, and I freeze at the sound of something falling.

I slowly place the hollow points in my gym bag as my attention is drawn to the sound of breathing. Its faint murmur trails towards a door to my left with the words "Manager's Office" labeling its front.

While slowly gripping my nine millimeter with both hands, I begin to creep towards the door. Each step I take causes broken glass and empty shells to slowly crack, making my presence less than discreet.

The heavy breathing now grows louder and more rapid as I get close.

I steady my aim ahead of me, anticipating the undead that will inevitably break through. As I take my seventh step forward, the sudden sound of a gunshot is heard followed closely by its round. The bullet exits the door at an upwards angle, far from my proximity, yet still cause for panic.

Smoke, sawdust, and small fragments of wood now rain upon me as I kneel down. Startled, I begin to feel my heart race as my gun remains clenched in-between my hands.

What the fuck just happened, I wonder? My mind now flees with thoughts of another survivor; that perhaps I'm not alone.

The loud thud of something hitting the floor causes me to slowly rise and take cover along the right side of the door. With my back against the wall, I hold on tight to my gun and pull back its hammer. My breathing, although deep, remains labored, my eyes focusing on the door handle near my right hand.

I hesitate for a moment as I watch a trickle of blood run down the door. Its red trail starts from the base of the bullet hole and works its way down, seeming almost parallel to the door's frame while creating a small puddle on the floor.

The sight of fresh blood is never a good sign, as I now know what just transpired.

I open the door and become startled as it forcefully swings open by the weight of a dead body. My eyes widen at the sight of the man lying on the floor, his eyes fixed upon me with his mouth left ajar. Soon blood begins to pour from the back of his head, the look and sound of which is that of a milk gallon being emptied. Smoke slowly escapes from his mouth along with more streams of blood. Its sight makes me wince and seems different than the undead, its freshness unmatched as I notice the gun lying by his feet.

The name tag etched on his camouflage jacket says Richard. This must be Richard's gun. The black forty-five millimeter I pick up is still warm, its pearl grip, although smooth, remains stained with blood.

Poor Richard, he must have assumed that the undead found him from the noise I was making. Like my brother, he ended his life before the monsters could; only this time the monster was me. It could be worse though, for if old Richard had aimed a little bit lower he would shot me as well. At the same time I wonder if I could have saved him by merely acknowledging my presence.

His eyes remain fixed towards me as I clean his forty-five millimeter with a nearby rag, still in shock as to what just happened, yet able to quickly move on.

I'm starting to realize the fine line between humanity and not giving a damn, as well as which way I'm straying. Maybe it has to do with all that I've been through in the past day or the losses I've suffered. All the blood, violence, and terror, all things that lead to the fact that I'm truly alone in the world.

Whatever it is… it's beginning to change me.

I'm personally not fond of stealing from the dead, but I doubt that Richard will be making use of the gun harness he wears.

I slowly slide the straps off his shoulders and turn him around to completely remove it, only to expose the large exit wound on the back of his head.

After dragging his body back into his office, I now make my way back to the counter and place my newly acquired items on the table.

1:25 p.m. as I light another cigarette and realize that it's going to get dark soon. Fortunately for me Richard and I shared a similar stature, as the harness that belonged to him fits me perfectly. Its black leather straps hug around my shoulders while its holsters rest comfortably at my sides. Like a glove my semi-automatics slide easily in its slots, forcing me to stow away my magnum within a separate holster at my hip.

I take another drag of my smoke as I stand and get a feel for the slight increase in weight. Once accustomed to the harness, I put out my cigarette and continue to search for extra clips.

Twenty minutes go by and the store is now completely empty. I've searched every possible rack and counter, only to find one extra clip that will fit my nine millimeter and two for my forty-five. Given the circumstances, the amount of ammunition proved a decent haul.

After loading up my gym bag, I bid farewell to Richard as I exit Gods and Ammo.

1:47 p.m. and once outside the warmth of the sun begins to fill my body. Its rays bring a sense of acceptance to why I'm here, as I look to my right to were the boardwalk begins. I take my shoes and socks off and place them in my truck after grabbing a bottle of water, in preparation for walking the beach.

These being one of the trivial things in life which help me stray from madness.

My bear feet take a few moments to get accustomed to the sizzling asphalt as I hop my way towards the sand. I take notice to the seagulls that peck at the lifeless undead. Its body, now broken, lies mutilated after dragging it onto the street. To which the birds ignore me while cleaning out its skull through its eye sockets.

My flesh relaxes and cools down once I reach the soft sands. Its gentle touch is much needed while less than a block away from Gods and Ammo. The beach is deserted with no signs of any life, showing only the endless ocean and shore that spans beyond what the eye can see. I find a nice spot underneath the sun to sit down, seeking comfort as I bury my feet within the warm sand.

The thought of running into another survivor still swirls through my mind, plaguing me with a sense of hope, as I try to relax and block out the image of Richard's dead body. His demise and my failure to save him, brings about a strong emphasis to my dreaded reality.

In an attempt to escape, I pull out and light one of the joints that I rolled earlier. Its long drag and quick inhale instantly tickles and forces me to cough. Each uncontrollable gasp feels like a punch to the throat as I hold back from dry heaving. My bottle of water however, helps soothe my throat, calming my spasms and teary eyes as I take a smaller hit.

Eventually I begin to feel my brain glow as I exhale and become lightheaded. I crack a smile as I'm now overwhelmed by warmth, yet still chilled by the gust of the ocean breeze. I slowly start to feel as though I'm dreaming; the same sensation I get while asleep, although now aided with consciousness. As much as I would like this all to be one big nightmare, I know in my heart that it's not.

My stage of denial has ended.

While enjoying my smoke, I open my gym bag and begin to load my extra clips with the rounds I obtained. Once finished I prepare to clean my guns, starting with my nine millimeter.

Time seems disorientated now.

Seconds last minutes and minutes to hours, and in state of panic, I stop at the thought of how much time I've wasted.

2:31 p.m. and I sigh with relief as only forty minutes have passed.

My mind is playing tricks on me; a brief sense of paranoia undoubtedly due to the intense high I now feel. I'm not even sure where I'll sleep tonight, worst comes to worst I'll look for a secluded spot to rest in my truck.

I set my forty-five millimeter on my lap and light up one of my cigarettes. Unaware of the make and model of the gun, I refrain from dismantling it after merely cleaning its exterior. While trying to familiarize myself with my new piece, I stand along the beach and fire towards the ocean. Its recoil is a little more than I expected, so much that it causes me to stagger back; a minor setback which will remind me next time to keep better footing.

My suicide gun, I think to myself as I stare at the forty-five, seems a fitting name for how I acquired it. Its increase in power from my nine millimeter gets me excited to an extent. My anticipation, although limited, makes me dread the inevitability of having to use it again.

While holstering it away, I take a moment to stretch my arms as I hear and feel a subtle growl in my stomach.

Shortly after storing the gym bag in my truck, I continue back down the boardwalk and arrive at the first shop of many, which happens to be a clothing store called Moses's Beach Gear. The sacrilegious store bears a sign with the biblical figure, sporting shades and surfing atop the stone commandments, which I find incredibly amusing.

With my forty-five in hand I walk in and search the small store. To my surprise, its interior seems to have no signs of struggle or remnants of the undead.

No blood, nothing broken.

I look around for a few moments, finding nothing but a pair of neon green sandals that I take while exiting the store.

2:49 p.m. and after searching through four stores with no undead, I finally come across a sandwich shop. My stomach rumbles and growls uncontrollably as I make my way inside Alfrado's Sub Stop.

The meats and vegetables on display are covered with flies from being left unattended, and now produce a moldy order. If it isn't my intense high, than it's my ongoing hunger that causes me to ignore the sight and smell. Its overwhelming effect does nothing to my senses as I walk towards the freezer in the back.

I lower my guard once I feel the cold escape from the freezer to find fresh ingredients inside. Only a few loafs of bread remain edible, as I now prepare a foot long on white bread. With what little I have left, I continue to put together my sandwich, which consists of ham, turkey, lettuce, mayo and mustard, all of which turned out to be close to what I usually order anyways.

I now sit down at a table outside Alfrado's and begin my eating lunch while sipping on a juice box. My frantic hunger causes me to bite the inside of my mouth. At first I continue eating until the metallic taste of blood becomes too much to handle. With a napkin I apply pressure to my wound, occasionally having to spit out fragments of cloth that stick to my mouth.

Once the bleeding stops, I toss the rolled up napkin a few yards ahead and continue eating. It remains balled up and stained with blood as it rolls along the wooden planks of the boardwalk. Soon the silence around me is interrupted by the sound of something running in the distance, something with more than two legs.

I instantly recognize the sound; its familiarity causes me to stop amidst chew. Within moments, a large dog appears from the corner of the store and attacks my bloody napkin, its voracity similar to that of Presley.

The one hundred pound bull mastiff immediately bites my napkin, almost swallowing it whole as it furiously shakes its head.

It takes no notice to me as I slowly pull out my .357 magnum.

The dog's hair coat is now painted black from being covered in blood. Its right ear is partially torn off while the skin folds on its face seem full of puncture wounds.

I remain seated as I aim my gun with both hands and slowly pull back its hammer. The subtle click my magnum gives off instantly causes the dog to stop and stare directly at me. I can always tell when a dog is about to lunge as my animal intuition now kicks in. Without giving it the slightest chance, I squeeze the trigger and fire off one shot through its skull, causing its head to pop and fall to its side.

The .357 round quickly puts an end to the dog, tearing apart its skin folds while exposing the right side of its shattered skull. The recoil from the blast forces me to fall back on my chair, bringing about a sharp pain as my head hits the floor. Its sting, although throbbing, is nothing compared to the ringing in my ears.

While pulling myself up, I take a moment and wait for the pain to fade. Its intensity drifts with the sound of the waves, as I now continue eating my lunch.

3:25 p.m. as I enjoy another smoke after my delicious meal. I feel a lot better now, both physically and mentally, as I leave Alfrado's Sub Stop. Most of the stores I come across are either locked or deserted along the boardwalk. Their independent branches stretch far and wide until I reach the end of the strip and arrive at Zeke's Bar and Grill.

Thoughts begin to flood my mind of the times I've been here with friends to watch bands play. All the laughs, the music, the drinks, all the fun we use to have during the few times we came here, now seem like a distant memory.

The tinted glass door at Zeke's main entrance is unlocked and feels heavy as I pull it open. I'm not entirely sure why I bother exploring this place, for there is nothing of value here. Call it out of boredom, nostalgia, or the fact that I'm still slightly stoned, I can't help but be curious.

Once inside, my surroundings become dark with only the sunlight shining through a few windows, similar to that of Gods and Ammo. I step forward to see that I'm in the restaurant section of Zeke's, its venue and main bar lies beyond the dining area ahead.

This place has seen better days, for there are obvious signs of struggle. Broken chairs and tables lie scattered throughout the floor, with some of the booths torn open and spoiled entrees lying about. No signs of any corpses though.

I slowly make my way around the restaurant to check and see if the patio section is open. It remains locked, and I suddenly feel something moist beneath my sandal. I look down to see my foot surrounded in a puddle of blood, its clots apparent with strings of hair wrapped around my big toe. A shiver runs up my spine as I pull out my nine millimeter and shake the hair off my foot. My disgust is repeated with each step I take, all while I try my hardest to stop the end of my sandal from smacking the bottom of my foot.

I finally reach the red double doors that lead towards the bar and venue, only to find them barricaded from the other side. I know from the past that there is a back entrance that leads to the stage. The notion of being denied access only makes me curious as I make my way outside.

The bright sun causes my eyes to squint again as I continue my way towards the back parking lot. Only two abandoned cars are left in the empty lot that connects to Shell Blvd, which if I recall, will take me back to the freeway.

While following the building, I come across a back entrance labeled "Staff Only". Its door is left slightly ajar, only darkness is seen beyond its opening as I notice the blood along its handle.

I carefully open the door as light reveals the hallway before me. Its end remains shrouded in shadows yet reveals a thick trail of blood along the floor. I step inside only to have it slam shut behind me, causing me to now be surrounded by darkness.

The door remains locked as I grip tightly around my nine millimeter. Figures that out of everything I packed for supplies, I forgot to grab a fucking flashlight.

While armed with my green lighter, I begin to feel the bottom of my feet moisten as I slowly make my way down the darkened hall. For fear of stepping on broken glass, I drag my sandals across the floor, shuffling along the trail of blood. I flick my lighter a few times so that I can see were I'm heading, and eventually see that the hallway leads towards the venue. I pause and kneel against the wall I follow, now able to vaguely see that I've reached its end and am facing the stage.

My heart throbs as terror ensues by the sudden sound of movement, as well as the familiar moans and violent chews.

I'm now fucked.

I've put myself at a serious disadvantage and I have no idea if the undead can see in the dark.

While putting away my lighter, I recall watching them last night through Eric's night vision camera. From what I can remember they merely walked aimlessly down the street. I want to believe that I saw them occasionally run into things, but in reality, I'm not sure.

I now panic, and although I manage to steady my heartbeat, I cannot overcome the feeling of sheer terror.

As my eyes adjust to the darkness, I begin to see a few shadowy objects that lie along the stage. Everything that I now see appears extremely vague; subtle blurs within the darkened mist, as I slowly slip off my sandals and step forward.

With my nine millimeter holstered, I cautiously creep towards the end of the stage, feeling my surroundings with both hands. Whatever calm I maintained has now diminished, as I try to tread lightly in hopes of going unnoticed. With a bit of luck there'll be another hallway at the other end of the stage, and with it, an exit.

The sounds of the undead eating are more noticeable than ever, and by the sounds of it, there must be many. Suddenly, my right foot slips into something hard yet moist. Its texture is stout and bears fragments of God knows what in-between my toes. I tell myself that it's just some jelly that I stepped on. Knowing all too well that it's not, I try to regain focus and refrain from vomiting.

Then it all comes to a head.

With one step forward all my efforts of discretion become spoiled, as I slip and fall hard on the ground. My outreached hand brushes across some guitar strings, causing the instrument to fall along with a few other shadowy objects.

Loud cracks and slams, along with the strum of the guitar cause me to panic and run towards the opposite side of the stage, which to my dismay, has no exit.

With my back against the wall, I cover my mouth with both hands to keep hidden, as I now listen to the undead scream.

I can hear them scurrying around the floor, confused and amidst search, along with the ones on the balcony above. Their cries echo and intensify within the venue, seeming more terrifying than before as I slowly move to my right.

My movements are put to a halt as my head suddenly hits something metal attached to the wall. As I try to focus on what I hope to be a circuit breaker near my head, I become drawn towards the sound of something climbing the stage.

My fear takes over as I watch a dark figure stagger its way up ahead. Now barely able to make out its shadowy features, its body sways from side to side as its fingers run across the keys of a nearby piano.

I desperately feel for the switches on the circuit breaker with my right hand, which to my surprise, I find.

Suddenly the horrid smell of decaying flesh hits me again, as I hold my breath and mouth with my left hand and come face to face with the undead. Its hot rancid breath hits me in waves with each pant it takes, which I can tell is much taller than me as its shadow looms over my head.

Seconds seem to last decades as it continues to stare, all the while my leg fidgets as I fight to hold my breath. With its hands against the wall and slightly above my head, I tremble at its closeness.

My will is now broken as it begins smelling my hair. Its body stands inches from pressing against mine, as the fear of fainting causes me to hold on a bit longer. I tighten and clench my neck so as not to have it twitch as I'm now in desperate need of air. The feeling of which becomes unbearable, even more so as I begin to feel and smell the decaying tongue of the undead.

Its moisture is cold and presses firmly against my left temple, slowly dragging itself along my cheek and flicking the tip of my earlobe. My disgust holds no bounds as it now slithers its way into the dark reaches of my ear.

While nearing the brink of passing out, I desperately gasp for air and shove the undead away. The darkness does little to help my cause, yet my hearing tells me that it falls on its back. With my position now made, I quickly flip the switches on the circuit breaker and shed light to the venue.

Brightness shines and blinds me as all the lights and audio devices turn on. My vision, although obscured, slowly pieces together while The Smiths "Sweet and Tender Hooligan" begins to play. The seven undead scattered throughout the floor of the venue become instantly drawn to my presence. Their intent ever so clear, as the one I shoved on the stage earlier finally gets up.

I waste no time as I quickly grab a keyboard off its stand to my left and swing it at the undead before me. The sound of the keys getting smashed across its face vibrate through some nearby speakers, creating a muffled yet static like noise. Its impact causes the undead to fall off the stage and join the others, as I now pull out my nine millimeter and open fire.

While slowly making my way towards the edge of the stage, I reluctantly blast through my hesitation. I manage to take down the two that draw near, as the first shots I fire miss, I follow up with two more that pierce their skulls.

I try to refrain from panicking as the undead rush towards me, their eyes red and bulging with rage. My mind reacts as I now take a deep breath, and aim for their legs.

By the time I cripple one of them with two shots to its knee; another suddenly reaches out and climbs the stage. With the benefit of having the high ground, I use my left leg and kick it back down while pulling out my forty-five millimeter.

The undead are persistent.

The four below me continue to reach out and attempt to climb the stage, as I now rapidly fire upon them with both guns. Each shot I take pushes me further away from death, and after taking one of them out while wounding the rest, I slowly back away and replace the empty clips in my guns.

With only a moment to catch my breath, I watch the two undead that I knocked off the stage earlier join the remaining three. All five of them now begin to climb the stage. Their approach, although relentless, drags on as I holster my nine millimeter and aim my forty-five with both hands.

With a twitch of my finger, I squeeze off two rounds directly through two of the undead's skulls and lay them to rest. The remaining three however, are now on the stage and advancing towards me. Their speed seems somewhat heightened as I once again pull out my nine millimeter, and rush to meet them.

While running I blindly fire at the undead, causing them to stagger as I push through and jump off the stage. Somehow along the way I manage to stall and weasel my way past them and gain some distance.

My jaw remains tense though I stand with both guns at my side, no longer aiming, yet surrounded by corpses. Even the hesitation I feel begins to fade, as I now wait patiently while the three undead drop from the stage.

They fidget and twitch as they move. All three of them walk along side each other while blood drips from the many bullet wounds on their bodies.

Yet they still smile.

The one in the middle looks down at me with a wider grin as it constantly licks its lips. My anger suddenly interrupts my patience, as I recognize the familiar height and wound on its face. Its cheek bears the indents of a keyboard's keys, which is that of the undead that tried to get fresh with me earlier.

With quick succession I fire a round from each gun through the heads of the undead that occupy its sides, their approach quickly put to an end while I cripple my initial target with two shots to its thigh. Now immobilized it falls to its knees, only inches away as I press my gun to its head.

We are now the same height, the undead and I. Blood pours around the barrel of my forty-five while its eyes widen as I shove my gun in its mouth. My eyes, however, twitch at the sight and sound of its teeth break and chip away. Yet the horror of it all does little to stop me, as I twist the barrel further in, and pull the trigger.

Blood splatters the floor that the undead lies lifeless upon, as I wipe the stains off my gun and holster it away. I take a deep breath and relax my jaw after seeing that I came out of this fight alive. The smell of blood and death surrounds me as I now take in what I've just done, and light a smoke.

Soon the harmonic sounds of The Smiths end as the track changes within the venue, and I suddenly become startled by a glass pint shattering near my foot. I look up towards the balcony but I'm forced to duck and dodge another incoming glass.

While turning away, I stare at the undead that linger above.

The upper level of Zeke's remains littered with them, ten from what I can see, and not including however many tread on the stairwell. As I check my surroundings, I steadily inhale more nicotine while dodging the glass and debris that the undead throw at me.

Near the bar to the right side of the venue is a stairwell that leads towards the balcony above, while across lies another yet smaller bar. Behind me are the barricaded doors that lead towards the restaurant section of Zeke's. Their red frame lies darkened with blood which stands directly across from the stage.

After ensuring that the entrance to the stairwell is locked, I find relief with the extra time I have as I head back towards the stage. The undead above continue to scream and throw bottles at me. Their accuracy lessened with their decaying state, makes dodging them easier as I backtrack and slip on my green sandals.

Their eyes follow my every move as I wander below them, desperately scurrying to keep me in sight. Eventually I lead their gaze to the larger bar near the stairwell, as I now sit down to have a drink.

5:47 p.m. as I sit back with my feet propped on a bar stool and enjoy my pint. The taps here have yet to run dry, such that I did not hesitate to fill my glass with my favorite dark beer. The small canopy above the bar prevents the undead from throwing objects at me. Its limited amount of cover, however small, provides me with a sense of safety and puts me at ease.

My body still shivers at the sight of the undead I just killed. Although many, it comes down to the one that I rearranged with the barrel of my gun. For I can still feel its tongue run along the side of my face, as I light up another cigarette and indulge in my drink.

6:17 p.m. and there are now two empty glasses on the bar near me. The undead have become restless, occasionally jumping from the balcony and breaking their legs. Three of them made this attempt while I was drinking and ended up eating rounds from my nine millimeter. I begin pouring my fifth pint from the bar's tap only to find myself swaying from side to side.

I wish I had some more cocaine.

The subtle craving lingers even though I tell myself that it won't help me sleep tonight.

I suddenly feel more fluid as my intoxication creeps up on me, bringing a slight haze to my vision as I stumble towards the entrance to the restaurant.

The screams behind me are now muffled and distant as I remove the barricade. Broken chairs and tables lie stacked upon each other which make up the blockade that I pull apart. Soon the cool ocean breeze from outside flows within the venue as I free and open the double doors. Its chill is crisp and welcoming, which quickly sharpens my vision and brings me to focus.

I slowly turn back and glare at the undead above, their screams somewhat louder as if able to read my intentions. The thought of finally making my escape gives me comfort, however leaving the undead alive does not. I fear the risk of them overwhelming me at night.

I have no choice but to take them out.

From within the bar I begin to grab and throw bottles of liquor at the undead above. The splash of booze and shattered glass causes them to scatter. I hate the sound of their cries yet I continue to pour alcohol throughout Zeke's, saturating its venue and restaurant to ensure that it will go up in flames.

My surroundings now reek of booze, gunpowder, and death. Its combination feels strange to me, as I finish my pint and prepare my leave. With the last bottle of vodka left, I douse a nearby rag in alcohol and shove it back in the bottle.

I light myself another cigarette along with the rag.

Its flame quickly catches as I watch my makeshift Molotov glow while The Misfits "Last Caress" begins to play.

My double vision soon becomes one as I lock eyes with an undead above and hurl my bottle at it. The flaming cocktail bomb spins quickly through the air and breaks upon its chest, instantly setting it ablaze. It runs hysterically while screaming, spreading flames throughout the upper level of the venue until it falls over the edge of the balcony and hits the floor.

Its flames rapidly erupt and begin to surround me, forcing my legs to now run and make my escape. The intense heat follows me closely and catches my heels. Its sting licks upon my bear feet while melting away the soles of my green sandals.

Fire burns... and with it comes its spread and imminent chase.

Once outside, I let the cigarette fall from my lips as I bend down to relieve my exhaustion. I now realize how close I got to being trapped in the fires. The thought of which seems frightening, as I don't know which could be worse, being burned or eaten alive.

With my recovery I move towards the beach and sit upon its sands. My fatigue, although lingering, bears little importance as I watch the flames dance. I take a drag from my smoke and smile at how I can still hear the music play, along with the slight hint of the undead's screams. Small explosions continue to spew from within Zeke's Bar and Grill. Their arrival becomes less frequent, as the fires burn brighter and light up the boardwalk from the night sky.

7:10 p.m. and the fire rages on. Although the music has stopped, the screams that echo within have only intensified.

While taking in the sight, I light up one of my joints and feel my body give way as I inhale its smooth high. The fire distracts me during my dreamlike state, as I now begin to feel myself blend within the sand. A part of me wonders if the flames will attract the undead, and if I unintentionally screwed myself over. The thought of which I take in stride, for I rather bask in my small victory.

I remain seated while watching the inferno, exhausted, stoned, drunk, and lonely. Eventually their mixture begins to grow on me and make me tired. It brings about a need for rest as I now walk back towards my truck.

The heat from the fires remains present while passing Gods and Ammo, and although faint, it still causes the back of my neck to sweat. I approach my truck and take notice to the undead that I dragged on the street earlier today. Its corpse has been picked clean by the seagulls, only bone and chucks of flesh now reside upon its body.

I discard my sandals which remain stained with blood, and after washing my feet, I begin to change. My shoes provide a much needed comfort after enduring my endeavors while bare footed. With the off chance of the boardwalk catching on fire, I feel it best to sleep on the beach tonight.

After putting on a poncho that my dad kept within his truck, I drive a few blocks along the boardwalk and park in front of Alfrado's

Sub Stop. The black and green poncho and nearby fires will help keep me warm at night, as I now make my way along the sand.

While trying not to stray far from where I parked, I begin to head towards a lifeguard tower that looms ahead. Its structure faces the ocean and is completely surrounded on all sides. Its stands are made of steel while the post itself is that of some type of plastic. Duplicate lifeguard towers run alongside the beach every mile or so, which will keep me well hidden from being attacked at night.

Once inside, I rest my head against my gym bag full of ammunition and stare out into the ocean. My eyes grow heavy as I light another cigarette, for the view of the stars and night sky above the dark ocean now dwindle my insomnia.

I place my nine millimeter on my lap to keep it close by, fearing the worst in preparation of resting. I do however feel well hidden and safer here as opposed to sleeping in my truck. The ocean air along with the sound of its waves sets the scene for the illumination of fire which reflects off the darkened water. It proves to be everything that I need.

My presence here is calming.

9:02 p.m. as I take the last few drags of my cigarette and struggle to fall asleep. The thought of my nightmare last night now causes me to fear my subconscious. I think to myself about how long this day dragged and what tomorrow will hold for me. Will every day from here on out seem longer than the last? Each day forcing me to live out an eternity.

The sight of the ocean grows dim as I let out a yawn and find myself slouching. I'm too lazy to see what time it is, let alone move. I've completely molded into the rigid comfort of the lifeguard tower, slowly fading into my fears as I shut my eyes, and finally fall asleep.

Day 3

10:29 a.m. and I awake to the sound of seagulls in the distance. A terrible feeling corrupts the lining of my throat as I now find it difficult to breathe. The sky is overcast and bears thick purple clouds which stretch beyond the ocean in front of me. The aroma of fire and ash now taint the fresh air that the beach once provided.

I jump off the lifeguard tower only to find myself collapse to the ground.

My body aches after my legs give way as I now to cough into the sand. Each of my limbs feels as though they weigh a ton, as I slowly pull myself up and begin dry heaving. While trying to clear my throat I instinctively throw up, as bits of phlegm, tar, and ash now splatter upon the white sand.

I must have slept through my alarm after constantly waking up throughout the night. My head is in a lot of pain, and I realize that breathing in the smoke from the fires all night must have taken its toll.

I stare at the sun which is slightly red from hiding behind the smoke and clouds, my gaze slowly trailing towards the ruins that was once Zeke's Bar and Grill. The fires seemed to have been contained within Zeke's, as the few buildings that stand by only suffer minor burns.

As I arrive at my truck, I sit upon its bed while lighting a smoke. Its taste is anything but sweet, and now heightens the thick film and softness felt on my teeth.

I then look up to see the undead approaching.

My headache and fatigue cause me to sigh with their inconvenience, as I toss my cigarette aside and pull out my nine millimeter. I immediately begin coughing again. Phlegm and ash continue to spew from my mouth after the cigarette worsened the soreness in my throat. I try to stop myself but I can't, for the spasms that cause me to gag now leave me vulnerable.

Four undead slowly advance down the street while the closest one approaches forty yards away. Their arrival couldn't come at a worse time.

I raise my nine millimeter with both hands and aim towards the nearest one, my chest now hiccupping from holding in coughs. The gun trembles within my grasp while trying to maintain focus. My hesitation remains limited to fear, as I clear my throat, swallow some phlegm, and open fire.

Suddenly, the loud sound of the gunshot sends a sharp pain throughout my skull, causing me to instantly fall to my knees. Its ringing pitch swirls in my head and forces me to drop my gun and cover my ears.

A sad attempt to block out the excruciating pain I feel.

The vibrations pulsing within my head nearly cause me to scream, yet I hold back as the undead draw near.

My ears begin to pop and the ringing soon fades after seeing that my initial shot missed. With the pain now tolerable, I quickly pull myself up and grab the fire axe from within my truck. Both hands curl tightly around its wooden handle as I walk towards the undead, my pace quickening to match their speed.

The bravest of the four is now dangerously close as I approach with confidence and swing. I wield my axe as if it's a sword, swiping it to my left with such speed that it surprises me. Its blade reaches out and slices through the undead's neck, causing its throat to split open and shed blood over my head. Within seconds it falls to its knees, its head hanging back and held by a strand of what remains of its neck.

I suddenly start coughing again, the adrenaline now overwhelming.

Unable to control my spasms, I bend down and unwillingly spit up more bile and ash.

The three undead that remain are equal distances apart and now only thirty yards away. Their stride quickens as they advance towards me. I try to force out my irritation by coughing more violently, for my sore throat leaves me exposed. The inconvenience of it all now reflects off the female undead that approaches.

My ears continue to pop as I pull myself up and panic at the proximity of her quick arrival. Feeling my opportunity escaping, I recklessly lift my axe and hurl it directly at her. Its red handle now a blur quickly spins in the air, gradually losing its height from initially aiming at her head.

To my surprise the axe connects with the undead. Its blade plunges deep in-between her breasts, causing blood to spew as she falls on her back. I look up to find the other undead, which also happens to be a woman, now only ten yards away and closing in fast.

With my weapon lying between us, I sprint towards the axe embedded in the undead's chest. Her attempt to grab me, although futile, proves distracting as I pry it from her body, leaving smears of blood along my jeans from boney hands and broken fingernails. I quickly stomp on her face as she then gives way, breaking flesh and cheekbones while moving on to the next.

We are now only a few feet apart, the undead and I. To which I use the force and leverage from pulling out my axe to swing it around bring it upon her head.

Blood slowly trickles along the wooden handle as my axe remains wedged halfway into the undead's face. Her body twitches for a few moments, only briefly until I see whatever life she had escape through her eyes, as she gradually goes limp.

While holding her body up, I watch her left eye protrude from her socket as I suddenly feel something tug on my leg. The undead I impaled earlier has now dragged her way to me. Her arrival is swift, given her recent wounds, as she prepares to bite my leg.

In a state of panic I kick her aside and desperately twist and pry away my axe.

Once free, blood flows in volumes as she collapses to the ground. My attention now drawn towards the one I failed to finish off.

With my blood soaked axe held high, I bring it down upon the undead, causing a streak of blood to stain the road from my downward swing. The blade cuts through her neck with ease, breaking bones and chipping the ground beneath her. My head however, continues to throb and sting at the sound of its steel hitting the asphalt.

A pain that is most unwelcoming.

My migraine consumes me as the last of the four undead approaches. Its faded image is that of a blur until I notice its small stature.

A ravenous young boy, no older than eleven or twelve, now sprints towards me. His dirty blonde hair covers most of his face yet sways as he runs. Only his bloodshot eyes are seen through his narrow yellow strands. Even at a distance I can hear his grunts and pants, similar to that of a rabid dog.

I have no choice but to put him down.

I position my axe so that its blade rests near my feet as I grip the end of its handle with my left hand. Its image is that of a sickle.

With my mind now clear I charge towards the undead, holding my axe back in preparation to strike. I begin to feel the urge to cough again as we close in on each other. Its timing proves to be a constant annoyance, as I'm forced to swallow it back down.

The boy's screams suddenly pierce my brain and make it feel as though it's bleeding, so much that I'm forced to block it out as I turn away and deliver an upwards swing with my axe. The blade effortlessly tears its way up his chest while meeting his chin, causing blood spray as he staggers back.

Blood slowly drips from the tip of my axe and onto the street as I now watch the boy. For a moment he stands with his back at an arch, the laceration up his torso steadily splitting open. The tips of his exposed ribs slowly conceal as he pulls himself forward, forcing more blood to spew out of his body.

We then lock eyes.

Our moment, however brief, seems to quickly fade as he attempts to scream, yet this time his cries are cut short as his jaw is now split open.

Again the boy tries to scream but only the gargling of blood is heard, along with the clicking sound of his severed jaw. Every attempt he makes causes more blood as well as teeth to fall on the ground. His body sways as he stands in place, desperately reaching for me as I pace around him.

Like a trained boxer I dance in a circle around the boy, his hindered movements giving me the advantage. I size him up while amidst strides, finding multiple openings as I chop away at his body with my axe.

The undead's blood is now the boy's blood, so much spilt for such a time spent.

10:47 a.m. and the undead is now terribly weakened. His body lies face first on the ground while hyperventilating, his shoulders shrugging with each rapid breath he takes. I watch the blood spread and seep from his chest as I slowly raise my axe high. His labored breathing swiftly put to an end by my sudden fit of rage.

With my axe lodged halfway into the back of his skull, the boy remains still, seeming far less threatening now that he no longer faces me.

I then close my eyes and take a moment to collect myself. My illness now apparent after all the excitement I've endured. My head refuses to stop throbbing as my throat feels as though I've swallowed a handful of razorblades. Its irritation is thick and its scratches remain deep.

While dragging my axe behind me I walk back to my truck, my pace now similar to how Jimmy's was two days ago. I begin to question if I did the right thing by letting him live. His past innocence, although not seen during his attack, made me unwilling to finish him off. Yet I had no problem hacking away at the young man I just killed.

As I arrive at my truck, I hastily drink some water while lighting another smoke, which I'm instantly forced to put out. Its initial drag causes me to cough and vomit again. My frustration is now heightened as I can no longer satisfy my cravings. Their occurrence, however frequent, makes me realize that today isn't going to be easy.

After starting my truck, I turn off my MP3 player to help with my headache, in hopes that the silence of the road might offer me comfort. I no longer feel the need to linger as I drive off. While approaching Shell Blvd, I take one last look at the ruins of Zeke's Bar and Grill. Smoke constantly creeps from its shambles while the hint of fire dwindles in the air.

There is nothing left for me here anymore. I got what I needed from Gods and Ammo which is all that matters. I can only hope that my escape goes unnoticed, for I'm now in desperate need of rest.

11:02 a.m. and I'm back on the freeway heading West. The fighting I've done has taken its toll on me and left my body weakened.

I recall spotting a hotel off the freeway yesterday, which will prove an ideal place for me to lay low. Finding shelter within its higher floors will help me rest easy without fear of being ambushed. But before any of that can happen, I must find a pharmacy in hopes of salvaging anything to overcome my sickness.

I continue westbound until I spot the hotel in the distance, and realize that I'm now in French Valley. The city seems well populated, a large mall lies near the hotel along with various fast food franchises and banks. All this tells me is that they're out there waiting for me. I must tread lightly if I'm to avoid the undead.

While making my way through the city I continue past the hotel, and in less than a block away, I stumble upon a grocery store. Below its sign hangs a large white banner which states "$5 Generic Prescriptions".

11:31 a.m. as I pull into the parking lot of Lucky's. For a moment I stop to witness the few undead that wander around the empty lot, currently unaware of my presence. All I want to do right now is to take some cough drops and a shower, for I don't have the energy or desire deal with these monsters.

That's all that I see them as now... nothing but monsters. I'll have to play it smart while their attention is drawn elsewhere, and take them out quickly with my truck.

With my windshield wipers on, I wash away the blood that sprays on my truck as I drive around and run over the scattered undead. The trail of blood that follows my tires soon comes to a halt as I pull up to the front of the grocery store.

While scanning my surroundings, I shut off the truck's engine and ensure that I've left no stragglers behind. All the driving, swerving, and sharp turns I took have left me nauseous again, as I now begin to vomit.

With my legs spread widely apart, I brace myself against my truck after nearly throwing up on my shoes. Each time I vomit I end up with a worse headache than before, and after ten minutes of puking, I finally stop. I take a deep breath and a few moments to relax, gargling water while arming myself with my axe.

My truck is now a darker red from being stained with the undead's blood. It stands littered with fragments of hair, clothing, and flesh, which remain stuck within the creases of its frame.

I now tremble at the thought of what terrors await for me inside.

My fear constantly builds, as I grip tightly around my axe and continue towards the store.

11:55 a.m. and I now stand before the entrance of Lucky's. Its automated doors seem to be broken, yet are open barely enough for me to squeeze through. Once inside, I immediately hear the groans and chewing sounds of the undead and crouch to stay hidden.

While scanning the area, I find that the only exit within the store is the one I came through, as well as the ten checkout stands before me. Beyond them are seventeen aisles filled with various goods, along with a produce section to the left side of the store.

I step gently along the white tile floor, keeping as low as possible as I slither between checkout stands. The sound of chewing leads me towards aisle thirteen which contains spices, as I'm suddenly forced to back up against a rack of gift cards.

While still crouched, I slowly peer through the aisle to find an undead on the floor with its face buried within a corpse. Its head twists and jerks within the body, tugging on organs while cracking bones with its teeth. The horrific sight becomes numb to me now, as my attention is soon drawn towards the pharmacy located behind it.

My intent is to play it smart and remain quiet, for the less attention I draw the better off I'll be. No time for heroics.

I stay low and sneak my way around near the produce section and brace up against the first checkout stand. My heart now beats out of my chest after getting by unnoticed.

As I peek around the corner, I watch an undead with its back towards me smell and grab at a pile of oranges. I grip my axe so that the base of the blade rests upon my right hand, and begin sneaking up behind it. Slow and light I make my footsteps, gradually making my way closer and closer to the undead. My body hesitates but my mind reacts as I now approach it, feeling the fear that I must unwillingly overcome.

An orange then falls from its hand as I swiftly pull back its hair and run the blade of my axe across its neck. Blood sprays on the pile of oranges in front of us, as the undead falls to its knees and attempts to scream. It is however, unable to make a sound, for I retain my grip on its hair which causes the slit on its throat to tear open. As it struggles,

I.carefully place my hands around its head and twist, making sure to stray from its mouth so as not to get bitten.

Its resistance comes to a halt at the snap of its neck breaking. Yet it still remains alive, nearly biting my finger off as I gently set its body on the floor. Its gaze is focused upon me as it begins to choke on its own blood, its body now paralyzed.

A blow to the head, although ideal, might draw too much attention. My options, however limited, hold no weight over me, for whatever threat the monster posed has now been severed.

While sneaking around the stands of fruits and vegetables, I quickly take notice to another undead. It as well remains distracted while feasting on a corpse, as I now draw near and hide behind a stand of melons. I keep low and wait patiently while enduring the wet and sloppy sounds it makes, slowly anticipating my moment to strike.

The stack of melons is now all that stands between us.

I suddenly hear the undead gasp for air as it abruptly stops eating and stands. While frightened, I press my axe against my chest and attempt to stay hidden, hoping that the melons obscure its vision.

I watch as it now stands looking over me, sniffing the air as if searching for something. Its head moves from side to side while scanning the area, as if aware of my presence, yet unable to see me below.

I now know that I will have to attack head-on with this one and make my initial strike count. My swing will have to be both swift and powerful if I intend to take it out quietly.

I wait and faintly hear the crackling sound of its mouth open as I make my move.

In one quick motion, I stand while swinging my axe to the left, causing it to thrust halfway into the undead's face. My eyes widen at the sight of the blade occupying the space between its ears while wedged alongside its mouth. Small subtle gasps for air are all that is heard as the undead fidgets against my axe, which I then begin to move away from the pile of melons.

While slowly sliding to my left, I hold the monster up with my axe as we move away from the stand. My fatigue now limits my strength and makes it difficult to support the weight, as I try to remain silent and avoiding hitting the melons.

The sudden urge to cough overwhelms me while setting its twitching body down, forcing me to lean against the axe embedded in its face. The undead, although unable to scream continues to struggle, to which I keep at bay by pressing my foot upon its neck.

Tears fill my eyes as I massage and rub my throat and am forced to swallow the urge to cough. Eventually I come to relax, regaining my wits as well as my focus which draw me to the undead below.

While pressing my shoe upon its neck, I apply enough pressure to keep it quiet as I twist on my axe. The slight cracks of its jaw breaking are subtle, yet still cause me to cringe. After eliminating any chance of it screaming, I slowly pull out my axe and tap it firmly upon its forehead. Like using a hammer, I gently pummel its skull until it cracks and its body goes limp.

A somewhat meek and refined way to meets ones end.

The sounds of the remaining undead in the distance now cause me to crouch as I recall hiding. I'm in no shape to take them all on at once, and must remain hidden if I'm to come out of this alive.

From the produce section I start to zigzag in-between aisles in hopes to sneak up on another undead. Unable to recall where exactly they lingered, I proceed cautiously. It isn't until I reach aisle seven, the chips and sodas section, that I stumble upon another.

As I peer inside I find the monster walking aimlessly towards me, its feet dragging with each sluggish step. I quickly press my back up against a stack of sodas to remain hidden, in hopes that the undead didn't catch my glance. While listening to its footsteps, I notice that they remain steady and realize that my cover is not blown.

Yet the sound of its pace draws closer and closer.

My fingers curl tightly around my axe as I wait for my moment to strike, once again anticipating my next move. Soon its steps begin to decrease while its dragging becomes more drawn out. A thick drop of sweat runs down my nose as I now feel its presence, not only by the smell of decaying flesh, but that of the sheer terror that overwhelms me.

While kneeling against the stack of sodas, I watch a shoe creep around the corner to my left. With its arrival, I quickly stand and raise my axe high, turning to face my enemy while bringing about my intent.

More blood showers the white tile floor as my axe now lies wedged within the undead's head. The blade rests vertically between its eyes, causing its face to split apart from using such force. Within moments it slowly fades from existence, gently falling to the ground with my undying support. Blood rapidly escapes from its wound as its eyes roll back after pulling the axe from its head.

A quick end followed by a deafening silence.

The sensation to cough suddenly builds up again. Its anticipation is that of a sneeze, as I bend down and fight to remain silent. It isn't until moments later that I manage to swallow the urge back down.

Being stealth is now proving more difficult than fighting the undead.

12:24 p.m. as I hold my axe with my right hand and move on to the next aisle. My sore throat now makes it difficult to breathe and remain hidden while journeying through the store. I begin to consider myself fortunate that so few undead occupy Lucky's as I approach aisle thirteen, for within it holds an array of canned goods along with a trail of blood. Its thick coat slightly elevates from the white tile floor, which coincidentally leads me towards the end of the aisle.

The pharmacy now lies directly ahead; its large red font hangs over a small white countertop. To my right stands the dairy section while to my left holds the meat and seafood department, where in which another undead lies.

My right eye squints as I focus on the monster along the meat section.

It stands facing away from me, hunched over while vigorously tearing apart packages of ground beef. Loud chews are heard as it continues to shove raw portions of meat in its mouth. From the looks of its attire, the two hundred pound undead must have once been the butcher of the store. Its white bloodstained apron hangs loosely by a single strap, along with a small white cap which rests behind its head.

I listen to it struggle in-between chews as its cheeks are full of ground beef.

It remains occupied, yet I tremble as I slowly creep alongside it, trying my best to keep clear of its peripheral vision.

The sight of its obesity is terrifying. Its ability to consume so much in such a short amount of time is most unsettling. I try to imagine myself being weightless, as if treading on clouds while carefully making my way closer.

Small portions of raw meat now fall to the ground as I draw near. Their chunks bring about a sense of disgust while I wait for the undead to stuff its face again. I seize my opportunity as it chokes on its own gluttony, using the distraction to see past my fear, and strike with my axe.

My strength, however, is not enough.

The axe tears through the fat and becomes lodged within the back of its skull.

Yet it still stands with my cover now blown.

My initial strike fails me as the undead suddenly turns and flails its arms. Its impact causes me to let go of my axe as I get knocked backwards while it gives chase. Such speed it has for its size seems to defy all logic as it now reaches out for me. Its fat sausage-like fingers graze my hair as I side step away, trying to use its width to my advantage. It's no use however, for its reach is too vast as it grabs a hold of the back of my leather jacket.

I come inches away from the axe embedded behind its head before it tosses me aside. My body hits the ground hard and slides across the floor as the undead follows, each step it takes causing the ground to now tremble.

I'm left with no choice but to pull out my nine millimeter and open fire.

My vision blurs and my mind disorientates with each round I send off.

The pain is without a doubt… excruciating.

I expel an entire clip in the undead's legs which now keep it at bay. My anguish soon heightened at the sound of its screams. Its roar echoes within the store and causes me to wince and drop my gun. The sound waves of its cries hinder my advance as I now stumble my way behind it.

Although crippled, the monster lashes out in anger as I grab hold of my axe. With my right foot pressed firmly against its back,

I frantically tug and pry away at the blade wedged behind its skull. Blood spurts and seeps along the top of its head once I free my weapon, and in one quick motion, I plunge it back into its cranium.

For safe measure, I rip my axe out and repeatedly bring it down upon its head.

Again and again I chop away at its skull, each time causing a thick layer of bone to crumble. Blood splatters upon me until I grow tired of hacking away at the undead, and with one final swing, I bury my axe within its gaping wound.

Silence now fills Lucky's as the giant no longer struggles, yet the pain in my head lingers as I kick its body away to free my axe.

The butcher now lies butchered within its own seeping blood, its mouth forever full of raw and decaying meat.

12:38 p.m. and to my right lies the pharmacy. My mind remains scrambled while desperately looking around for anymore undead. Relieved after seeing that I'm alone, I'm shocked at how none remain or rushed out of the aisles I failed to search.

With my back turned to the butcher, I finally release the cough that I've held in for so long. The built up phlegm that's accumulated in my throat now escapes and helps regulate my breathing.

While hunched over from dry heaving, I turn and stare at my nine millimeter that lies on the floor. I brace myself up with my axe by the time my throat settles, my movements now slow and frail from being tossed around.

Then I hear the screams.

Although my mind's not ready, my body reacts on instinct as I turn to face its source. A loud crash is suddenly heard as another undead rises from behind the pharmacy. Its rabid and feminine demeanor strengthens my poise, as she shoves a computer and cash register aside and rushes towards me.

Frightened, but more or less surprised, I immediately approach her while swinging my axe. Yet the female undead has speed, quickly evading my initial strike while following up with a lunge of its own.

I hit the ground hard on my back as I now come face to face with her.

I quickly hold my axe sideways to keep her at bay, eventually able gag her mouth within its handle. Her bloodshot eyes draw closer to mine as she continues to bite down on my axe, slowly chipping away teeth and accumulating saliva. Her white lab coat covers our bodies as she straddles upon me, and I soon begin to feel the pressure of her thighs squeeze tightly around my pelvis.

The undead now grinds vigorously against me, each powerful thrust forcing me to loosen the grip on my axe. She grunts heavily while in sync with her rapid rhythm, causing my strength to fail as I let up and watch her pull the axe from my hands.

Like a woman in sheer ecstasy she arches her back while tossing my weapon aside, pressing back and forth against me as she screams and moans. I seize the moment and pull out both my forty-five and magnum and open fire.

The sickness and violation of it all, ends with its inevitable climax.

A round from each gun now puts a stop to the undead pharmacist. The first of which enters her stomach while the second pierces her skull. Her body soon collapses on my chest, her hips slowly rubbing against mine until her rhythm finally dies off.

My eyes remain closed from the painful aftershock of firing both my guns. The sound caused by the higher caliber rounds produces a ringing pain which is far worse than before. I begin to feel my brain throb as if it had a heartbeat, to which each pulse forces my skull to crack from the pressure.

Blood seeps from the monster's head and trickles down my collarbone as I push her body away. She lies on her back while staring blankly at the ceiling, the name Sarah embroidered across her lab coat.

While still lying next to her, I holster away my guns and wait for my migraine to subside. My discomfort distracting me from what just happened between Sarah and I.

After a few minutes my headache becomes tolerable, as I slowly pull myself up and observe the undead I just put down. Both the butcher and pharmacist lie lifeless as I walk towards my nine millimeter and fire axe. My pace now quickening after acquiring my weapons.

As I approach the pharmacy, I immediately notice a rack of nonprescription medications that rest on the white countertop. While scanning its contents, I grab a bottle of Advil Extra Strength and scramble to get it open. No water is necessary, for I swallow the pills whole, in hopes of some instant migraine relief.

While continuing my search, I set multiple bags of cough drops aside, along with some Band-aids, Neosporin, and more Advil. Like a child during Halloween, I tear apart one of the bags of cough drops and stash a few in my pocket after eating one. My throat instantly feels at ease, more or less numb as I savor the cool breeze coursing down my mouth. Its feeling is that of a tiny blanket covering the many lacerations on my throat.

After taking a deep breath, I pull myself over the countertop and into the pharmacy, but am forced stop at a corpse lying on the floor. While slowly moving around it, I can't help but stare at the tear within its stomach, for its entrails are left exposed with what I believe to be its liver. I think of how Sarah must have been feeding on the body during my struggle with the butcher, which I carelessly overlooked before coughing. Yet another mistake that nearly cost me my life.

I now realize that I have to stay sharp if I'm to survive, and in order to do that, I need to get some rest.

With a nearby shopping basket I now raid the shelves of prescription drugs. The first ones I stock up on are antibiotics: Amoxicillin, Augmentin, Cefalexin, Clindamycin, and Tetracycline. I then move on to the other essential and recreational drugs: Prednisone, Valium, Oxycodine, Vicodin, Xanax, Adderall, Ambien, Dolophine, and Norco's.

Once finished, I climb out of the pharmacy and place the rest of my medication within the basket, and as I prepare my leave, I stumble upon a shopping cart near aisle fourteen.

While on my way out, I stroll through Lucky's and grab supplies while placing them within the cart. I make sure to take a case of Sprite to help with my throat, along with a vast variety of canned foods. Keeping breakfast in mind, I grab some bread and eggs which have yet to spoil, as well as some ham and bacon. A few flashlights and an abundance of batteries finish my shopping as I now approach the store's exit.

Everything I've endured makes this day seem extensive, and yet it is far from over.

1:03 p.m. and my head now feels better as I drink one of my Sprites. Its crisp carbonation awakens the numbness in my throat while chasing two Amoxicillin 500mg capsules. The beginning of a regiment that I can only hope sees me past my illness.

While leaning against my truck, I stare at the hotel that lies across from me. Its structure seems to hold only seven floors, yet I'd rather not imagine how many rooms it contains. Either way I'll have my work cut out for me, and the sooner I clear out the hotel, the sooner I can rest.

1:07 p.m. and I pull up to the front entrance of The Royal Resort. Its high class and blood splattered exterior is anything but welcoming.

As I enter the hotel, I see my way past its golden automated doors and catch the sound of a vacuum cleaner in the distance. The sound of which, although faint, grows obvious with my arrival.

With my bag of ammunition on the floor, I grip tightly around my axe and begin scanning the area. I now stand in a large lobby. In its center rests a tall fountain surrounded by love seats and sofas, all lingering below a giant swaying chandelier. To my left lies the check-in counter while to the right holds a restaurant and bar which remains locked. Their ends meet alongside two identical hallways that lead to the elevators and stairs.

I then spot a power cord stretching towards the hallway to my left as I approach its outlet and listen. The sound of the vacuum, although loud, is not consistent, but is that of someone moving it along the floor. Its black power cord trails along the ground while occasionally swaying from frequent tugs.

I begin to follow it against the wall, gradually making my way further until it eventually wraps around the corner of the hall. With my head slowly peeking out, I watch the undead pushing the vacuum look up and stare into my eyes.

Its hellish gaze instantly petrifies me.

An effect I thought I outgrew, yet I'm stuck while forced to endure its screams.

The undead's cries echo through the hallway and radiate with force as I stand to face it. Its light blue and white uniform makes me assume it was once a housekeeper.

My paralysis takes me by storm yet quickly fades as it now sprints towards me.

While holding my axe with my left hand, I grab a nearby decorative vase and hurl it at the undead. The white flower painted vase instantly shatters across its head, forcing it to stagger back and turn away.

Its screams now of a higher pitch cause me to react faster by moving in on my stunned foe. Although fast, it proves inferior to my reach as my axe drives itself into the left side of its head.

My clean swing causes it to stagger back again as I follow up on my assault.

While building momentum, I continue to swing relentlessly on the monster's face, each time forcing it to back away. Its jaw hangs by a thread of flesh, swaying loosely as I put an end to its suffering by bringing my axe down upon its head.

I now feel the small pieces of the broken vase crush beneath my shoes as I stare into the housekeeper's eyes. Blood covers its face and drips down on its white apron as it fidgets against the wall. Its dangling jaw sways with each spasm as I observe its many lacerations.

Eventually it stops twitching and lays silent.

The deafness of it all now complete, as I shut off vacuum that vibrates along the floor. My fear and anxiety also ended with the flip of a switch.

While searching its body, I come across an all access keycard that belongs to Deborah Monroe, which I claim as my own.

Poor Deborah, I think to myself. Her demise proved necessary for my well being, yet could have been done in a less vigorous manner. However I do not dwell on this, given my current state of affairs.

While back in my truck, I unload my camping bag along with some of the groceries I took from Lucky's, and after setting them inside, I look back at the exposed entrance to the hotel. Its opening, although not large, remains unsettling, as if inviting an ambush. The overhead that hangs over its golden doors is not held by any poles, which makes life easier as I park along the walkway.

With the front half of my truck now blocking the entrance to the hotel, I shut off its engine and shimmy my way out through the passenger door.

1:35 p.m. and while sitting on one of the sofas in the lobby, I begin to reload my guns. Ideally I'd rather not use my firearms, for my headaches are now numb and tolerable from the Advil. However, I'm unaware of what lies await for me so I feel it best to be prepared.

While hunched over the sofa I massage my head and clear my throat. The meds I've taken have helped, yet I still feel like shit. The feeling of fatigue and illness weighing over me will lead to my death if continue without rest.

After holstering my guns and placing their spare clips within my leather jacket, I begin my search and walk towards the hallway to my left.

I wait and watch the numbers above the elevator descend to the lobby.

I suppose I could always head straight to the penthouse suites without securing the floors, yet I don't feel comfortable with the possibility of getting ambushed.

Confirming my isolation is the only way I'll sleep tonight.

The subtle sound of a small bell goes off as I grip my axe and watch the elevator doors slide open. My eyes now appalled as I stand in horror at the sight of two female undead on the floor. Both of them lie half naked while chewing on each other's flesh and amidst grind.

They remain facing me as they continue to spoon.

The one closest has the arm of the undead behind stretched across her face as she bites into its forearm. Their bodies sway as the other wraps her legs around one before me, squeezing ever so tightly as she begins thrusting. Her hand suddenly squeezes the woman's exposed breast, slowly digging her nails into her flesh while pulling out portions of her shoulder.

I stop and listen to their moans as they both look up at me with bloodshot eyes and smile. The feeling of disgust overwhelms me, as I raise my axe high, and enter the elevator while its doors shut closely behind.

1:58 p.m. and the light stating that I've arrived on the first floor shines as the elevator doors now open. I walk out stained with fresh blood, leaving the remains of the two undead behind me. I don't even bother looking back at the blood splattered elevator as its doors slowly close. For within it holds the severed heads and limbs of the undead I spent hacking apart during my short ride here.

While calming my rage, I try to block out what I just did by sucking on a cough drops. The vivid imagery of my wrath now similar to that of the monsters I've killed.

I then make my way around the first floor to ensure that I'm alone, and to observe its layout. Its perimeter is that of a giant square with identical sets of elevators on either side.

Although I don't believe that the undead can open doors, I do recall the one that managed to get into my car two days ago. With that in mind I begin my search of the first floor, entering the first of many rooms to come.

2:29 p.m. as I return to the elevators after clearing the first floor. With my axe ready and expecting the worst, I now wait patiently for the lift to arrive. I'm relieved as the doors open to reveal the emptiness before me as I hastily make my way inside. The first floor of the hotel proved uneventful, for every room within bared signs of vacancy and desertion.

With my mind still feeling out of sorts, I lean up against the wall of the elevator and massage my head, desperately trying to fight my sense of nausea. A good start I figure, as my effortless search ended quickly, the notion of which gives me hope for the floors to come.

As my head rests against the cold steel of the elevator wall, I now warily stare as the numbers above ascend to the second floor. My dread seems limitless, for the fear I feel never ends and adds to my anxiety for what's yet to come.

3:25 p.m. and I'm back at the elevators after clearing the second and third floor. I must have searched well over two dozen rooms with no signs of the undead. With a little luck, I can only hope that my entire search will continue as such.

While anxiously waiting, I spit out the saliva that accumulates in my mouth, growing more and more impatient until the lift finally arrives.

As I approach the fourth floor, the elevator doors open to reveal an undead facing away from me. It stands while running with its hand against the wall, the sound of the elevator's bell instantly drawing its attention. Its tall and slender stature seems almost alien as it now turns to face me. The bellboy attire it wears is tattered and torn, splitting at the seams while its vest hangs loosely around its waist. An open wound occupies its left ear, spreading infection across its face as it stares and smiles.

Its bloodshot eyes remain fixed upon me as it stumbles down the narrow hall.

With my cough drop now diminished, I feel the sudden urge to gag as I'm forced spit out more saliva. The timing is such that it leaves me impaired, handicapped and grateful that there is only one undead.

Without hesitation, I pull my axe back and swing it across the undead's right knee, instantly causing it to shatter. Its hand arrives inches from my face as the blow causes it now to kneel before me.

The phlegm in my mouth builds as my saliva constantly keeps up.

Unable to keep myself from drooling, I spit on the monster's face while bringing the blade of my axe sideways upon its neck.

Skinny, filthy, bloody fingers scratch at my leather jacket and soon lose interest as the undead goes limp. Its demise followed closely by its head rolling on the floor, the force of my swing so powerful that it pins its body against the wall.

Small bits of dust and drywall now fly from where my axe was stuck after pulling it free. Its mist trails my movements as I continue my search of the fourth floor.

The first room I enter holds no signs of the undead, only the scattered personal belongings of its previous tenants. Each of the rooms I come across seem to share an identical layout, small and basic, which makes searching them a breeze.

Once finished, I make my way down the hallway to check the ones that remain, using Debora's keycard for unlimited access.

4:01 p.m. as I face the last room to be searched on the fourth floor. For a few moments I stand patiently at its entrance, watching a pool of blood creep from underneath its door. With my right ear pressed against its frame, I find myself listening to what sounds like static from a television within. After taking a moment to pop in another cough drop, I follow up with a deep breath, and carefully make my way inside.

Like the previous rooms I've searched, the heavy door in which I enter slowly shuts behind me. This time however, making me feel uneasy.

As I look around I can't help but feel the darkness loom above me, for unlike the other rooms, this one seems smaller. A hint of death lingers with the humidity in the air, causing my skin to now leak. The soles of my shoes become damp as the entire carpet is moistened by what appears to be blood.

A television at the far end of the room broadcasts static while shedding light to the darkness around me. Its sound, although slight, causes my head to pulse as I'm forced to shut it off. While turning away, I follow the peeking light that shines from the bathroom ahead. Its door slightly cracked open is anything but inviting.

I tread lightly as I make my approach towards the bathroom, each step causing more blood to seep in my shoes and dampen my socks. The sound of running water is heard as I open the door and stumble upon a flooded restroom. Its once attractive interior now tainted by my surroundings.

A pool of blood fills the white bathtub to my left. Its running faucet causes the blood within to spill throughout the floor. I stare into its void after shutting off the water and wait, unable to see what lies beneath all the blood.

Death holds many faces, yet whatever rests below will prove most unwelcoming.

With my axe in hand, I quickly distract myself and grab the newspaper that rests atop a nearby sink. I stand while facing away from the tub, taking the moments I need to scan the front page of the paper.

Terrorist Attack the United States! November 6, 2007.

That's when it all started.

As I continue reading I focus half my attention towards the mirror ahead, which now begins to show movement within the bathtub behind me.

Suddenly, a small slender hand slowly rises from the tub and latches on to its edge. Seconds later another hand appears. Its arrival seems prolonged with the steady rise of the head and shoulders of a woman.

I can hear the blood and water trickle down her naked body as I watch her reflection in the mirror. The young woman must have been in her twenties before she turned. Her shoulder length blonde hair is saturated with blood while parted down the middle. Her porcelain white skin is that of the bathtub she rests in, as I now watch the red trails of blood run down her long and slender legs.

Her intact and striking beauty does not distract me from the fact that she's an undead. It only takes away any satisfaction that I will have from killing her.

My hand grips tightly around my axe as she finally stands. Her large breasts stained with streaks of blood now expand with each breath she takes. I watch her bloodshot eyes widen as her mouth begins to stretch open. The blood that follows is that of a thicker texture. It pours like sap and continues to drip down her chest, which soon reveals the torn off portion from where her tongue use to be.

The grotesque sight is anything but attractive.

The sound of the undead gargling its own blood now causes me to break from my trance and make my move. While turning, I lift and bring my axe down upon her head, causing my newspaper to drop and float on the flooded floor. Blood overflows from the bathtub and creates small waves as she drops to her knees, twitching only slightly as she finally passes on.

She stares blankly into my eyes. Her expression that of disappointment as I pry out the axe plunged between her parted hair. She slowly begins to sink back into the bloody bathtub, her gaze ever focused upon me until she's no longer visible.

What a waste, I think to myself. What was once a thing of beauty is now forever lost within her porcelain tomb.

4:43 p.m. as I yet again wait for the elevator to arrive. After clearing the fifth floor which held no undead, I watch the elevator open to reveal the damp newspaper that I left behind.

As I ascend to the sixth floor, I begin to feel the effects of the Advil wear off, for my head now throbs harder than before. I anxiously wait while tapping my foot on the ground, dreading the thought of having to clear yet another part of the hotel.

Suddenly, my stomach turns as the feeling of imminent danger hits me. Its arrival comes in waves as the lights around me begin to flicker, a sensation now heightened with the elevator's hesitation to ascend.

Once I arrive, I become startled as the doors slide open to reveal the undead before me. All of them are scattered about the hallway, such that I'm unable to count how many there are. Their attention is now drawn to me by the subtle chime that the elevator gives off.

While panicked, I repeatedly press the button to shut the elevator doors. Its delay increases my desperation, as I count six undead rushing towards me. My confidence is consumed by terror as they approach, and I'm now left with no choice but to pull out my nine millimeter, and open fire.

My eyes are forced shut as each blast I give off causes my head to sting.

Louder and louder the ringing in my head becomes, eventually leading me against the wall of the elevator while unleashing rounds. The six undead, however, continue their advance, their screams now in unison as the doors slowly close inches away from their grasp.

All I can hear now is the sound of an empty clip overlapping the ringing in my ears. Its faint click is distant, yet apparent over the vibrations surrounding my skull. My body sinks to the floor as I sit while pressing my hands against my head. The agony seems everlasting, while the fear of it never ending causes me to scream.

The pain is unlike anything I've ever felt before. Worse than any hangover I've had, worse than any blow I've endured... worse than any losses I've suffered. My mind feels somewhat damaged and I'm surprised that I've been able to maintain focus while feeling this way. Let alone still be alive.

Phlegm and ash spews from my mouth as I begin coughing again, causing my brain to pulse with each uncontrollable hack. Its severing repetition slowly reopens the many lacerations in my throat. My spasms gradually subside once I reach the fifth floor. Their remnants leave the roof of my mouth raw as I grab my newspaper and exit the elevator.

I slowly regain my balance while walking down the empty floor, and I soon remember to replace the empty clip in my nine millimeter. I make it apparent to never underestimate my enemy, although from my experience so far, they are anything but clever. My plan is simple and is that to flank them, as I now make my way towards the second set of elevators on the fifth floor.

While waiting for their arrival, I pop in three Advil's which I regret not taking sooner. The familiar sound of the small bell going off breaks my hesitation, as I holster my nine millimeter and make my way inside.

If I remember the layout correctly, the elevator should bring me to the opposite side of the sixth floor, far from the group of undead.

My only concern is what lies await for me now.

As I wait for the elevator to rise, I clench tightly onto my axe and find myself accustomed to the inertia that the lift provides. Fueled by anger and the lingering pain in my head and throat, I now take a deep breath as the doors slide open.

In a state of fury, I sprint out the elevator and turn towards an undead to my left. The handicap of my fatigue proves no hindrance, as I use the element of surprise to hack it apart. Suddenly, two more undead advance behind me. Their arrival is quick as I look over my right shoulder and rush to meet them.

The narrow hallway has only enough space for them to run side by side as I now draw near. My rage gives me the energy I need as I jump towards them, swinging my axe across the undead to my right.

The force of my swing heavily lacerates its face, creating a deep wound that stretches from ear to ear. Blood sprays upon me as it twists and falls to the ground, instantly forcing the remaining undead to stagger back.

With the brief moment I have to regain my footing, I step forward, using my momentum to stomp on the monster below and crush its skull. I strike at the undead before me three times, each time bringing my axe upon its neck, each time causing more blood to spray upon me, until eventually its head tears from its body.

I now look down at the undead twitching below, its shattered face still caved in beneath my foot. Not much is left within its subtle animation. It lies breathless, as if capable of such a thing.

I waste no time as I lift my axe high and put an end to its struggles.

While running through the halls, I cautiously look behind me while I have energy to spare, quickly anticipating my next encounter. As I approach the elevators I initially took, I stop at the sight of the undead.

Four of them now stand waiting for me, all violently pounding and scratching at the door of the lift I was in earlier. Regardless of my recent actions, they remain oblivious to my arrival.

Blood drips from my hair and along the tip of my axe as I step out to greet them. They continue fighting amongst themselves while trying to get through the elevator, unaware of my presence until I stomp my foot to grab their attention.

The undead turn their heads and immediately huddle together, gaining space as they push each other away while rushing towards me. I keep my eyes focused on them while winding my axe back, pulling it far along my right side as I then hurl it towards them.

My head instantly turns as the blood along its edge streaks across my face.

While spinning sideways before me, its trajectory is quickly cut short as it impales an undead in the chest.

With my hands now free and the monsters staggered, I pull out my forty-five and magnum and take aim. My brain already stings with the anticipation of the hurt I'm about feel.

I relentlessly open fire, expelling bullets as fast as I can so as not to endure too much pain. Their numbers dwindle in a matter of seconds as they all meet their bitter end.

Silence now surrounds me as smoke slowly seeps from the barrels of my guns.

The four undead, now lifeless, fall on the ground, while at the same time I drop my guns and fall to my knees. With my jaw locked I snarl as I massage my head, desperately trying to ease the pain that the gunshots caused. For a few moments I'm suddenly left to my thoughts, staring down at my guns as I wait for my head to clear.

My craving for a cigarette now reaches its peak.

Within seconds, my brief moment of peace becomes interrupted by the sound of screams. One after another, doors begin to burst open from the rooms surrounding the floor, each time causing a loud bang to echo throughout the halls. The screams intensify as I hear the undead flood out of the rooms, the sound of their footsteps now drawing near.

There's no way in hell I can deal with this shit right now, my will is literally drained and I have yet to reload my guns. My fear causes my body to respond, forcing me to holster my guns and stand to grab my axe from the undead's chest on the floor.

I desperately press the button to call down the elevator as its doors finally open before me. The undead arrive as I make my way inside, their presence once again forcing me to backup against the elevator wall.

Just like before, they sprint towards me with outreached arms.

They approach screaming while only a few feet away, the sight of them slowly diminishing as the steel doors close before me.

5:29 p.m. as I arrive at the seventh floor. My head now in constant pain from all the madness I've endured. While dragging myself out of the elevator, I stop to observe my surroundings. The top floor of the hotel holds only six rooms which are all penthouse suites. Its hallways are slightly wider yet seem desolate, as if the entire floor was unoccupied by the hotel's recent tenants.

I claim the first suite I come across as my own, quickly making myself at home with the help of Debora's keycard. While still cautious, I observe the intact suite in all its luxury. A large living room with assorted couches lies before me. Its décor is sleek and matches the stainless steel appliances within the kitchen to my left.

I slowly tread past it all while carefully making my way towards the bedroom. For within it holds a white king size bed, its image ever so inviting as it waits patiently for my embrace.

As much as I need to lie down my urge to urinate takes precedence, to which I quickly head towards the bathroom to my right. A large porcelain bathtub and double headed shower rest nearby, along with the surrounding white marble tile and countertops that make the room seem brighter than it really is.

While back in the bedroom, I find solace within the bed as I throw myself upon it. Its pillows are soft and its sheets are smooth. Its feeling offers me bliss as I bask in the cool chill that its emptiness provides.

After a few moments, I pull myself up and head back towards the living room, walking past the furnishings while approaching the balcony that overlooks French Valley. The sun is still slightly red as it looms behind the clouds, slowly setting against the overcast sky. An empty city now spans before me, its streets naked with an unwelcoming silence.

I remain exhausted as I lean my body against the railing and light up a smoke. Its sticky and sour flavor hits my tongue with each drag, creating a film that latches onto the phlegm lingering in my throat. I soon become aggravated, crushing the cigarette within my hand while ignoring the pain it causes. My disappointment is expressed as I slowly let its remnants fall, stretching my palm out in dismay while watching the tiny embers burn away at my skin.

My relief and satisfaction now ruined by my bad habit.

5:46 p.m. and I'm back in the elevator heading down towards the lobby. In my mind I know that I should search the other penthouse suites, yet I find myself not caring. I feel confident that the undead on the sixth floor will remain there, but as for the seventh… I'll have to wait and see.

My stomach growls as I reach the lobby to find my bags where I left them, along with my truck still blocking the hotel's entrance. After loading my supplies in the elevator, I can't help but feel out of breath as I head back to the seventh floor yet again. Exhausted and feeling worse than I did this morning, I finally arrive back in my room.

Two Amoxicillin capsules rest in my mouth which I quickly chase down with one of my Sprites. Although the Advil helps with my headaches, a cigarette would do me much better. My frustration builds with my increased cravings as I now set my weapons aside. Near the front door my gun harness lies with my bag of ammunition, along with my blood encrusted axe which leans up against the wall.

After finishing my soda, I kick off my shoes while walking towards the bathroom. I slowly peel off the black shirt I wear, its fabric sticks to my skin from all the blood and sweat that saturates it. It doesn't take long until I'm completely nude and begin to feel lighter, as if all the stains and blood that covered my clothing were weighing me down.

Like yesterday, I stand in front of the mirror and faintly recognize my reflection, unable to comprehend what's causing me to question my appearance. Spots of dirt and blood now cover my naked body, as well as the ash that has smeared around my neck and arms. My hair has now crusted with the massive amounts of blood and sweat that I've endured. For every movement I make causes flakes of dirt and dry blood to fall on the bathroom floor.

Although my headache is slowly fading, my body remains extremely sore as I lean up against the sink. The rancid taste of vomit, phlegm, and ash has been difficult to stomach today, as the bile I've been excreting has now made my teeth raw.

A mixture of blood, ash, and toothpaste pours from my mouth and spirals down the sink's drain. Its collage of colors shows the variance of my struggles as I vigorously brush my teeth. No amount of flossing can rid me of the taste of death that I've nearly grown accustomed to.

6:11 p.m. as hot water runs from the shower and builds up steam. I stand staring at my reflection in the mirror, its gaze ever haunting while slightly unfamiliar. Three dry streaks of blood stretch across my face and span from my cheek to ear. My black hair now stained with blood hangs forward, making it seem darker than usual. Malnutrition while feeling ill has made my skin pale, for my lips remain raw and bleed from being chapped. My eyes are slightly red from irritation and exhaustion, their pupils dilate from my constant strain and fear.

Then it hits me, a sudden epiphany that causes me to snarl at the mirror.

My eyebrows hang low while anger forces my nostrils to flare. Its sensation fills my body as I now come to see the resemblance of the monsters I've been killing. Pain and rage is all that is seen in my eyes, the very same look of wrath and anguish that I stare into every time I kill an undead.

My hands ball into fists and I finally feel the burn of the cigarette I crushed in my hand. The steam around me slowly builds and begins to fog the mirror. Its haze conceals my counterpart as I turn away and step into the hot shower.

My muscles relax as hot water trickles down my body, rinsing off blood and dirt while causing it to spiral down the drain. Eventually my sinuses begin to clear. The steam from the hot shower alleviates my congestion as I wash my body with soap. The pain I feel causes me to flinch while detangling the crusted blood off my arms and chest.

For no matter how hard I try, no amount of strength or vigor can wash the hate off my body.

I will never succumb to the undead… let alone become one of them.

6:35 p.m. as I step out of the shower and dry myself off. I find myself feeling better with my cleanliness, uplifted, if not renewed. My head, however, still aches from feeling like shit and lack of food.

The white pair of boxer shorts I put on feel much better than the briefs I've been wearing for the past two days. Their looseness and fabric is soft against my skin, providing a nice sense of airflow as I head back towards the kitchen.

Now half naked, I proceed to pull out the groceries that I picked up from Lucky's earlier today. The suite is equipped with skillets and plates that I set aside to make my late breakfast. It again consists of two eggs, this time sunny side up, with five slices of bacon, one piece of ham, and two slices of toast.

Once finished, I sit upon the dining table in my underwear and indulge in my meal, overlooking my newspaper which has now dried.

The paper doesn't tell me much more than what Eric's letter did. Same old shit with the media, covering up the truth with propaganda of terrorism and biochemical weapons. It must have never occurred to people that perhaps the human race has run its course; that maybe this is what we get for taking our lives for granted. I obviously can't speak for everyone but maybe, just maybe, there is no explanation as to why this is all happening. Perhaps this is all a part of evolution, the final chapter in human existence.

I would give anything to see the newspaper headline read "The Dead Walk Among Us!", but I suppose that's too much to ask.

However, there is always the possibility that there wasn't enough time to admit the truth.

Where this all originated from is not stated, although it seems that the entire world became affected at around the same time. I suppose I should be grateful that the world's leaders didn't have enough time, or the balls, to nuke the hell out of everything.

The inevitable fate of what we all feared might come to pass; only now drawn from sheer terror and not terrorism.

I can only hope that some government officials remain tucked away in some underground bunker, strategizing a last attempt to rid the world of this filth.

Halfway through my meal, I read an article involving religious activists regarding the situation as "Hell on Earth". A photo of the Pope, priest, or pastor... one of which is shown alongside a dozen children within a lake, most likely the rape victims of the so called man of the cloth.

I've never been much for religion, but if I was I'd assume that we're all condemned to hell, and I have no idea how many Hail Marys will get me out of this predicament. Nor do I care.

7:17 p.m. and as I finish my meal, I pop in another cough drop. The craving for a cigarette hits me hard now that my stomach is full. Yet I know it won't do me any good, as I fight the urge and finish reading the headlines of arsonists and riots.

Darkness floods the sky as I once again stand on the balcony and overlook French Valley. Only a few streetlights remain lit within the city, which seems to provide a safe haven from the surrounding shadows. The half full moon is barely visible behind the clouds drifting up ahead, while the stars lingering above are no longer present. It's as if with all the wrong that is happening, they feel it unnecessary to grace me with their presence.

The night is cold as I stand with my arms crossed, now fully clothed in my brown Dickies, white undershirt, and leather jacket. The Ambien I took earlier is starting to make me feel tired, even more so while listening to the complete silence throughout the city below.

8:09 p.m. and I'm back at the dining table with my guns and ammunition laid out, my rounds now separated into groups. I grin at the abundance of bullets I have as I begin cleaning my guns, starting with my nine millimeter. A fair amount of sand and residue remains lodged within them, and after some experimenting, I figure out how to dismantle my magnum and forty-five.

My head begins to feel better and clearer by the time I finish loading my extra clips. The sound of their rounds snapping together quickly overlapped by my incessant yawns.

I now listen to my subconscious and slowly make my way back to the bedroom. My body instantly molds to the soft mattress of the king size bed, bringing me comfort as my tension gradually gives way.

Everything I've endured today has been for this very moment, the bed, the pillows, the sheets, all of which is my reward. A great feeling of satisfaction overwhelms me as I finally get to rest after another long day.

My eyes soon grow heavy as I lie on my side and look through the haze of my vision. I stare at the clock before me which resembles nothing short of a blur. The obscurity of it all brings me to the brink of unconsciousness, as I finally give in, and everything goes dark.

Smears of blood and dirt splatter across the ceiling above as I now lay on my back. Its sight brings about a sense of delusion while emphasizing the warmth and dampness on my head. As I run my fingers through my hair I begin to feel a wound on the top of my skull. Its opening remains jagged and its surroundings moist.

I sit up and instantly feel the rush of cold air flow through the hole underneath my chin. Its chill, although faint, causes blood to drip from my mouth. I feel weak yet strong as I finally manage to stand, my legs uneasy and similar to that of a newborn.

I'm dressed in the same clothing that I had on two days ago, only now completely stained in blood... my blood.

While looking around, I soon realize that I'm back in my brother's house, back in his dreaded bedroom. The only thing different is that his corpse is no longer present.

I slowly begin to lose feeling throughout my body.

A haze of red, thickened in mist, now drifts like a surrounding cloud and fills my vision. Within minutes I no longer feel the pain from the wound on my head and jaw, nor can I feel the breeze upon my face. Everything around me is tinted red as I unwillingly grind my teeth. The pressure from my whittled away enamel now causes me to succumb to my blinding rage.

I then abruptly turn towards the door which is slightly left open, my attention now drawn to the sounds of laughter.

Blood trails behind me as I stumble my way out of Eric's bedroom and down the hall. My brother's house is still filthy, and soon a muscle spasm causes me to quickly jerk and burst into the bathroom to my right.

Fragments of flesh and clotted blood now hang off the bottom of my chin, slowly revealing the bullet wound that exits the top of my head.

My mind no longer has power over my body.

It takes a will of its own as I'm forced to watch my reflection grin at me through the shattered mirror. Its intent remains unclear, yet sinister in its lustful gaze.

I turn away only to be drawn to the blood flowing down my left leg. Its sight bares the teeth marks from where the little girl bit me, as I now realize that I must be dreaming.

My eyes water as a tear trails down my face, cleaning off the blood and dirt on my skin as it reaches my chin. I've now completely lost myself, and in a fit of rage I suddenly scream and bash my head against the mirror, causing it to shatter.

I have no control over what I'm doing.

I'm now seeing red while watching myself run out of the bathroom and towards the living room. I then stop at the sight of my family eating at the dining table ahead. Their contentment and purity is anything but real.

More tears run down my face as I know all too well what will happen next, yet I'm unable to stop it.

The eyes on my mother and father's face widen as I rush over to my brother's back and grab onto his head. My nails dig deep into his flesh, piercing his skin while blood squirts out of the ten tiny punctures. I can't help but scream as I twist and break his neck, causing his head to now turn and face me. His final look of despair does nothing to stop my onslaught.

The terror expressed by my mother is unforgettable as I'm suddenly tackled by my father. His body pins me down as he restrains my arms, struggling to maintain dominance behind my mother's screams.

Soon his tears begin to rain upon me, his face suddenly pale at the sight of the wound underneath my chin. He hesitates and loosens his grip on my right hand, which I free and immediately shove in his mouth.

While holding onto his jaw, blood begins to drip from his lips as he bites down on my fingers. His desperation reaches new heights as he now tries his hardest to break free. It is however no use, for I no longer feel pain as I slowly pull his face towards mine.

His eyes tell the story of who he once was, a hardworking man, a loving husband, and a proud father. All of which stands for nothing, as I unwillingly pull myself forward and bite off his nose. His desperation quickly put to an end by the blood that follows, and his collapse to the floor.

By the time I stand my mother is already in the bathroom screaming. I listen to her frantically try to escape from the bathroom's window, but I know she can't.

My mouth now waters at the sight of Eric's corpse, his fresh cadaver and ripened flesh. The insatiable appetite proves too much for me as I begin feasting upon him. I ravenously start by tearing off portions of his shoulder. My teeth sink easily into his skin while causing me to relish my meal.

So much pleasure overcomes me as I continue to eat my brother, a hunger that at this moment can never be satisfied.

Within moments my father begins to twitch and rise from the floor. His nose now completely torn off sheds blood that covers the bottom half of his face. Without hesitation he shoves me aside and starts tearing through Eric's corpse, viciously pulling out organs while breaking off ribs.

I have no choice but to share.

The sound of my mother's screams now grabs my attention. It quickly pulls me away as I sprint while tripping over my father. More blood smears and paints the bathroom door as I continue to scream and pound upon it, and within seconds my father soon joins.

Over and over we smash against the door, each time echoed by screams until we finally breakthrough. I try my hardest to close my eyes as to not have her look of terror imprinted on me. But it's no use. There is no explaining the pain I feel as I now watch my father and I murder and tear her apart. Her screams fade away as more blood sprays upon us.

All the blood, all of her blood... then everything turns red.

Day 4

9:04 a.m. reads the clock near my bed as I awake in a state of panic. My body is now saturated with sweat as I lie exhausted and out of breath. While wiping away the dry tears that have crusted on my face, I begin to feel the dampness of the bed sheets upon my skin. The likes of which moisten my mind with the terrors I've constantly dreamt.

I look around to find myself still in the penthouse suite of The Royal Hotel. Relieved at my current reality, I lie back down and rest my head, thinking about the nightmare I just had. Eventually I finally decide to get out of bed. The clammy feeling of the sheets peeling off my skin is most sickening.

While standing I stretch and come to realize that my throat now feels better, that along with my headaches. Nevertheless, I sit down and take two Amoxicillin capsules with some water that I set aside last night.

Now unwilling to move, I stop to wonder what my dream was all about. Was it just a nightmare from feeling ill, or is there some meaning to it all? I saw myself kill my family, and even worse... I saw myself as an undead. It's as if I can still taste the flesh from my brother's corpse in my mouth. I'm in constant fear for my life yet it seems I should be more afraid of myself... of becoming one of them.

The dream seemed to have had some connection with the one I had three nights ago, which can't be a coincidence. But I don't dwell on this, considering how much better I feel today.

10:12 a.m. and I'm back out on the balcony after taking a shower. I now feel more comfortable in my brown Dickies and black undershirt, as I stand overlooking French Valley.

The sky is still cloudy and overcast with the same hint of red which makes it seem as though it's on fire. I feel stronger and more at ease, and although my sickness has yet to diminish, it is now manageable.

Nothing more Advil and cough drops won't fix.

While leaning against the railing of the balcony, I brace myself as I light up a cigarette. My brain instantly floods as I warily inhale the smoke, and I then crack a smile as I can finally enjoy my bad habit. My throat now only slightly irritated can tolerate the smoke without coughing up phlegm and tar. Although not as enjoyable as I would hope, I bask in the buzz that the sweet nicotine provides.

With my cigarette near its end, I grab my nine millimeter from the dining table and fire out towards the sky. To my surprise, the loud sound of the gunshot doesn't faze me one bit. No sharp pain, no headaches, only the startling shock from the blast that I forgot about after neglecting my guns.

10:43 a.m. as I finish eating some chicken noodle soup for breakfast. Its warm steamy broth keeps my lingering illness at bay, all the while providing a fair amount of sustenance.

I begin to pack my bags and prepare my leave, bringing them out one at a time to the elevators down the hall. With one final look around the suite, I slowly strap on my gun harness while heading out the door. But not before I pause to admire my brief sanctuary.

So much effort made to get here for such a small time spent.

My blood encrusted axe now stands leaned against the door with my leather jacket hanging off its handle. Proving too warm to wear today, I throw it over my left shoulder as I grab a hold of my trusty weapon.

The axe feels familiar in my hands.

So much blood we've shed together, and although I take it, I don't plan on using it. My firearms will now take way if I'm to run into anymore undead. I risked a lot by not using them yesterday, and yet I wonder if it would have been worse if I did.

The elevator ride down to the lobby seems longer than before as I bid farewell to The Royal Hotel. I'm done with this town and plan leaving it behind me. The remaining undead here are of little importance, however I will not hesitate to take out any that cross my path.

With my red truck still blocking the entrance to the hotel, I load up my bags and start up its engine. Taking caution not to overextend my stay, I waste no time as I punch on the gas and drive off.

What will today hold for me I wonder? Whatever it is couldn't possibly be as grueling as yesterday proved to be.

12:04 p.m. and I'm now at another gas station to refuel. My surroundings remain abandoned as stare at the trash littering the streets. Oddly enough, I've spent almost an hour driving around town with barely any signs of the undead, only the occasional few that I quickly disposed of with my truck.

As I look down Magnolia Avenue, I focus on an undead that approaches twenty yards away. I remain calm and slowly let up on the gas pump, anticipating its arrival as I now take aim. From a distance the shirtless undead rushes towards me, its tattoos spread across its body now scratched and smeared with blood.

With my aim focused, I fire two rounds from my nine millimeter, causing them to pierce the undead's legs and bring it to the ground. It lies face down while only a few feet away, blood trailing behind it as it slowly drags itself to me.

The name "Castellanos" is imprinted across its back. Its ink is surrounded by blood and dirt which covers the portrait of a phoenix.

I wait for it to get close before I remove the gas pump from my truck. With my shoe pressed against its head, I keep the undead at bay, stalling it momentarily before pouring gasoline upon it. It screams as I continue to bathe it in fuel, gradually washing away the blood off its body while saturating it in gas.

After replacing the gas pump, I light up another smoke and watch it struggle. Each attempt it makes to pull itself towards me is short lived as I kick it away, each time causing more of its ribs to break. While nearing the end of my smoke, I smile as I flick it at the undead and watch it combust in flames.

Its screams are music to my ears. No longer painful as I watch its body become engulfed in flames. Unfortunately I don't have time to enjoy watching it burn, though finding amusement in such a thing now seems less unsettling. My nerves only become shaken at the sight of the burning undead lying dangerously close to the gas pumps.

I quickly drive off in my truck, leaving the undead behind as I watch it roll around on fire through my rearview mirror. Although it is still very much alive, I made sure that it will suffer a long and painful end.

12:35 p.m. as I approach the freeway on-ramp that heads north. My intent is to make my way back to Sovereignty, my hometown, in an attempt to rid it of the undead. I then recall the city that I passed by on the way to Eric's house a few days ago. Its buildings lay in ruins while in flames, its streets scattered with the undead. With nothing left for me to do today, I figure it worthwhile to check it out.

One more stop until I'm back home, but what happens after that? The way I see it is that this nightmare started there and will eventually end there.

What happens after now seems... irrelevant.

1:13 p.m. and my truck comes to a screeching halt. I've now arrived at the ruined city of Corona, its smoke still bellowing from the streets below. The whiplash from my abrupt stop nearly causes me to head butt the steering wheel, as I slowly look up at the undead before me.

A hoard of monsters now floods the road ahead, creating a wall of flesh that steadily rushes my way. There's no way around them as I'm stopped at the suspended part of the freeway. My chest caves in as they run towards me, and it is then that I realize that there's no going back.

Within moments of my distraction, I take notice to another crowd of undead develop behind me. Their arrival is ever so quick as I watch them funnel up the on-ramp.

There has to be hundreds of these things surrounding me, all of them quickly advancing their way closer. I'm trapped and I cannot win this fight, for there are too many of them. Trying to run them over would now be futile, and I will not die by these monsters... not today.

My truck remains stuck the middle of the three lane freeway, as I now blend in with the abandoned cars around me. To my right holds the road going south along with the spot I urinated off three days ago, while to my left holds a steep mountainside leading down towards the city.

As the undead surround me, I frantically place some essential supplies within my gym bag. A flashlight, pills, water, ammo, and smokes, along with whatever I can fit inside as I now pack it full. Soon the endless supply of undead arrive and press up against my truck, as dozens of faces pound and smear blood across my windows.

I'm now frightened.

The terror I feel outweighs any nightmare I've had. How I ended up here I do not know, or let alone how I will get out of this one alive.

My wits can only get me so far, yet I have to try.

I quickly strap on my gym bag and take hold of my axe. The screams from the hundreds of undead make it difficult to concentrate, as my truck slowly begins to sway from side to side. Its windows shielding me now crack in preparation to shatter while the monsters fight to breakthrough.

I have to act fast before they flip over my truck.

I have to make a run for it.

Without thinking, I immediately stomp on the gas pedal which causes my truck to pull forward, only slightly as it becomes blocked again by the crowd. My truck, now slightly lifted, rests upon a few of the undead, while the force of its acceleration causes the ones surrounding me to back away. With only a few seconds to spare, I burst open my door and begin to quickly climb my truck.

Once atop, I stand holding my axe while overlooking my surroundings. Hundreds upon hundreds of undead now flood the freeway; all of which form their way around the wrecked and abandoned cars on the road.

Within moments of scaling my truck they begin to climb and reach out for me. Their bloodshot eyes share a constant gaze, along with the sound of their screams that echo off the mountainside. I feel more trapped than ever now, and after fending off two undead with my axe, I take notice to the wrecked cars nearby.

Without a second to think or hesitate, I jump towards a crashed Honda that lies sideways a few feet away. I manage to clear the jump while landing on its passenger side door, using my axe as a sort of balance beam as I sway from one leg to another, fighting to gain my footing.

A multitude of torn and bloody arms reach out and graze me as I'm now closer to the undead. They grab and pull on my pants as I kick them away, fighting the urge to look down until I spot the cars ahead.

My eyes widen at the distance I'll have to cover next.

The two compact cars that seemed to have crashed into each other are roughly ten feet away, while beyond lies the edge of the freeway. I dance for a few moments atop the shifting Honda, taking caution to watch my footing as I step back and leap towards the two cars ahead.

The weight of my gym bag along with my axe impairs my distance as I soar over the undead. I can't help but feel that time has suddenly slowed down again. Steadily drifting over the monsters below, I then feel the hand of one of them grab onto my pants and pull. Its sudden force causes me to instantly fall forward, breaking my flight as I hit the hood of the car before me with my chin.

I cry out in pain.

My delusion conflicts with my reflexes, as I desperately pull myself onto the hood of the blue compact. While now disorientated, I turn around and become pulled by the many hands of the undead. Their mouths hang open as they prepare to indulge on my legs.

I panic and desperately kick away at the crowd. What should be my life flashing before me is suddenly tainted by the vivid imagery of my death.

I fight to pull myself to escape but there are too many.

The amount of undead is too vast.

I quickly come to my senses and pull out my nine millimeter and fire blindly at the undead. Their sheer mass hinders any chance of accuracy as I expel rounds towards my legs. I kick like a child until I empty the clip in my gun, finding relief with the sudden release of the monster's grasp.

As I stand on the hood of the car, I'm put to a stop by a sharp pain coursing up my left leg. Its piercing sensation rushes my body and brings me to my knees. I block out the pain as I manage to get back on my feet, and attempt to ignore the blood now dripping from my leg.

While holstering my nine millimeter, I turn to face the edge of the freeway which resides along the mountainside. Its steep drop seems painful and uninviting, yet far better than the alternative.

I can sense the undead behind me atop the car after throwing my bag and axe over the freeway's edge. Its presence is familiar to me, to which I turn with my magnum upon its face and fire.

The small shockwave from the blast causes the pain on my leg to throb as the undead flies back into the crowd. While on the verge of my leg giving out again, I waste no time as I limp across the collided cars, and throw myself over the edge of the freeway.

My body now flies over the lingering undead and turns inward as they rush along the freeway's edge. I can't help but feel the slow motion again as I remain airborne, most likely due to the anticipation of my upcoming impact.

More pain inflicts upon me as my back smashes against the jagged mountainside. Its sting is severe and rough as I begin to roll down its steep hill. A multitude of rocks, bushes, and branches repeatedly bash against my body as I roll sixty feet down. The continuous pain prevents me from protecting my head and limbs, as I eventually topple my down and end up face first on the ground.

1:31 p.m. as I awake to find my face buried in dirt and in excruciating pain. My body feels damaged as I slowly pull myself up, for the ache I endure now intensifies with each joint that bends. I'm relieved to see that nothing seems broken other than my pride, which in reality, no longer amounts to anything.

My axe and gym bag lie a few feet away as my leg suddenly gives out and I collapse to the ground. Its blood continues to seep through my pants as I sit and examine my leg.

A three inch flesh wound runs deep along the right side of my calf. Its shock is unlike any wound I've endured, to which I soon panic while trying to find something to stop the bleeding.

My attention becomes drawn towards the crowd of undead that stares at me from the freeway above. Their screams still reflect and radiate off the mountainside behind me. With nothing left for me to bandage my leg, I bite down and tear the bottom portion of my black undershirt.

While wrapping the tattered strip of cotton around my left leg, I'm forced to stagger back as an undead suddenly falls from the freeway above. Its body hits the ground hard and lands ten feet away from me. Shocked by their persistence, I grunt in pain as I tighten the wrap firmly around my calf.

The undead ahead of me now lies on its back, both its femur bones protruding from its thighs as it struggles to turn over. I continue to watch it while relishing the brief moments I have to catch my breath. Eventually, it slowly begins to drag itself towards me, its exposed bones scraping along the gravel now causing me to cringe.

My body continues to throb in pain, such that I would welcome the discomfort I endured yesterday. Though I should be grateful that my mind remains clear, I still suffer from my lingering ailments. Along with the cause of my wound still in question, I find that my survival now seems bleak.

By the time I pull myself up and strap on my gym bag, I look up as the screams intensify. Such horrors I've never thought imaginable than to watch the undead fall from the freeway above. One by one they drop while crashing to the ground, breaking limbs and skulls along with the earth beneath them.

I run towards the ruined city ahead as the undead rain from the sky. Their screams remain constant during their plummet, yet fall silent as they hit the ground. I continue to limp my way forward, dodging the bodies that fall upon me until I reach the shadow of the freeway above.

The pain from my leg now pulses as the numerous undead that are able to walk from their plummet advance towards me. They gradually gain speed while those that cannot simply drag their bodies and fall behind. My pace decreases as I near the city and become cut off by more undead. Their bodies arrive in clumps and continue to drop from the opposite side of the freeway ahead.

Eventually I spot Sixth Street, a long stretch of road which spans before me while surrounded by smoldering buildings. By the time I make a break for it, the undead behind me are at full chase.

Dozens of them lie broken along my path, all struggling to get up while reaching out for me. The sound of their skulls crushing is heard. Each crunch carries my feet forward, as I relentlessly stomp upon them while limping my way towards the city.

With my forty-five in hand, I stumble down Sixth Street while the hoard of undead closely follows. The wound on my leg causes me to slow down as they give chase, with now only twenty yards standing between us.

I continue to run for what seems like ten minutes until I come across Ermitage Lane, a small alleyway to my left to which I proceed towards. The alley is dark and narrow with two large apartment buildings surrounding its sides. Splashes are heard as my feet stomp along puddles on the ground, and I soon turn back to see that I've lost the undead.

Before me lies the many dumpsters that occupy Ermitage Lane. Their stained and yellow coloring shines as a safe haven as I approach the nearest one. Swarms of flies escape from within as I lift its hood to reveal the grotesque amount of maggots that dwell inside.

I stifle the vomit back down my throat as the putrid smell of garbage is that of the undead's flesh. Before I can even attempt to climb inside, an undead suddenly falls from the rooftop above and onto the dumpster, forcing its lid to slam shut on my hand.

I scream as its weight now presses the cover on my left hand, causing a sharp pain to instantly course through my fingers. Within moments it drops to its knees and grabs onto my shoulders. Each movement it makes now causing my fingers to crack while inflicting unbearable pain.

With my right hand still free, I swing my forty-five millimeter across the undead's face. The agony I feel guides my hand as I hit it again and again. Each pistol whip forces its head to turn right, while each time it slowly looks back and smiles.

Soon the left side of its jaw becomes exposed.

Blood steadily drips from its mouth and onto my hand which remains wedged underneath the dumpster's lid. The fear for my life outweighs the chance of letting this undead live, and with one final swing, I plant the barrel of my gun against its cheek and squeeze the trigger.

My hand is released and now throbs once the undead's body falls to the ground. It trembles along with my digits as I caress my hand to see that no wounds are present. All that is left is the brittleness of my now crushed joints.

The sound of the gunshot echoed throughout the alley and summoned the undead, as the hoard now arrives and begins to funnel their way inside. The undead I shot lies on the floor and twitches as blood pours from the side of its face. Its screams amplify within the alley followed by those of the ones that now approach.

I quickly holster my forty-five while picking up my axe and limp my way out of Ermitage Lane. The dread of it all bears weight on me, as I run from the undead yet again.

Forth Street now lies ahead as I turn right and continue down its path. Its asphalt remains stained with blood and corpses, along with a few undead that scatter about. My body feels fatigued as I begin to get lightheaded from losing blood. I now know that I can't keep running for very long, but I have to try.

I continue down Forth Street with the weight of my gym bag and axe bringing me down. The pain of it all brings me to new heights, as I can no longer carry on and prepare to make my last stand.

Then I see the church in the distance.

2:02 p.m. and the undead follow me by the hundreds. The further I go the closer they get while their screams now grow louder.

The castle-like church in the distance stands three stories tall. Its darkened atmosphere and looming shadows prove most sinister. The stone it's made of is old and falling apart while most of its windows remain boarded shut.

This less than inviting structure is my only way out, yet I push myself to keep running, in hopes that its doors remain unlocked.

The army of undead is now ten yards away and gaining fast. Their persistence seems limitless as I approach the church and open its double doors, narrowly escaping while closing them behind me.

While out of breath and with my hands pressed against the ten foot wooden doors, I kick down the small golden pegs below in hopes to keep them shut. Within seconds, the undead outside smash against the entrance and nearly cause it to break open. Their force and sudden impact catches me off guard while shoving me away.

A small beam of sunlight now blinds me as the doors crack open, yet remain shut by their pegs braced upon the ground. In an attempt to buy me some time, I push a nearby pew up against the church's entrance. The screeching sound of it dragging along the white marble floor seems to heighten the strain on my leg. My heart races and skips a beat with each bang caused by the undead outside, their continued attempts to breakthrough now forcing me to back away.

I bend down for a moment to apply pressure to my leg, feeling exhausted and weak, I then turn and become shocked at what lies before me. The overwhelming stench of death finally hits me as I gaze at a pile of corpses lying before the altar. Its mound of flesh glistens with the surrounding light, bringing about fear and despair to what was once a house of God.

Two long rows of pews stretch before me along with a red carpet leading towards the ten foot pile of bodies. My heart continues to race as I walk further away from the undead outside and more towards the altar ahead. The red carpet I tread on remains soaked in blood, squishing beneath my shoes with each step I take.

The inside of the church is large and bright. So bright that it's as if the nonexistent sun is penetrating through its roof. Its white marble floor rests chipped and stained with blood, bearing the tragic remnants of a past struggle. Numerous candles lie burned with their wicks depleted and long strands of wax hanging from their stands.

The decrepit smell of death is now intolerable, forcing me to stand away from the pile of bodies in order to keep from tearing. Men, women, and children, all dead lay stacked high with their limbs folded across each other. As if the neglect of their corpses has molded them together. Blood streaks along their bodies while flies mist around them, their final expressions are that of sheer terror.

I turn to the sound of the undead hitting the doors outside, its wood nearly breaking off its hinges as the pegs now begin to give way. In an attempt to keep them at bay, I reluctantly make my way towards the entrance and slide my axe in-between the handles of both doors.

A final act and means of escaping my impending fate that awaits outside.

2:23 p.m. and I remain lightheaded while sitting alongside a pew, my left leg now stretched out before me. My pants remain moistened with blood, my blood. Its fabric rests thickened on my skin as I roll them up and untie the bandage around my calf.

While clenching my teeth, I slowly peel the black strip of cotton from my wound and toss it aside. The three inch gash across my leg is too deep for comfort and will require sutures. It continues to bleed as I pull out one of the few bottles of water from my gym bag, along with my Vicodin and Amoxicillin.

After chasing the pills with some water, I pour the rest upon my wound. Its cold sensation floods the deep laceration and sends a sharp pain up my leg. The likes which burn as I wash away the small black strands of cotton stuck along my torn flesh.

Once clean of fabric and looking fresh, I tear apart a portion of satin from the foot stool below to use as a bandage. Lucky for me I'm already onboard with antibiotics, as I've upped my dosage to ensure that no infection contaminates my wound.

While keeping it snug to enforce pressure, I roll the purple strip of fabric three times around my calf before tightening it with a knot. Its pain causes me to inhale through my teeth, yet I'm relieved to see that blood no longer seeps through.

The continuous sound of the undead outside still startles me as I lay back and light up a cigarette. Panic hits me as I stare down at my leg while exhaling smoke, now coming to the realization of what might have caused my wound.

I'm not entirely sure how I got injured, and I begin to question if I shot myself by accident, or worse. It all happened so fast, being overwhelmed by the undead, proving that firing blindly towards my legs was undoubtedly unwise. The width and diameter of the wound however seems to have been caused by a nine millimeter round, its clean cut margins don't seem that of a bite.

At least that's what I keep telling myself, for all I know they finally got me.

There was so many of them on the freeway that I couldn't focus, I should have been more prepared. Even if I did shoot myself by mistake, who's to say that some of their blood or saliva didn't enter my wound?

Not knowing how one turns into an undead only makes things more dire.

I keep replaying the scenario over in my head, reliving the terror as I watched the crowd of undead pull me off the hood of the car. I begin to wonder if I did in fact narrowly escape death, or if I'm now forced to wait for its arrival.

The wound on my leg is similar to that of the one I had in my nightmare three days ago. It all seems too familiar, too much of a coincidence. Which begs the question... how long do I have? I cannot die like this, I refuse to. I will not become one of them and will gladly kill myself if it comes to that.

My nicotine buzz now blends with the Vicodins which have finally kicked in, slowly mixing while putting my pain at ease.

I can't help but wonder what it will be like to turn undead.

Will it be like my nightmare? I can only hope that it doesn't as I recall the painful sensation I felt.

All I can do now is wait.

2:40 p.m. and the screams outside now intensify. I remain seated alongside the pew, chain smoking while waiting to turn undead. I've unfortunately come to realize that I'm left with no options but to simply see what happens.

The forty-five resting on my lap now waits patiently to end my life.

My suicide gun.

I feel hopeless and scared. In my mind I've already lost, wondering what the point of trying to survive is anymore.

For a few minutes, I sulk in my inevitable death until I hear the subtle sound of footsteps. My depression, along with the Vicodins must have blinded me from the undead behind me, as I now turn and am left with no time to react.

It wastes no time as it grabs me by the shirt and tosses me aside, causing me to fly ten feet away while knocking over three rows of pews. My head spins as the ringing in my ears overcomes my hearing again, slowing my progress as I pull myself up and focus on the undead. The mammoth three hundred pound clergyman has a muscular build to him and towers over me by at least a foot. Its white robe is tattered and smeared with blood, exposing the torn flesh beneath while a silver rosary hangs around its neck.

Now furious, yet delusional from hitting my head, I aggressively pull out my magnum while holding my forty-five and take aim.

My blasphemy hits me in more ways than one.

It guides my faith as I fire a shot from each gun.

Both rounds instantly miss the clergyman's head and connect with its neck and chest, leaving it unscathed as it continues to rush towards me. I quickly fire two more shots to its right leg which halts its approach, only briefly as I gain my footing and run away.

I feel the blood seep from my wound again as I stagger towards a flight of stairs. The undead follows closely behind me, sluggishly as we both now suffer from our lameness. Its screams push my body forward as I turn back and watch it give chase.

The crazed look in its eyes is that of death itself.

Its rage and anger made clear by the rows of pews it flips over with its advance.

It struggles halfway up the stairs once I reach the second level of the church, my surroundings now similar to below, although confined with limited seating. I quickly brace myself up against the wall near the stairway and wait. To my surprise, the giant undead runs past me and stands overlooking the balcony ahead. It stares down at the pile of bodies below, unaware of my presence as I now make my move.

I slowly step towards the giant undead, taking caution to remain silent as I place my forty-five upon the back of its head.

My faith now finally lost as I pull the trigger.

The gunshot roars throughout the church as blood shoots out of the monster's head, causing it to lean over the balcony's edge. I take a step back and prepare to fire again, but hesitate as it slowly turns to face me.

It somehow manages to pull itself up and stare down at me. Its body swaying from side to side causes the smoke to drift from the wound on its head. Blood soon follows and trickles down between its eyes as I watch it branch around its nose. The suspense is enough to make tensions flare, its build that of an impending lust without the climatic end.

I excrete my fear by firing off another round from my forty-five.

Again and again I fire upon its face, each time causing me to step back until I've reached five paces, and expelled my rounds.

The undead stands dazed with six shots plugged into its face.

Shocked by its perseverance, I rush forward and push it back towards the edge of the balcony.

The moment our bodies connect, I become caught within its grasps as we both tumble off the second floor. Blood drips from its disfigured face and rains upon me as we plummet twenty feet down.

My body now aches as I lie atop the lifeless undead. Its massive build along with the pews below ended up breaking my fall. I remain lying atop its body, out of breath and hyperventilating as my leg begins to throb.

Is it finally happening I wonder? Am I about to turn undead?

I start to panic at the thought of my wound being the result of a bite begins to cross my mind. I haven't the faintest idea of how it works, how one becomes an undead. All I'm left with is from what I've seen in films or heard in stories.

Within moments the pulsing from my leg subsides, and I hear the screams of the undead echo within the church. The sound of which is that of a stampede, forcing me to move and look for a place to hide. I'm left with no options as I now notice the mound of rotting flesh before me.

With my gym bag lying near the undead clergyman, I holster my guns and reluctantly limp towards the pile of corpses. The foul smell of the dead bodies is unbearable, yet I have no choice but to try and blend in. The ten foot high pile of death is tightly packed with bodies, such that I'm forced to quickly thrust myself in so as not to be seen.

While watching the second story above fill with the undead, I quietly shimmy my way into the mound of flesh. I leave my face exposed as it rests against a few of the corpses heads, their dead eyes now stare ahead as I try to mimic their gaze. The taste of rotting flesh exuding from the cadavers rolls off my tongue with each breath I take.

Soon my vision becomes hazy and my eyes water while staring at the gym bag ahead. My body, now moistened beneath the corpses, continues to make me nauseous as I grow lightheaded.

I vaguely watch the bottom level of the church fill with the undead, undoubtedly due to the many exits I failed to check when I arrived. I can only make out ten that walk aimlessly in front of me, along with the groans of many more that surround the pile of bodies.

This is by far the worst endeavor I've endured.

I'm now more frightened than ever, forced to assume that the undead will mistake me for the surrounding corpses.

Within minutes of hiding, I begin to feel sick while breathing alone becomes unbearable. The weight from the stack of bodies contorts my spine as I suffocate on the putrid smell around me. My dilemma now brings me to the brink of sanity, until eventually... everything goes dark.

My eyes open to reveal the gritty haze around me as I lie wedged within the pile of bodies. This time however, I am unable to move as I struggle to break free.

The undead that lingered within the church are now gone, where they went is unknown as I'm forced to endure the surrounding silence. My immobility causes me to panic, as I now find myself caught within the grasps of the corpses around me.

I can no longer feel the pain from my leg as well as the nausea that consumed me. Its strange development and release from my subtle torment, makes me realize that I must be dreaming.

Either that or I'm already dead.

Within my struggles, I stop as I faintly feel what I believe to be a hand coursing up my right leg. Its pressure is light and firm as it runs along my calf, causing heat to trail its path while it gradually works its way higher. I slowly feel its fingers curl around the inside of my thigh, squeezing tightly as another hand begins traveling up my left leg.

I begin panting and my breathing becomes heavy, unable to move as I now feel a multitude of hands upon my body.

The flicker of a cold tongue against my neck causes me to gasp.

Its familiar sensation is unwelcoming, as the trail of saliva that is left behind crystallizes on my skin.

My black shirt being pulled begins to tear as more fingers run along my torso.

Two cold and slimy hands travel up my chest and slowly run down over my stomach. Their jagged nails press softly on my skin as they reach my belt and hastily pull. Their impatience clearly shown as they frantically tug on my pants.

I steady my breathing to no avail, as I see the faces of the corpses around me begin to smile, no longer bearing the look of terror upon them. They intensely gaze into my eyes while working me over, patiently watching as if trying to get a rise out of me.

I continue struggling yet I'm unable to move, trapped underneath the weight of the many undead. Their hands and movements become more aggressive and rapid, eventually losing patience as they ravage and tear my clothing apart.

I wince while in my immobile state, now feeling the initial sting of chipped nails digging into my skin. The pain and agony I feel is beyond intolerable as they tear into my chest and thighs. The squeezing, licking, nibbling, and scratching, all coincides with the soft touch of the cold hands upon me.

Yet I'm unable to scream.

Part of me holds back from the pain the undead cause while the others continue to caress my body.

The fine line between pain and pleasure is now nonexistent.

While lifting my head, I watch the undead on top of me slowly raise her face up to mine. Her short black hair hangs over her left eye as she grins, our faces now only inches apart. Her bone structure is that of a unique quality which emphasizes her plump and luscious lips. What once could have been a striking girl is now reduced to a decrepit and less attractive state.

Her gaze is not of hunger but that of allure, and her smile stretches wide while saliva strings from her lips and touches mine.

The intense heat overwhelms me along with the pain.

Its effect stalls my breathing as I become aroused at the feel of being fondled.

She quickly pulls her face closer to mine. Her breath, although rancid, weighs heavy upon my lips. The undead surrounding me however continue their advance, digging their nails into my collarbone and shoulders while causing blood to trail my body. All the pain forces my throat to clear as I prepare to scream, but I'm cut off as the undead on top of me presses her lips against mine.

Her short black hair feels dry upon my cheek as she kisses me softly, her surge of intensity slowly building. Within moments, she quickens her lust along with the remaining undead. Their desire now driven while matched with my labored breaths.

Without giving any resistance she gradually meets her tongue with mine.

Its taste is metallic and that of blood, along with a grotesque and bitter tinge of decaying flesh. Regardless of its flavor, it doesn't come close to the ache I now feel.

I give in to the pain as I close my eyes and run my hand along her waist. Ashamed of my lust, yet unwilling to refuse as I find myself tearing off her rotting taste buds with my tongue.

More blood seeps from my body as the undead scratch open my back and stomach. The pain, although excruciating, seems slightly less with my arousal.

The undead kissing me suddenly slows down, only briefly to suck and pull on my bottom lip. Our heat causes my head to pull back in ecstasy as my breathing now trembles. All the pain and pleasure conflicting with each other now unwillingly brings me closer to the brink.

It all comes to an end as she suddenly bites down on my bottom lip. Its torturing sting causes my eyes to water as blood sprays upon us.

For all the bliss I felt is instantly taken, as my lip bursts open and I finally scream.

3:33 p.m. as I awake frightened while still buried within the pile of corpses. A stretch of vomit lies smeared alongside my jaw, crusted and now stuck upon my skin.

I'm starting to lose touch with reality.

Unable to fully cope with what's real or a dream, I begin to adhere to my surroundings. At first I hear the undead chewing and grunting in the distance. Their distraction makes me aware of their presence, as I feel more of them pull on the corpses that rest above.

The weight of the bodies that lie upon me has now greatly decreased. Its pressure remains nonexistent and livens my breathing as the undead feast on the mountain of flesh.

I remain silent and still, playing possum while the undead ahead have yet to notice my breaths.

The pile of corpses resting on top of me is rapidly getting smaller, such that I only have mere moments until they reach my body.

With my gym bag lying across from me from where I left it earlier, I observe the undead while planning my next move. I have no idea how many them surround me, but I have no choice but to act while I have the element of surprise.

The four undead ahead are too busy ravaging corpses to notice my movements, as I slowly shimmy and grab my nine millimeter and magnum. The entrance to the church is still closed and barricaded with my axe, and I soon realize that I'll have to find another way out. My heart races at the thought of underestimating the undead around me, a mistake I've made numerous times, yet fail to learn from.

I take a deep breath and get ready.

With only a few corpses now lying on me, I use all the strength I have to pull myself up while pointing my guns ahead. While rising, I push the bodies that rest upon me and cause them to fall onto the monsters behind. The abruptness of my actions catches them off guard and pins them to the ground.

Within seconds, I fire off a round from each gun into the heads of two undead before me, instantly causing them to drop to the floor. The recoil from my magnum proves too much for me to currently handle, as I quickly holster it away and fire at the undead to my right.

Three nine millimeter rounds dispose of the two monsters to my right, to which I turn to face another with outreached arms. As I near its embrace, I take a step back and pin it down with one shot to its leg. Its agonizing cries bear little remorse, and force my hand to end its life with a single round between its eyes.

The undead behind me now pull themselves up as I grab my gym bag and run. Their screams echo while I desperately limp towards a corridor to my left, banking away from the altar before me in hopes of finding an exit. My adrenaline masks the pain from my leg as I continue down the dimly lit hallway followed by the five undead.

Their cries a constant reminder of what is yet to come.

After gaining enough distance, I turn and aim my nine millimeter with both hands and prepare to fire. The narrow hallway crams the undead in as they rush towards me, single file which now makes for easy pickings.

With a deep breath I lock onto them and open fire, one by one causing four of them to drop and lay dormant. Only one remains as it stumbles over the bodies of its predecessors, and with the rounds in my nine millimeter now depleted, I pulled out my magnum and take aim.

I quickly let off two .357 rounds that penetrate the undead's chest and head, finally bringing it to its end. The intense recoil from aiming with one hand impairs my marksmanship, even more so with my body feeling weak.

I take a moment to catch my breath and replace the empty clips in my semi-automatics, along with the rounds in my magnum. Intentionally drawing out the time I have before continuing down the hallway.

As I reach the end of the dark and narrow path, I come to an opening and stop at the sight of confessional booths. The large marble room is enclosed with two rows of wooden booths that run along both sides. Each stands parallel to another while leading up towards an ascending hallway.

I can hear the sounds of moans and scratching surround me as I slowly walk down the rows, my anticipation building with an impending attack. Now growing impatient, I fire a shot blindly into the booth to my right, causing the undead behind me to jump out of hiding.

Its startling arrival is heard as it breaks out of its confessional booth and grabs a hold of my gun harness. It nearly sinks its teeth into my shoulder as I turn and break free from its grasp, and while too close for firing range, I deliver a straight kick to its chest which applies strain to my wound.

The pain fuels my intentions as I put an end to it with a shot to its pelvis and face. My emotions run wild with hesitation, and yet I ready my aim towards the booths before me as their doors suddenly break open.

The four undead that escape from within now rush to greet me, only to get gunned down with the rounds left in my nine millimeter.

A pathetic attempt to an almost effortless means of disposal.

The craving for a cigarette hits me hard as I replenish the rounds in my empty clip. Each bullet snapping into place coincides with each step I take. I can't help but notice my distractions from the death I inflict; all the while I walk down the white marble room which is now splattered with blood.

My pace quickens as I finally ascend the hallway and feel the cold breeze of air upon my face. A small wooden door is left ajar at the end of the hall, to which I lower my aim to cautiously peek outside.

Where I intend to go once I leave the church I do not know. All that matters now is that I'm alive and away from the dreaded pile of corpses.

4:13 p.m. and I see no signs of the undead through the crease in the door. All that lies ahead waiting for me is the bleak sunlight and a vacant street. The church no longer seems safe for there are too many entrances, too many opportunities to become trapped again.

I ready my aim as I open the door and walk outside, but gasp at the sight of the undead to my right. The crowd that wanders around the empty street before me is nearly as vast as the one that chased me here. Within moments of stepping outside, they immediately take notice and sprint towards me.

I have no choice but to run.

I now continue down Jefferson Avenue, running as fast as my leg can bear until I pass the church's entrance to my left. My legs suddenly buckle as I nearly trip at the sight of the hoard of undead greeting me by its doors. Their presence is all too familiar as they immediately give chase.

They now come at me from all sides.

The ones I evaded earlier eventually join the crowd behind me, creating a massive mob of monsters.

I'm no match for the speed of the undead.

Their mass in numbers seems limitless compared to solitary, as I occasionally turn and fire blindly towards the crowd.

The purple clouds above cover the dimly lit sun as I watch its darkness follow, covering the ground between the undead and I. Their endurance never ending as mine now begins to dwindle.

I run for what seems likes hours yet only minutes pass, fighting through the pain as my wound slowly tears open. Part of me feels that my attempt to escape is futile, that I should perhaps stop and put an end to my suffering. Another part of me however, gives me the strength to press on, fueling my stamina to maintain speed.

I run by a few scattered undead along my path, drawing their attention as they join the hoard behind me.

Their arrival brings my morale down to even lower depths.

All the buildings I pass by are either on fire or in ruins, as the smoke in the atmosphere now causes my throat to tingle. It seems my streak of luck has run its course as I desperately look for a means of escape. Yet the desolate town provides none.

There is nowhere left for me to hide.

4:28 p.m. and while on the brink of collapsing I run down Jefferson Avenue. The undead are now so close behind that I can almost feel their presence pushing me away. Like two positive sides of a magnet refusing to connect.

My breathing becomes heavy and raspy while in desperate need of rest, and my left leg now goes numb from the constant pain I feel. Blood saturates my pants and renders my bandage useless, bringing about the sudden fear of going into shock. My survival appears bleak as the hundreds of undead continue to chase after me; their persistence holds no bounds as they gradually draw near.

What started off as a thirty yard lead has now diminished to ten, and I soon find myself disappointed for prolonging my inevitable death. Suddenly, my desperation fades as I spot Orange Creek High School in the distance, home of the Bisons.

My legs now try to get me to run faster, pushing my will to survive as I sprint towards the school. A large football field lies ahead and beyond is the campus, its massive buildings and ruined structure is that of a prison. The gate entering the field is open yet I haven't the time to close it, for the undead closely follow with their ravenous intent.

As I reach the fifty yard line of the grassy field, I almost give up as my legs start to give way. My body feels broken beyond repair, and as I run I watch a smaller crowd of undead approach to my left.

They now surround me on all sides.

All seems lost until I notice the double doors leading towards the gymnasium ahead, and while hoping that they remain unlocked, I find the strength to press on.

The wound on my leg causes me to stumble as I run backwards and fire at the undead. Blindly shooting at the crowd now closing in, I skip backwards, clenching my jaw from the strain that each step takes.

No point in picking my shots anymore, no point in aiming. All I can do now is channel my pain through the barrel of my guns. I don't even bother counting my rounds anymore, for soon I will empty my clips and most likely be fucked.

I prepare for the bitter end while saving the rounds in my magnum to end my life, yet pause as I feel the doors to the gymnasium press against my back. While staring at the hoard of undead rushing towards me, I holster my forty-five and fumble my hand in search for the door's handle.

To my surprise the entrance is unlocked.

Its sanctuary gives me hope as I quickly crack it open and escape inside.

4:37 p.m. and my head rests on the door of the gymnasium as I brace myself against it. Unable to figure out how the doors lock, I now breathe rapidly while anticipating the undead's arrival. I can steadily feel the tension build, my fear increasing with the delay of their approach.

My jaw then drops as I turn to find an Olympic size pool spread out behind me.

I didn't notice it while entering the gym, I had no time, and this might be my only means of escape. Its calm blue surface seems inviting as I admire its length and depth. A tranquil sight that brings hope soon proves distracting as I'm suddenly startled by undead.

The force of the massive crowd outside almost knocks me down as they smash against the doors. While still maintaining my footing, I put all my strength and weight upon the doors to keep them shut. It's no use however, for I can soon feel my body give way as they slowly begin to push through.

Six monstrous hands now appear before me and curl their bloody fingers in-between the double doors. They slowly begin to pry them open, revealing their eyes as my arms now tremble from keeping them at bay.

I can only hope that the undead forgot how to swim.

Their numbers, although many, remain heightened by my many failures. Their wrath comes in waves as I stare at them one last time, and let go.

Within seconds of releasing pressure, I'm pushed back as the doors burst open followed closely by the swarm of undead. Their intent now emphasized by their heightened speed.

My body reacts instantly as I turn and run towards the pool.

With the undead only a few feet away, I drop my gym bag while pulling off my gun harness and t-shirt along the way, forcing the monsters to draw near as I throw myself into the water.

A sharp cold sensation fills my body as I slowly let myself sink deeper into the pool. Its feeling is that of a giant bowl of jagged ice cubes, in which every movement causes my skin to pinch and sting. The intense cold gradually fades as I float in the middle of my endless blue surroundings. My ears gently pop while sinking past the depths of ten feet.

For a moment I forget where I'm at and what's been happening. I simply let myself float underwater for what feels like hours. I bask in the color of its bright blue haze, only briefly until the blood from my leg forms a small cloud that courses its way up to the surface.

I follow its trail for I'm in need of air, pushing my way through the endless blue as I now notice the dark figures along the edge of the pool. Their shadows loom above and shed darkness to my once peaceful surroundings.

Small bubbles of air slowly escape my nostrils as I suddenly hear and watch the undead jump in the water. The first of which quickly sinks to the bottom of the pool, roughly ten feet below while unable to swim. The anger expressed on its face remains constant, as I stare down and watch it desperately try to rise.

One by one they jump in the pool and immediately sink past me, as if tethered by stones. A few of them manage to stay afloat, only briefly until their inevitable descent.

Their cries forever muffled by the surrounding water that now fills their lungs.

I now frantically swim towards the surface to get some air, all while the bodies of the undead continue to plummet like torpedoes. The blood trailing from my leg marks my path as I follow it all the way up, gasping for air as I cautiously scan my surroundings.

The undead all stand along the edge of the pool, throwing their bodies into the water while falling short of success. Over a hundred of them surround me as their numbers begin to dwindle. Not to mention however many struggle and reside within the depths below.

My teeth start to chatter as I stay afloat in the center of the pool, circling around while keeping a safe distance from the undead that join me. A cold breeze brushes across my face as my legs now grow tired from staying afloat. The fatigue I feel weighs heavily on me, as I take another deep breath and submerge underwater.

4:52 p.m. and the bottom of the pool is now full of undead, some of which attempt to swim up yet end up sinking moments later. I stay a safe distance above them while watching the remainder drop down like bombs.

My body continues to slightly ache, not only from the wound on my leg, but from my fall down the mountain and within the church. Not to mention my endless running. Yet the water helps as it no longer feels sharp or cold, only numb.

I now feel relaxed, and my mind drifts with the more I stare at the blood seeping from my leg. I can't help but wonder what it would feel like to drown. Does it hurt? How long it takes?

It would be so easy right now, to just not go up for air, and let myself die.

Bubbles now surround me and fill the pool as air escapes from the many undead below. It is unlike anything I've ever seen before, almost surreal. Their spheres of air instantly pop as more undead drop into the pool and sink below, their gaze ever upon me during their short descent.

I once again surface for air while evading the sinking undead, embracing the chill from outside the water as I now look around.

There are only five of them left alongside the pool. They hesitate momentarily, as I watch them closely and swim towards the water's edge. With my body still weak, I use the arm of a corpse lying nearby to pull myself out of the pool. Its weight anchors me down until I come to see that there are six undead left standing, not five.

The corpse I use as leverage suddenly reanimates and pushes us back into the water. Our struggle ensues as we descend further down the pool, my eyes now glancing at the number of feet we sink to.

At six feet I loosen the undead's grip and keep it at bay. At eight feet I begin to panic at the thought of reaching the undead below. At twelve feet I flip myself on top of it, our descent now decreased by my dominance.

With only five feet above the undead below, I separate myself from the monster's grasp by pressing my feet upon its stomach and prying myself free. No longer tethered by its grasp, I desperately struggle to stop from sinking.

While face down I flatten my body at the fifteen foot mark, my arms and legs now spread apart in order to keep from sinking. The undead that attacked me slowly reaches the bottom of the pool, no longer recognizable as it joins the rest of its brethren.

The undead now sway together beneath me, trying their hardest to reach out while attempting to swim. There has to be over a hundred of them below. Each one that relentlessly chased me now resides in the bottom of the pool.

A multitude of bloodshot eyes stare up at me in anger while

a plethora of teeth begin to snarl. A rush of bubbles continues to drift upwards as I watch them escape from the undead's lungs. The remnants of whatever life they had now lost within the water.

While in desperate need of air, I quickly turn my body upwards and swim back towards the surface. By the time I ascend past the six foot mark, four undead suddenly leap into the pool. The closest of which sinks five feet away while the others vainly plummet to their watery tomb.

I cough and gasp again as air consumes me after finally surfacing. My lungs, although tattered, have pleasantly surprised me as I struggle to swim towards the edge of the pool.

After three failed attempts, I manage to muscle up the strength to pull myself out of the water. A loud smack of my back hitting the concrete floor is heard, the sound of which brings relief to my undying fatigue.

Unaware of what lies ahead, I roll myself over towards my gym bag and gun harness. Exhausted and now panting for air, my eyes try to focus on the last undead making its way around the pool.

The small slap of its feet stepping on the wet floor seems amplified within the empty gymnasium. Its approach, now more of an annoyance, causes me to sigh as I watch it twitch and pull itself with each step it takes.

Blood continues to seep from my wound as the pain becomes unbearable, and while reaching out for my gun harness, I begin to feel lightheaded. With my left hand I grab a hold of my nine millimeter and open fire, but am daunted by the sound of its empty clip.

The undead is now uncomfortably close and shares a sinister grin while quickening its pace. Within seconds I pull out my magnum, which I have yet to use during the chase, and empty all six rounds on the undead.

The gunshots echoing within the gym bring about a sharp and familiar ring in my ears. Its sound painfully drags and dawns a gritty haze in my vision.

With the last undead finally gone, I now lie semiconscious on the cold and wet floor, steadily breathing with a small pool of blood forming around my left leg. Slowly fading away within the depths of my mind, until eventually... everything turns white.

7:12 p.m. and my eyes painfully open to reveal the ceiling of the gymnasium above. Now gasping for air, I frantically look around for any lingering undead, but none are to be found.

My body feels dry yet I still tremble as I rub my chest. The pain from my leg lingers as I sit up and question my consciousness. My mind feels strange and out of place, a sort of doughy sensation that puts me in a melancholy state. Which then begs the question if I nearly died from blood loss.

I quickly come to terms with where I'm at after seeing the dry blood around me. My body aches and I feel weak, for I've lost a lot of blood and will need to recover or I will surely die.

While pulling myself up I scan my surroundings once more, still no signs of the undead. Those that remain simply dwell within the dark depths of the Olympic size pool.

My socks remain damp as I now walk towards my gym bag, each step causing cold water to seep between my toes. Even though I'm dry the cold breeze from outside makes me shiver while putting on my shirt and gun harness. I begin readjusting the purple wrap around my left leg, pleased to see that the bleeding has stopped, yet regretting the pain I endure while tightening it in place.

I take some time to reload my guns and extra clips with the ammunition in my bag, which now proves difficult while my head constantly spins and aches. Once finished, I approach the pool to gaze at the undead below. The blue water now a brownish tinge makes it difficult to see, yet I manage to catch their eyes looking up at me through the haze of dirt, filth, and blood.

Ripples start to tremble along the surface of the calm water as the undead start to scramble, the sight of me reigniting their fury.

For a while I stop and stare, surprised at how I evaded the undead.

My survival, however bleak, proved no match for my will. My suffering and pain brought about my wits to survive, the evidence of which lies at the bottom of the pool. And after one last look, I exit the gym to face the darkness outside.

The city of Corona is quiet now, not even the sound of the wind is heard as I walk across the football field. Only a few streetlights remain lit along Jefferson Avenue, and underneath one I find sanctuary as I rummage through my bag of supplies.

During the initial struggle in my truck, I'm glad to see that I grabbed most of my drugs along with a few bottles of water. The gym bag alone already held my ammunition, which is why I grabbed it in the first place.

I panic for a brief moment until I find a pack of smokes within.

Unfortunately for me, I failed to grab some clothes as well as some more cigarettes, for it is now getting cold.

After downing an entire bottle of water and two Vicodins in one sitting, I proceed to light a cigarette while leaning back against the light pole. I watch the smoke slowly creep from my nose underneath the light. Its calming swirls carelessly twist and put my head at ease.

The night sky seems thickened with the smoke and ash that occupies the city. Very few stars remain visible as the moon continues to hide and peek from the corner of the clouds above.

I should feel victorious but I don't, I merely feel tired.

I managed to lure a lot of undead into the pool, perhaps all of them, and for that reason I should feel safer walking the streets at night. Yet I don't.

With my forty-five in hand I continue down Jefferson Avenue, looking at the few intact stores through the darkness. I need to find a place to rest and eat, for my body has lost a lot of blood and I must sustain myself. Yet the last thing I am right now is hungry, and although I can hear my stomach turn, the only thing I feel is fear.

Most of the stores I pass are burnt down from the fires, the smell of smoke and ash still radiating from their ruins. The only thing keeping me on edge is the deafening sound of silence. For its stillness is as if all existence, whether alive or dead, has been utterly removed.

I can only hope to find a store that holds some clothing, for my current shirt is torn as well as my pants and socks which remain damp. Most importantly however, I must attend to my wound. My worst fear at the moment is blood loss and the possibility of infection. The scenario is such that it's shocking at how I once only feared the undead, when there is so much more to be afraid of.

7:45 p.m. as I light up another smoke and stand in front of Rick's Army Surplus. Its bold yellow font is easily seen through the darkness. The one story concrete building is wedged between two ruined stores. Its windows are barred along with an impenetrable looking steel door at its entrance.

After many attempts to get through, I accept the fact it's locked and continue my way around to find an alternate way in. The concrete wall feels cold against my hand as I run it along the side of the store, up until I stumble upon a broken window. I feel relieved while looking up at its frame which seems large enough for me to squeeze through.

While atop a dumpster, I use my forty-five to chip away the jagged pieces of glass attached to the window. My muscles tense and strain as I slowly pull myself up, such an effortless feat now seems difficult with my fatigue.

With a little bit of maneuvering I manage to worm my way inside. Unaware of the emptiness below me, I become caught by the air and instantly fall to the floor.

Small pieces of glass now pinch my back as I wait in darkness, anticipating whatever might reside inside. I hear the moans of an undead close by, to which I press my forty-five against my chest and wait for my eyes to adjust.

The store itself is small which means that the monster is nearby, yet I'm unsure how many are inside. While slowly pulling myself up, I back against a wall and ready my aim, scanning the store for any sign of movement.

Soon the small pieces of glass begin to loosen and trickle down the back of my shirt, giving away my position along with my heavy breathing. The sounds from the undead continue yet I see no shadowy figures ahead. Only a long countertop and some racks, along with a large pillar that form vague obstacles within the darkened store.

After awhile I realize that the undead is gasping for air, as if choking. Its cries are frequently cut off and now seem more sporadic. With my right hand taking aim, I use my left to hold out my lighter, and with a single flick I light up the store.

There is no sign of the undead near me as I hear the broken glass crunch beneath my shoes. I figure if the lights still work then their switch should be near the entrance, and as I pass the pillar ahead, I suddenly feel something brush against me.

My light goes out as I'm startled and turn to face the large figure suspended behind me, now faintly visible in the dark. I tremble to ready my aim and hold out my lighter, panting excessively as I reluctantly release its flame and shine light onto the undead before me.

Its bulging eyes cause me to stagger back, nearly knocking over the rack behind me while I aim for its head. Within my brief moment of terror, I hesitate as I notice the noose around its neck. It is however very much alive, and after watching and ensuring myself that it can't move, I find the light switch.

Only two out of the four ceiling fan lights turn on and now struggle to stay lit, providing me with just enough light to get by. One of them shines above the hanging undead, its short noose remains tied around the base of the ceiling fan.

Its body casually sways from side to side, now acknowledging me as it attempts to break free. Its screams are faint and unclear, for the noose is wrapped so tight around its neck that the rope is barely visible. Blood and overlapped skin is all that is seen around the noose after digging its way into the monster's flesh. It continues to hang while gargling and choking in between broken screams and moans. All the while its eyes protrude on the verge of exiting their sockets.

By the looks of the camouflage it wears, I can only assume that it must have worked here. Its failed attempt at suicide shines brightly as I notice the hunting knife strapped to its leg. It kicks and struggles as I attempt to remove the knife, and after taking a few of its blows, I finally claim the blade as my own.

Once unsheathed, I begin to examine the knife. Its blade is thick and broad while roughly twelve inches in length. Its edge remains sharp as I slowly run my thumb against it, and without warning, I quickly plunge it into the undead's heart.

It barely reacts to its impalement as blood steadily drips down its shirt. Its end suddenly delayed, as I stop and take a moment to fasten the sheath around my right leg.

I now stand on a stool and come face to face with the undead, its hair thinning and almost gone along with most of its teeth. Its eyes still protrude to the point where I can see a hint of white around their bloodshot surfaces. Its gaze, although frightening, does little to stop me from passing judgment.

I press my left hand under its jaw to keep it shut while pulling the knife from its chest. Now looking into its eyes I try to see the man inside. The poor bastard that tried to hang himself and put an end to it all, only to be had by whatever turned him undead.

All I receive now is the crazed look of the monster before me, its intentions are clear and likes of which I've already seen.

Whatever shred humanity it had is long gone, as I now hold its face steady and rest the tip of my knife against its head.

I turn away as a stream of blood shoots out while sinking the blade into its skull.

The knife slowly digs into the undead with little resistance, and by now I've noticed that their flesh seems delicate and their bones weak from decay.

I stare into its eyes until they roll back with my blade halfway into its skull. Its struggling has stopped, yet I feel the cold blood and saliva pour from its mouth and onto my left hand.

Its body now hangs lifeless as I pull out the knife and clean it with its shirt.

Admiring my work for a few moments, I make my way off the stool and slide the blade into its sheath around my right leg.

Humanity seems to not come without its own sense of irony.

8:05 p.m. and after thinking this store is a godsend, I now realize how ransacked it really is. The racks of clothing only hold a few pair of pants, the likes of which are black and slightly too large, as well as some white thermals.

As I sit on the floor with my back against the counter, I begin to remove both my gun and knife holsters. The dry blood, pool water, and sweat soaked into my pants sticks to my flesh as I slowly peel them off. Taking extra caution while removing them around my wound, I toss my pants aside and continue to open a package of fresh boxers and socks.

Once changed into some dry clothes, I briefly bask in their warmth and continue my search of the store.

Not much is left to salvage yet I'm fortunate to find a few military rations behind the counter. Along with the food, I come across a bandanna, a flashlight, nine millimeter rounds, and a new pair of boots which fit perfectly.

While sitting atop the counter, I rummage through one of the military rations. Its main course is spaghetti and meat sauce which I begin to warm up. I don't even feel hungry as I force myself to eat the stale cracker, which comes with not nearly enough strawberry spread, although the Mars bar inside does prove delectable. Regardless of how I feel I must eat to regain my strength, for my body is still broken and weak from blood loss.

After finishing my appetizers, I pull my left leg upon the counter and slowly roll my pants to reveal the purple bandage. A slight stinging sensation grows as I remove the fabric from around my calf, its pain reminiscent of my carelessness.

My spaghetti continues to cook while I examine my leg, as the bag it boils in expands and grows with each passing minute.

The once three inch gash has now stretched two more inches and runs diagonally across my calf. The skin around it remains red and tender to the touch. Everything I've endured so far has caused my wound to bleed profusely, as I'm now hesitant to remove the jiggling clots that dwell inside.

My spaghetti has finished cooking as the aroma coming from its packet soon entices my hunger. Halfway through my meal, I begin to feel my strength return. Its warmth slowly dissolves my disorientation as I'm finally able to think more clearly.

With my thoughts now in order, I go back to how I might have developed my wound. My paranoia quickly overlapped by my ongoing distress. I soon recall that I've never seen anyone turn undead. In reality, I have no idea how long it would take for me to turn, if I was in fact bitten. I bury the notion inside and convince myself that if I was infected, I would have succumbed to the change by now.

I have yet to even come across any survivors. Not that it matters though, I have no desire to find anyone anymore. I no longer feel loneliness, for I'm now content with my isolation. The feeling of once enjoying company or companionship seems alien to me now. I wouldn't know how to handle it. I can't even remember the last time I spoke, I have no reason to. My thoughts are the only voice I now care to hear.

These past four days seemed to have lasted a lifetime. A new beginning leading me towards my questionable end. My only drive is to survive and to kill more undead, although I gravely underestimated them today. Yet I still came out alive. I managed to overcome impossible odds, and though I suffered dearly, I remain intact. I ensnared hundreds of undead, killed God knows how many, and disposed of a monster twice my size. All in all I bested the undead today.

8:42 p.m. and only moments after lighting my smoke I have to take a piss. I slowly drag my leg off the counter and walk towards the restroom, each step now causing small beads of blood to run down my leg. The black pants I wear prove too large around my waist which I adjust with a belt I found. Their bagginess only emphasized as they slightly drag along my feet. The white thermal I wear however, fits me well and keeps me warm.

Once inside the bathroom I begin to relieve myself, a much needed and elongated piss that causes me to brace myself against the wall. My leg constantly fidgets from putting weight on it, and while sitting back on the counter, I realize that I must suture it up soon.

Staying the night here will be ideal, yet I don't know how much longer I can leave my wound untreated. Even though I've gained some sustenance it isn't enough, and all my efforts will be in vain if I continue to bleed out.

After chasing two Amoxicillins and Vicodins, I prepare to wrap my leg. The wound looks dry yet fresh with its lingering blood clots. Its sting is ever so frequent as I now wrap it with the green bandana I acquired.

Using a light amount of pressure at first, I wrap the bandana tighter until I'm left with its two ends in my hands. After loosely tying a knot with its ends, I close my eyes, take a deep breath, prepare for the pain, and pull.

I grunt and bite down on my teeth as the intense pinch rushes up my leg. To which I immediately tighten with a double knot to avoid any hesitation, which causes me to scream.

9:05 p.m. and the Vicodin is beginning to numb the pain and lift my spirits. I put out my cigarette as I approach a rack of jackets across the store, which apparently has a clearance sale of thirty percent off.

I now feel wide awake from passing out so many times today, and although I mentally feel better, my body still suffers. My throat also feels dry and scratchy from being sick, which I find irrelevant compared to my many injuries.

My main priority now is to find a hospital or veterinary practice, anywhere that might hold suture material. I know how to stitch a wound from assisting in surgeries during my time at my old job. The depth of this procedure should prove no different than what I'm used to.

I fear that without proper suture for closing my wound that I might risk further infection. Considering what my laceration has been through, I figure the only thing saving my leg are the antibiotics I've been taking. It shouldn't be hard to find somewhere with medical supplies unless they are all burnt down. Either way I can't sit and wait to bleed to death, for if that's the case, I might as well hang myself next to the undead here.

Only a few jackets now remain in the store, one of which is a dark green trench coat which I instantly put on. Its sleeves are a bit long and its length tails behind me. But I don't mind much. I brush the discomfort aside as I load my gym bag with the remaining military rations and ammunition.

After ensuring that my guns and clips are loaded, I holster them in my harnesses which hide underneath my trench coat, as well as my knife strapped to my right leg. Now armed with a flashlight and food in my stomach, I pull my gym bag over my left shoulder and sluggishly walk towards the store's entrance.

I sigh like an irritated child as I unlock the door.

Exhausted and afraid to sleep, I casually exit Rick's Army Surplus and enter the darkness outside.

9:31 p.m. and the air feels cool against my face. Its chill does little to daunt my path, as I've now grown accustom to the smell of fire and ash. Yet I continue down Jefferson Avenue, adjusting my gym bag to relieve its weight upon my leg.

I haven't the faintest idea where a hospital might be, and if I'm to quicken my search, I'll have to find some wheels. After numerous failed attempts at hijacking abandoned cars, I come across Sixth Street. While turning left and walking down the road, I suddenly realize that I'm right back to where it all started.

If I'm correct then what's left of my truck and supplies lies behind me on the freeway. Through the darkness I'm unable to see the suspended bridge that I jumped off of earlier. Unaware of how long the journey lies, I decided to venture deeper into the city.

I can't worry about that now, I figure once I get my bearings, perhaps then I can recover my things.

The uncomfortable silence still surrounds me while walking down Sixth Street, that and the sound of the long trench coat dragging behind me along the road.

9:54 p.m. and after walking a few blocks, I stumble upon a black Toyota Corolla. It rests underneath one of the few streetlights that remain lit, surrounded by darkness and begging to be commandeered.

I anxiously rush towards the vehicle and within twenty feet of it; I halt at the sight of the undead inside. Unaware of my presence, I watch the woman in the driver's seat slowly rock her body as I draw near. Our eyes finally meet once I approach, my arrival fueling her rage as she rocks back and forth even faster.

Her movements abruptly stop as I lean close.

Her patience does little to calm my nerves as I find myself staring directly at her.

Only a thin sheet of glass now stands between the undead and I. Her bangs which are dyed black hang low along the sides of her face, along with the rest of her natural blonde hair which is tied in a ponytail. Her makeup surprisingly remains intact along with the rest of her face, for there is only the faint hint of tears that might have smeared her eyeliner.

A small bite mark is visible on her left shoulder that branches out trails of blood down her chest. Her bloodshot eyes glare at me as she begins to lick the glass, smearing two parallel streaks of blood along the split portions of her tongue.

The likes of which is that of a snake.

A slight grin cracks my lip open as I stare at the eyebrow, septum, and many other piercings that the girl has.

The result of what happened to her tongue now obvious.

My eyes focus downward at the securely buckled seatbelt, which follows its gray strap up across the undead's stomach and in-between her large breasts. Now feeling confident that she's restrained, I pull on the door's handle only to find it locked. My actions however, instantly break the undead's trance as she suddenly rocks back and forth again, desperately trying to release herself from the seatbelt's grasp.

One way or another I'm taking this car, which is one of the few I've seen that might start and possibly contain its keys.

While watching the young female undead struggle, I slowly move to the passenger door to my right and pull on its handle. To my surprise it opens, and with the door left ajar, I take a seat behind the undead.

The girl shows no intention of stopping as she continues to thrash about in her seat, unable to comprehend the complexity of a seatbelt as I now bring out my magnum. With its hammer pulled back I point my gun behind her head, and after letting her struggle for a while, I squeeze the trigger.

Her body goes limp moments after the .357 round exits her skull, and to my dismay ends up hitting the windshield. Feeling slightly disappointed that I fucked up the car, which was easily avoidable; I sit back and light up another smoke.

My many failures now build as I stop and stare at my half empty pack of cigarettes. A problem I will have to deal with soon, but for now I exhale a sigh and lay my head back on the seat.

10:13 p.m. and the abrupt sound of the car's horn going off startles me. I sit up in a state of panic; unaware of what's happening until I see the undead's face leaning on the steering wheel ahead.

My smoke rests tightly between my lips as I pull myself forward to unlock the door. While grabbing a hold of the undead's ponytail, I pull her head off the steering wheel and relieve my ears from the incessant sound of the horn. It's alerting pitch causes me to move as I exit the car and open the driver's side door.

The undead slouches while now lifeless.

Its bullet wound adds variance to its blank expression, as I unbuckle its seatbelt and pull her out of the car. With her back upon the street she stares up at me, blood pouring from the wound on her head which forms a puddle that stains her blonde hair.

I pause for a few moments to look her over.

Her orange low cut shirt places emphasis on her cleavage as one breast is now slightly exposed. Before I could even become slightly aroused, I come to my senses and turn away, shaking my head in shame.

What has become of me I wonder? First my explicit nightmare and now this. Each day I carry on seems to push me further away from who I once was. All while molding me into this harsh reality. However damaged I am psychologically is nothing compared to how broken my body is.

With that said, I bury all feelings of guilt and longing deep inside, and move on.

Once inside the Corolla I find its keys within the center console, but am suddenly forced to cringe at the smell that occupies the car. The moistness of the saturated driver's seat begins to seep through my clothes, while the stench of death, piss, and shit now surrounds me. Yet I don't bother getting up, for I know that the undead must have let loose all its bodily fluids while trapped in the car.

The small and sudden roar of the engine starting makes me smile.

Its sound, although uplifting, bears little pleasure as I try to find space within the shattered windshield to see the road ahead. After adjusting my seat and mirrors to gain some sense of normality, I brush aside the fragments of skull and tissue that lie on the dashboard, and drive off.

10:52 p.m. and I now wait quietly in the Corolla, its engine's off while parked underneath another streetlight. The lit cherry of my cigarette brightens as I inhale more smoke, for my eyes wearily focus on the hospital before me.

The four story building is one of the few structures left standing from the fires. Various lights shine through its many windows while the sliding glass doors at its entrance are left open.

A numbing pain shifts up my leg after exiting the car.

Its sting, although numb, weighs heavy as I flick my cigarette in the distance and limp towards the hospital. Soon small droplets of blood trail behind me, for the bandana around my wound is now soaked in blood.

I once again feel lightheaded.

Before coming across the hospital, I was on the verge of giving up after driving for half an hour. It wasn't until I found an ambulance flipped on its side that I finally regained hope. Unfortunately for me the ambulance contained no medical supplies, only broken-down equipment and a few lingering undead.

I made short work of the monsters in EMT uniforms. All four of them met their end within five rounds of my forty-five millimeter. It was then that I knew I was close to a hospital, and only by pressing on would I achieve my goal.

The shining blue cross above the entrance flickers to stay lit as I follow a trail of blood towards the hospital. Once inside, I ready my forty-five and check my surroundings. To my left stand the elevators and a flight of stairs, while to my right is the receptionist desk within the lobby, along with a pair of bloodstained double doors that lead to the cafeteria.

The bright lights within the hospital now cause me to squint.

My eyes, still adjusted to the darkness, slowly begin to piece together a severed head in the distance. The mangled, unrecognizable structure of the decapitated head faces me at the end of the hallway before me. Beyond it lies another pair of doors labeled "Emergency", which I can only make out once I approach the severed head.

For a few moments I roll the head around with my right foot, playing for a bit until I give it a hard FIFA style kick towards the doors ahead. Its eyes carelessly stare at me as it soars through the air, gaining speed during its flight as it slams against the doors leading towards Emergency.

Shortly after the echoing sound of its impact, both doors suddenly burst open followed by an undead. The monster rushes towards me in a surgical cap and gown, dragging along a crash cart which is tied around its waist. Only its red piercing eyes are exposed above its mask as it now screams and runs down the hallway.

My right eye twitches and enhances my aim.

Its focus brings about death as I fire off a round into the surgeon's head.

The blast pushes the undead back onto the crash cart behind it, slowly causing it to roll its way back through the double doors from whence it came. I pause and watch the doors swing to a close and abruptly open as four more undead begin rush through. They frantically advance while in surgical scrubs and gowns, only making it halfway down the hall as I gun them down with six rounds from my forty-five.

I feel no emotion, satisfaction, or fear. Perhaps maybe a hint of boredom which I imagine is due to my body on the verge of going into shock.

While taking care not to stumble over the corpses of the undead, I now carefully make my way into the ER.

My ears now ring and my body sways from the gunfire. The stress of it all weighs down on me, and only after shaking my head can I finally make out the room I'm in.

The ER is surrounded by many beds and treatment tables, along with curtains that separate each patient from one another. Broken syringes, scalpels, and various instruments litter the room, all floating atop the blood and clear fluid that floods the floor.

I can't imagine the destruction and chaos that must have broken out five days ago, nor do I want to. Evidence of panic lies everywhere, its desolation is apparent, yet it's as if the screams of those that died here still linger on.

I quickly replace the nearly empty clip in my forty-five while making my way around the undead surgeon. Its back lies sprawled over the cash cart with its arms and legs swaying above ground, the blood dripping off its head now adding to the puddles on the floor.

I take caution in my search and keep my aim ready, pulling away at each curtain separating the beds in anticipation of finding more undead. Once assured that I'm in the clear, I holster away my gun and begin to ransack the ER.

11:21 p.m. and after desperately searching every cart and drawer for supplies, I remain unsuccessful. A slight buildup of anger consumes me, yet I'm unable to lash out, for the adrenaline from my recent encounter with the undead has long passed.

My mind is still unable to accept that there is no suture material within the ER. To my dismay, I rest my head on a nearby counter as the room begins to spin.

I've lost a lot of blood and now fear losing more.

Proof of my fatigue lays on the dry portions of the white floor, as numerous streaks of blood trail my search throughout the ER. The sight of which only adds to my distress and subtle longing for help.

My dizziness hits me in waves.

Nausea overwhelms me in sporadic jolts while now obscuring my vision.

With my strength failing me, I stumble my way towards a cart I found earlier at the far end of the room. The contents of which contain IV catheters and bags of fluids. Slowly but surely I press on, sluggishly walking while dragging an IV stand I grab along the way.

11:27 p.m. and I now sit on one of the many beds in the ER. My mind, although jumbled, provides me with enough clarity to desperately open and hang a one liter bag of Sodium Chloride on my IV stand. Once setup, I let the fluids run freely through its line, and after ensuring that no air lingers within the extension, I prepare my catheter.

I use a thick yellow rubber tourniquet and tie it firmly around my left arm, slightly above my elbow and wait for my veins to show. It takes a few moments for my blood pressure to rise, but soon my forearm branches out with three blue veins that stretch across my arm.

With my right hand steady, I carefully place a twenty gauge catheter into the center vein. The Vicodins, along with my exhaustion, mask the small pinch the needle makes as it pierces my skin.

A fair amount of luck and skill makes things less difficult with my vision now a blur. A small pool of blood slowly creeps up the flashback chamber of the catheter once I'm in. Its steady arrival confirms my approach, as I slide the rest of the catheter through my vein and secure it with some adhesive tape.

While connecting the IV line to my catheter, I already begin to dread having to remove the tape from around my skin. Its sting to remove seems trivial to my alternate pains, yet it's the trivial things that keep me sane.

The fluids feel cold as they now enter my bloodstream, and I give it just a moment to run freely to ensure that my catheter's working. I set the bag at a high drip rate so that I can re-hydrate myself faster, taking caution to not run the risk of hypothermia or heart failure.

I then take a moment to replace the blood soaked bandana wrapped around my leg. Utilizing what I have, I grab the bandage material that lies in the drawer next to me.

Once finished, I lie on my back while sprawled out on the bed. I find comfort with my forty-five resting on my chest, as I now close my eyes and wait.

12:00 a.m. and my eyes open towards the bright ultraviolet lights that shine above me. Unable to sleep during my time of rest, I was merely left to my thoughts until the room finally stopped spinning.

My back cracks as I sit up and my head now begins to feel clear. The sensitivity of the light seems severe and that of my many hangovers. I'm no longer sure what to make of my thoughts anymore, for all I recall is emptiness and visions of my bad dreams.

The half empty bag of fluids still hangs and maintains its fast drip, to which I slow down to one drop every two seconds. I feel the strong urge to urinate as I stand to find the restroom across from me. Its distance will make walking difficult.

With my forty-five held in my right hand and the IV stand in my left, I make my way towards the bathroom. I sigh as I relieve myself for nearly three minutes, all while the power of the fluids flushes through me.

While washing my face and hands, I begin to notice the color returning to my skin. My face no longer looks or feels pale as my vision now seems sharper than ever. My body on the other hand remains broken and sore. The blood and grime that stains my hands and face refuses to leave after washing, as well as my hair that flakes small pieces of dirt with my every move.

Now feeling rejuvenated, I wheel my IV stand along with me and continue my search for suture material.

I find myself backtracking as I now stand in the hallway with the elevators, which to my surprise no longer function. A map of the hospital hangs along the wall which shows that the second floor holds the surgery rooms. Relieved that the surgical wing is only one floor above, I waste no time and continue towards the stairs at the end of the hall.

An endless spiraling stairway towers above me as I look up and scan for any undead. An attempt which proves difficult as the few working lights struggle to stay lit. Soon the sound of the IV stand hitting the concrete is all that is heard while ascending the stairs. The act of which seems strenuous, as I take my time with each grueling step.

Even though the stand could hinder my chances at surviving an encounter with the undead, I feel that any improvement in my overall health outweighs the handicap of being left one handed. Yet if it boils down to it, I could always remove the catheter and replace it later.

I use the stand as a cane by lifting it upon each step while pulling myself up, which eventually becomes tiresome by the time I reach the last set of stairs. My breathing becomes heavy and labored once I arrive at the second floor, which I quickly overcome as I notice the blood seeping through my bandage.

The door before me brings about a bad omen with blood staining its handle, the likes of which are painted along its frame. While bracing myself for whatever might lie ahead, I ready my forty-five with my right hand and lift the IV stand with my left. My fearful delay only causes more blood loss, as I push my way through and enter the second floor.

I now stand corrected by the emptiness of the second floor. Its desertion is surreal, yet welcomed as I wait patiently for any undead. The hallway before me is identical to the one downstairs, while the only difference lies with the corpses and body parts that litter its floor.

I follow the sound of an electric saw echoing in the distance.

Its noise takes me past the elevators as the hallway branches off into three sections. Each narrow path leading towards separate doors labeled surgery room one, two, and three.

I prepare for the worst as I ready my aim and slowly walk down the hall, its end bringing me towards the first room out of the three. The sound of the saw intensifies as I draw near, and soon the wheels on my IV stand begin to stick from the blood clogging its bearings.

A plaster saw lies running on its side along the blood splattered floor. Its image remains unsettling as I enter surgery room one. Its long extension cord trails along the floor towards an outlet to my left. Three dead surgeons lie mutilated across the room, their decaying bodies half chewed and sawed off show no signs of reanimating.

Within the first drawer I open, I find a sterile kit which contains thumb forceps, scissors, and suture material. My eyes light up with excitement at the sight of my findings, as I set aside four kits to take with me once I finish addressing my leg.

12:41 p.m. and after clearing out the last two rooms of a few undead, I sit upon the table of surgery room three. With my left leg stretched across my knee and the bandage now removed, I begin to feel the cold stale air breathe upon my wound.

Everything I need to tend to my leg rests besides me: my suture kit, bandage material, gauze, and a sixty milliliter syringe full of dilute Iodine. All the tools needed to repair myself seem faintly familiar of a time long since past.

I use an empty syringe to bite down on during my procedure. My anticipation for pain grows ever vigilant, as I now glove up and prepare myself. With my syringe full of flush in hand, I take a deep breath, knowing all too well what to do next, yet unaware of how bad it'll hurt.

The five inch laceration now bleeds as I flush it with Iodine. Its sting builds with the increased pressure while lathering it up inside. At first I use some gauze to gently scrub my wound, eventually working my way faster and past the pain. I vigorously continue to clean the inside. Using Iodine to flood its depths, I abrade the edges of the torn tissue with more gauze.

While breathing hard through my nose and the laceration clear of dirt and fabric, I notice a dark discoloration to the tissue surrounding my wound. Anticipating that this might happen, I bite down hard on the empty syringe in my mouth and prepare to debride its edges.

Using small surgical scissors, I begin to cut away at the dead flesh surrounding my wound. Blood seeps from the fresh and healthy tissue that is now exposed, on which I use more gauze to stop the bleeding. My bag of IV fluids however, bleeds profusely and nearly runs dry as I continue working on my leg.

By the time I finish cutting away the dead skin, the pain becomes so severe that the syringe I use as a gag falls from my mouth. Its trail immediately followed by a long string of saliva.

I suddenly lose all sense of sterility as I set the bloody scissors and string of dead flesh aside and light up a smoke. The gloves smell of latex and blood as I set the cigarette between my lips and rummage through my suture kit.

With my thumb forceps in hand, I open up a package of 0-0 nylon suture material. The size of the suture is thicker and would seem more durable and appropriate, given the tension of where my laceration is.

Smoke drifts past my face and spills ash on my chest as I now use more gauze to absorb the lingering Iodine. The cigarette helps distract me from the pain, to which I take one long drag before I stitch myself up.

While grabbing onto the skin's edges with my thumb forceps, I use my fingers to grip the needle at the end of the suture. Its pinch piercing my flesh is minimal compared to the abrading and debridement of the dead tissue, such that I find myself loosening up. I feel a tightening sensation around my calf while pulling the skin together, as I use a simple interrupted pattern to suture myself up.

Little by little I continue to close my wound, applying stitch after stitch at about a centimeter apart. My smoke has long finished by the time I tie the last suture in place. What remains is nothing more than a filter as I spit it out while blotting the stitches with more gauze.

I sigh with relief at my new found success, feeling more or less impressed by the straightness and cleanliness of my results. With my bandage material in hand, I place a piece of gauze over my sutures and begin to lightly roll elastic wrap around my calf.

Once finished I remove my catheter, its clear adhesive tape sticks to my skin and slowly pulls away at my hair. But I don't mind much, my excitement outweighs my strain as I stretch and take a deep breath. For I feel repaired now, and although my body still suffers, I get the sense that I'm going to be alright.

1:40 a.m. and the Vicodins I took earlier have worn off. My leg still hurts from putting weight on it but not nearly as bad as before, as I now quicken my pace to leave the hospital. Once outside, I embrace the silence and darkness of the night and continue towards my car, which still rests underneath the light provided by the streetlamp above.

The rank aroma within the Corolla makes me nauseous again, and soon the dampness of the driver's seat begins to soak into my clothes. After starting the car, I quickly pop in two Vicodins while chasing them down with my left over water, desperately relying on drugs to help with my recovery.

I now drive back to Rick's Army Surplus, the only remaining building in this city which can provide me shelter. Halfway into the drive, I begin to feel the Vicodins kick in as my eyes grow heavy.

No more detours or fucking around.

I've covered most of this city during my search and found nothing left for me here. My time spent in Corona has been longer than expected, for the events of today have proven most... undesirable.

2:12 a.m. as I pull up to Rick's Army Surplus. The drive back proved much faster after knowing where I should go, as well as not having to dispose of any undead.

With my gym bag strapped around me and my medical supplies in hand, I ready my forty-five and open the front door which I left unlocked. The hanging undead greets me as I walk in. Its lifeless body slowly sways while I lock the door behind me.

Darkness patches the corners of the store while the few remaining lights within struggle to stay lit. Everything seems to be as how I left it hours ago, and after a quick sweep of the store, I find comfort in knowing that I'm alone.

A warm fuzzy sensation fills my body as I no longer notice the pain from my leg, only the pleasant and peaceful high that I now thank the drugs for.

While using the remaining jackets and clothing from within the store, I form a makeshift mattress behind the counter, similar to that of a bird's nest.

I find comfort and security within my bedding.

Nestled against the warmth of the jackets, I rest my head upon a few rolled up thermals and sigh with relief.

What will come next I wonder? Each day so far has proven a challenge and I fear that I will eventually fail. I plan on leaving this hellhole of a city tomorrow, but for now I'll rest. My mind and body remain exhausted beyond belief.

I need to get some rest... I need this day to end.

Day 5

12:05 p.m. is shown on the clock above me as I now awake. My mind remains scattered and its pieces are nowhere to be found. I take a moment to visualize where I'm at, constantly unaware of my current consciousness. I can never tell I'm awake or amidst dream, and while pulling myself up, I become taken back by the sharp pain in my leg.

I now realize that I'm very much awake... and very much alive.

The blue bandage around my calf remains intact with no traces of blood seeping through. My joints crack and snap into place as I stand, yawning while searching through my bag for my drugs. The smell of chlorine and sweat now exudes from my body, which I can't help but feel from the hot layers of clothing that I wear.

While feeling much better physically, I toss aside the heavy trench coat I wear and adjust my pants so that they no longer drag. My thermal is drenched in sweat and sticks to my skin as I pull it off, which I replace with another that I find within the store. Shortly after taking two Vicodins and Amoxicillins, I ration the remaining water I have left by washing my mouth and eyes within the sink.

Daylight shines through the windows and now lights up the store, its radiance emphasizing the dust and humidity in the air. I sit upon a nearby counter and open up another MRE. It seems I'll be having cheddar potato soup for breakfast, and while letting my meal warm up, I partake in a morning smoke.

Two cigarettes remain in my current pack, a dilemma I will soon rectify once I reach my truck and get the hell out of this town. My only concern now is how many undead stayed behind with my truck, which I imagine is not many, considering the amount I lured to their watery grave.

My gym bag is now full and difficult to close after adding the supplies I gathered from the hospital. Its compactness forces me to discard an MRE, as well as a suture kit in order to make room. I can live without food for a few days, as well as some of the unnecessary medical supplies.

However my drugs and bullets I can not, and will not, go without.

12:24 p.m. and I've now finished my meal. It's time for me to get going before the day ends, especially if I plan on making it back to Sovereignty before nightfall. My current sanctuary proves only temporary like it did at The Royal Resort. I use it like I would a cheap whore, gathering my gear as I tighten my boots, strap on my gym bag, and head out the door.

Numerous purple clouds race across the sky which still block out the sun, revealing only a few small patches of the blue sky above. A few lingering undead wander aimlessly along the street, which I temporarily leave alone while loading my bag into the Corolla.

With my forty-five gripped tightly in my left hand, I unsheathe the hunting knife strapped to my right leg and get to work.

The undead closest to me lies to my right, roughly ten yards away and remains there as I dispose of it with a single round to the back of its head. The sound of the gunshot alerts the six remaining undead, and within moments they begin to sprint towards me.

I quickly take the high ground and gain the advantage by climbing atop the Corolla. The pain from my leg, now tolerable, slightly hinders my agility.

The undead's screams no longer have an effect on me.

I welcome the sound of their pain, as well as the inevitable silence that follows.

All six of them foolishly rush towards me, stumbling over each other while unaware of what's yet to come. With accurate succession I quickly take five of them out. One by one they near the edge of the car and instantly fall at the hands of my forty-five.

The last one remaining now continues its advance, oblivious that I will soon end its fate as it attempts to climb the car. Its blonde thinning hair and obese stature would have once brought about terror, yet all I feel is disgust.

While growling and snarling, the undead finally pulls itself onto the hood of the car, its bloodshot eyes constantly locked onto mine. I shake my head and chuckle at its pathetic attempt, and while now feeling a little experimental, I hop off the roof of the car, gain some distance, and throw my knife at it.

The large hunting knife instantly twirls in the air, gaining speed as it approaches my target, yet falls short of success as it bounces off its chest.

My eyes squint with displeasure after failing to pierce the undead.

My amusement cut short as I walk towards it with my forty-five in hand.

Now angry, the undead rushes to greet me, only to get dropped by a single round to its knee, followed closely by another to its skull.

It all seems so surreal, until I embrace the silence.

Smoke drifts from the barrel of my gun as I light up one of the few cigarettes I have. Its buzz brings about a sense of satisfaction while observing the mess I've made.

After putting away my knife, I stop to bask at the new found confidence I've gained. It seems only natural to relish after everything I've overcome, and while yesterday proved to be most terrifying, I still came out alive.

That alone speaks volumes.

12:55 p.m. as I approach the on-ramp heading north. The sight of the suspended bridge makes me cringe as I recall tumbling down its mountainside. I pull to a stop in front of my red Silverado, which remains standing in the middle of the freeway. Its front end is slightly elevated atop a few crushed cadavers. Its image reminiscent of the trauma I suffered, as I look towards the wrecked cars I used to hop scotch over the crowd of undead.

Relieved that I no longer have to endure the rotting smell of death within the Corolla, I quickly grab my bag and head towards my truck. All the blood and cracked windows along my truck shine as remnants of the terror I experienced yesterday, though the damage to the windshield is not nearly as bad as the Corolla.

Soon after loading my gym bag within the truck, I scrounge through the supplies I left behind to find a carton of smokes.

I suddenly become engulfed by warmth as the clouds break to reveal the sun that shines brightly upon my truck. A slight grin consumes me as I begin to pack my new pack of cigarettes. All the while the thought of light shining down upon me after finding my smokes seems too coincidental.

I take caution in checking my surroundings, searching underneath and around my truck for any undead that might be, for lack of a better word... alive.

Once secure I find myself alone, standing in the middle of a desolate freeway and staring upwards at the bright sun. I bask in the warm sunlight and exhale the smoke from my lungs, which is now more visible as it swirls and brushes against my body, like ribbons dancing in mid-air.

Only moments pass until the clouds begin to shroud the light and block out the sun, leaving me to dwell in the darkness yet again. Without further delay, I quickly jump in my truck and turn on its ignition, only to find that it no longer starts.

Fuck.

1:20 p.m. and I'm driving back through town, once again forced to endure the foul smell of the Corolla after my truck failed to start.

I suppose I shouldn't be surprised that its battery died after leaving it idle, for I was in a hurry to escape the hoard of undead. Nevertheless, I failed to secure some jumper cables during my travels, and I can only assume that the truck most likely ran out of fuel.

While driving through the ruined city, I make drastic attempt to find jumper cables, as well as anything I could use to siphon gas from the Corolla.

The compact is too low to the ground and not ideal for running over the undead, not to mention the unbearable odor within its interior. Its windshield, which I foolishly destroyed, has cracked beyond repair, for its spider web image now blocks my entire view. Ideally I'd rather not have to constantly look out the window to drive, and unless I can find what I need or another vehicle that's still running, I might just have to tough it out in the Corolla.

The day is still young however, and Sovereignty is not that far away, and as much as I hate having to linger in this dreaded city, I should at least try to get better means of travel.

1:39 p.m. as I pull to a stop on Ivy Street. I've now reached the residential side of Corona, and decide to continue on foot as to not waste my remaining gas.

I intend on traveling light during my search, as I'm no longer burdened with the gym bag that I left in the car. The oversized attire I wore didn't help either, as I now sport a clean set of clothing which consists of blue Levis, a black A-shirt underneath my red scrub top, and my leather jacket.

I'm not entirely sure how the scrub top got into my supplies, for I've always hated wearing them and found them to be uncomfortable. It must have snuck its way into my bag while leaving my house five days ago.

Either way I can care less what I have to wear, and recalling the events back then now seem... irrelevant.

As I step out of the car I find myself feeling more agile, more at ease. My gun harness is wrapped firmly across my torso while concealed within my leather jacket. Its pressure similar to that of the hunting knife strapped to my right leg.

The dark gloom of the sky above now casts its shadow over the suburban neighborhood, darkening the asphalt of the path before me.

I continue down Ivy Street in hopes of finding what I need, which if I'm lucky will entail another vehicle that I can confiscate. One by one I break into every intact car, truck, and van that I see, each time proving unsuccessful. Some unable to start and some without keys, and with no knowledge in mechanics or stealing cars, I begin to lose hope after my many failures.

My search seems grim as I continue down the neighborhood and observe the burnt down lawns and houses. The fragments of the city's infrastructure now fractured remain around me, leaving behind the whispers of its inhabitants.

I suddenly come across another house in ruins to my left, to which I instantly spot a hose attached to a water spigot in its front lawn. The green hose coils up and stretches across the half burnt lawn, its width seeming as though it would fit perfectly in the Corolla's gas tank.

Now excited, I quickly walk towards the house but pause at the sound of wheels turning.

The squeaking sound of unlubricated wheels now grows louder as I spot an adolescent undead. It slowly makes it way out from the side gate of the neighboring house to my right. It struggles its way forward while dragging behind a small radio flyer, all the while its wheels continue to screech with each forceful tug.

A half chewed and headless corpse along with a basketball lay within the small red wagon. Its naked limbs hang off the edge while causing one of its heels to drag along the sidewalk.

I pull out my nine millimeter and take aim while braced against a nearby tree, giving the boy a few more steps as I prepare to fire.

The undead sluggishly treads past me, its tattered clothing barely hanging on to its skinny body. Its demeanor, although unthreatening, heightens my wrath as I regain my new found confidence.

The likes of which the undead will see.

The little bastard never saw it coming, as the moment our eyes met was the moment he met his end. His body falls back from the impact which causes his radio flyer to stroll away, leaving a trail of blood along its path.

He now lies on his back twitching.

My rage remains wedged within the depths of the wound on his head, and without knowing, I bring the smoking barrel of the gun up to my nose. The sweet aroma of gunpowder fills my sinuses and distracts me as I'm suddenly pulled by my hair.

Its force causes me to wince while dropping my nine millimeter.

Another undead child has snuck behind me and now has its ravenous teeth inches away from my shoulder. Its approach was unknown to me and I remain startled by my negligence, its arrival quick and unseen.

I scramble with it momentarily, dancing in circles while the little monster remains latched onto my back. I can almost feel its teeth press against my leather jacket as I back into a nearby tree. Over and over I repeatedly smash the undead against the thick trunk of the tree, chipping away pieces of bark as its grip begins to give way.

While panicking I manage to regain myself, thinking quickly as I turn and press my forearm upon its neck.

Whatever advantage it had is now gone while braced against the tree.

The monstrous little boy screams while wrapping its legs around me, frantically trying to break free, yet unaware of my knife that I pull out with my right hand.

A loud pop followed by a blank expression now stares at me with my knife embedded in the boy's head. Its legs go limp and relieve the tension around my waist, while blood continuously drips from its nose and mouth after pulling out my blade.

I use the boy's hair to wipe the blood off my knife. Its dirty blonde strands scrape dirt along the steel which is now felt as I clean.

After cutting a four foot portion of the water hose and wrapping it around my shoulder, I leave the corpses of the two children to rot on the front lawn. Their demise bears little weight on me, as I now watch their radio flyer stroll away in the distance.

1:57 p.m. as I continue down Ivy Street and dispose of a few more rabid children. A task which up until now, grows easier with each killing blow.

Eventually I stumble upon two neighboring houses; their structures remain intact and left standing. Both of the two story homes seem to have survived the fires with only minor burns. Their exteriors lie charred yet sturdy and stable.

Now armed with my magnum, I approach the dry and overgrown lawn of the first house. Its front door appears to have been pulled off its hinges, as all that remains is the thin screen door that stands behind it.

I stare down at my feet which rest on a brown bloodstained welcome mat that reads "Wipe Your Paws". Its slogan, although clever, I find less than amusing, and within moments I'm drawn to the sound of footsteps.

The tiny tapping grows louder as I watch a small Yorkshire terrier trot its way towards me. My head tilts as I stop and stare the bloodstained dog sitting patiently, its tail carelessly wagging on the other side of the screen door.

All five pounds of it is dyed red and covered in blood, a similar color which matches its eyes that now gaze through me.

Its cute demeanor suddenly diminished by its unsavory intentions.

Our moment of peace soon falls to an end as I bend down and the dog tries to attack me. Yet I remain unfazed by its sudden aggression and simply watch, reminiscing my past along with all the dogs that hated me back at work.

The only difference now is that I'll be putting this one down with a shell full of lead.

Knowing that just one small bite from this little bastard could end it all for me, I quickly take aim and fire. The blast from the .357 round tears the little Yorkie apart, causing a small explosion of blood, bones, and hair. Its end suddenly met in the most inhumane way possible, as its fragments now splatter against the screen door.

I take a chance and hope that these owners only have one dog.

As I make my way inside I step on a heart shaped dog tag with the name "Precious" embodied upon it. Its name is typical for its ferocious intent, to which I casually kick aside and continue towards the living room.

I remain unfazed by my actions of late, and with my magnum now ready, I begin my search of the house.

Similar to the stores I've previously searched, the house remains ransacked with obvious signs of struggle. A fifty inch television lies shattered with a chair plowed into its screen, while the carpet and white walls remain torn and stained with blood.

Each step I take is over some type of debris, remnants of those that once lived here. Their fallen memories are a constant that trails my heels, and eventually I make my way past into the kitchen.

The white tile below me now chips and cracks as I walk.

Its sound follows me until I stop near a bowl of fruit sitting atop a counter. Rotting bananas, mangos, and oranges reside within the bowl, while on top lie some freshly preserved green apples.

Still feeling slightly malnourished, I grab one of the apples and proceed towards the sink. A mass of blood along with pieces of flesh and hair lie at the bottom of its stainless steel basin. The sight of which does little to dampen my appetite, as I take no notice and turn on the faucet.

The water stalls and soon a grumbling sound is heard within the pipes.

Its noise, although unsettling, makes it seem as if the entire house is coming to life. Suddenly, more blood begins to fill the sink as clot after clot spits out of the faucet, eventually leading towards a solid stream of darkened blood.

Feeling less than amused and with the expression to show it, I shut off the faucet and continue to eat my apple. It would have been nice to rinse the apple off, but no matter, I still manage to savor the taste of fresh fruit and the natural sugars it provides.

Once finished, I make my way towards a door at the far end of the kitchen, and once inside I become surrounded by darkness.

With my right hand I fumble for the light switch.

Its press sheds light within as a door slowly squeals and opens before me, revealing the cluttered mess that was once the garage. Old televisions, computer monitors, boxes, and over a hundred pairs of shoes now take up most of the space around me, with only a small opening to which a vehicle once occupied.

With a long sigh I move away from the wall and light up a smoke, already dreading the search I'll have to partake in to find jumper cables.

2:36 p.m. and I now leave the house through its garage, frustrated at my failure to find jumper cables. While walking across the lawn, I begin to expect the worst and realize that I might have to tough it out in the Corolla.

One last house remains standing, and is now my final hope in finding the means to regain my truck. It lies in shambles with its exterior slightly burned and its windows broken. The sight of which begs the question if I should even bother searching.

As I head towards its front door, I set my hose aside and reach for its handle.

Yet I find myself hesitating.

My stomach turns and my instincts make me cautious as to what might be lurking on the other side. The feeling is that of a light switch being turned on, frightening with its own sense of assurance.

I can now sense the ravenous hunger that awaits me, for that I am sure.

A familiar presence is felt, that which is not from me being alone.

With my right hand I aim my magnum towards the brown wooden door, following my senses which suddenly tell me to pull the trigger. The blast forces my head to turn as fragments of wood and sawdust race past, causing me to abruptly burst through the broken door.

An undead lies in front of me as I enter the house.

Blood seeps from the wound near its collarbone as it slowly struggles to lift itself up. With one more shot from my magnum, it now lies dormant with the right side of its face blown off. Blood saturates the white carpet around it and squishes beneath my boots, its noise that of a cartoon as I make my way around the undead.

After passing the multitude of chewed up body parts that make up the living room, I find myself at the base of a staircase. Its stairs lead upwards and turn right towards the sound of something struggling above.

Its subtlety, although imminent, increases in volume as I now draw near.

A slight sting courses up my leg as I ascend the stairs and ready my aim. Each step causes the floor to creak no matter how lightly I tread, and once I reach the top of the first flight of stairs, I stop at the sound of footsteps.

Within moments the sight of a naked undead appears. Its body glistening with blood causes me to hesitate as it rushes by.

I quickly fire a round from my magnum which misses as it crosses my path.

Now seeing that its legs are intact, I pull out my knife and prepare myself. My blade points to the left while braced underneath my gun, steady and without trembling as I strafe up the stairs.

Once atop, I follow the undead down the hallway to my left, tailing the distant sounds of grunts and slapping flesh. The heavy breathing becomes amplified as I draw near, forcing me to take caution with each step down the blood-splattered hallway.

While approaching the last door to my left, my stomach turns as I peer inside to find the naked undead amidst orgasm.

A large master bedroom now lies before me. Its king size bed rests in its center surrounded by the dim lighting that the few windows provide.

The horrid sound and smell of rough sex has unwillingly brought me to the undead ahead. It stands facing me on the edge of the bed, thrusting vigorously against a headless corpse. It grunts and screams with each plow as it faces the doorway, currently unaware of my presence.

I feel sick while at the same time intrigued.

For whatever reason, I'm unwillingly compelled to watch the undead get off as I stand halfway through the doorway and lower my guard.

The corpse being raped is too mangled and disfigured to make out what gender it is, for it as well remains covered in blood. Its naked body lies sprawled out on its stomach along the bed. All the while spurts of blood shoot out from its decapitated neck with each forceful thrust.

After watching for a few minutes, the undead begins to bite off portions of the corpse while maintaining its rhythm. The constant slap of rotting skin now overlaps the sound of flesh being torn off the cadaver's back and wrists.

I look up to find the undead staring at me as it relishes its meal.

Its perverse grin stretches across its face and sends a shiver up my spine, the likes of which reignite my fear as I watch it smear blood over its neck and chest.

With a steady hand I slowly raise my magnum.

Its elevation causes the undead to thrust harder and faster until I reach its head. Yet it doesn't stop. For my intent to kill now seems to fuel its arousal and increase its primal vigor.

While digging its nails into the corpse's hips it delivers one final thrust, and as its eyes grow large and its head tilts back, I open fire.

The .357 round rearranges the monster's face as it falls back and lays silent. Its naked body now covered in blood lies glazed within the small amount of daylight.

With a deep breath, I put away my knife and light up another smoke, feeling somewhat unfazed by what I've just observed. After all I've seen lately, I now realize how strangely accustomed I've gotten towards the undead's raw means of affection.

Another fraction of my humanity lost, and a notion that I choose not to dwell on.

Once clear, I finish my search upstairs and head back towards the living room. The air is thick within the house as I make my way down the stairs. A lingering aroma of regret, sex, and bad decisions now follows my path, up until I enter the garage.

With a flip of a nearby switch the darkness escapes around me and sheds light to reveal a black Toyota Tacoma. Now drained of my remaining enthusiasm, I carelessly enter the truck. Its tan leather interior holds no signs of the undead, along with the absence of its keys which are nowhere to be found.

Within moments of briefly searching the truck, I stop and catch my reflection through the rearview mirror. My eyes hang low and seem fatigued. Dark shadows of dirt and trauma surrounds their sockets, along with the blue color within which has now turned a grayish tinge.

After a few blinks I turn away and instinctively pull down the visor, and to my surprise, a set of keys fall on my lap. My jaw drops and my eyes widen to the point where their color regains. Still speechless, I remain unsure as I fumble with the keys.

The expression of excitement on my face now causes it to hurt, and after some trial and error, I manage to slide one of the keys into the truck's ignition. The sound of the Tacoma starting brings my mouth to a smile while exposing my teeth for the first time in days. Relieved that I won't have to resort to driving the Corolla or siphoning gas, I quickly step out and open the garage door.

Even the gray sky and desolate street now seems welcoming as I drive off in my new truck. I try not to falter after grabbing my supplies from the Corolla, for the anticipation of leaving nearly makes me forget my ammunition.

I continue down Ivy Street while passing the many undead I disposed of. Without even a glance I leave it all behind me, continuing down the road at full speed while heading back towards the freeway.

Nothing can stop me now.

3:53 p.m. as I pull to a stop in front of my old Silverado. Its red exterior now blends with the blood covering it as I regain my supplies. My bags remain within the safety of the truck as expected, and I soon waste no time in transferring them to my new Tacoma.

I almost forget my MP3 player again while loading my bags, my excitement now forcing me to double-check my supplies. Once settled, I look up at the cloudy sky to find that the sun no longer hides above.

Darkness will be arriving soon.

Its unavoidable shroud forces my hand as I hop back in my Tacoma and punch on the gas. Its tires scream while a trail of white smoke lingers behind. My actions now speak louder than words, guiding my path as I accelerate north on the freeway.

I put as much distance as I can between the city of Corona and I. Learning much from my mistakes after enduring another trial here, I make it a point to never let myself get trapped or overrun again.

While pushing speeds I now make my trip back to Sovereignty.

I don't know what I expect to find back home or why I'm going there, but I do know that the undead I left there will be waiting.

Perhaps that's why I feel drawn to go back.

I soon become engulfed by the sounds of Nine Inch Nails' "The Day the World Went Away". Its grueling and stimulating melody brings about unknown pleasures and purpose to my ambition; a feeling I never thought existed, yet ignited within the truck's speakers. A subtle remembrance of the person I once was, now guiding my path towards unknown ends.

Everything I've come to see, hear, and feel, all reflects off the deserted freeway ahead. Its sensory overload hits me in waves at the road that still occupies abandoned cars, corpses, and body parts alike.

I now begin to feel as though the world revolves around me.

Only I matter now, seeing as how the human race is endangered if not extinct. The thought of this no longer bothers me as it did before. For I've come to embrace my dilemma, and have learned to enjoy it.

4:21 p.m. as I exit the freeway onto Rainbow Drive. My new truck only had a half a tank of gas to begin with, which has now reduced to a forth of that by the time I spot the gas station ahead.

Without risking being stranded again, I pull up to pump number eleven.

The gas station served as a pit stop and rest area between cities, the one nearest being Sovereignty. The station itself is wide and includes a burger shop as well as a general store, the likes of which bring back memories of a life now lost.

Bunz N Fun was known for its good burgers and open hours for both late nights and hangovers alike. Its popularity made it a must stop while traveling, and proved a Godsend at times when my friends and I needed sobering up.

As I leave my truck to fill up with gas, I pull out my nine and forty-five millimeters and make my way towards the store. The Vicodins I took earlier are beginning to wear off, as each step I take now causes me to wince in pain.

I pause while standing five feet away from the sliding glass doors, just enough so that its sensor won't detect and grant me entrance. My hands tighten around my guns as I watch the undead inside.

They casually wander within the store.

Their attention is drawn elsewhere as they stumble along and bump into each other, currently unaware of the end that I'm about to bring them.

I take one last drag from the cigarette between my lips before I let it fall and bounce off my chest. My instincts and intuition finally take hold as I press on.

With my guns held down and my head hanging low, I enter the store through its sliding glass doors. My heart beats steady yet I find myself facing the undead. All ten of them surround me, slowly circling and advancing like a pack of lions stalking their prey.

If they only knew how the tables have turned.

Time seems drawn out when I'm facing the undead, as the mere seconds I have to I act now last an eternity. A few of the ones surrounding me are in Bunz N Fun attire, their teal visors and matching garbs remain speckled with dry blood. Their moans and snarls reflect off me at all sides, and with twenty rounds in the palms of my hands, I now know that I can get away with a few blind shots.

The lingering smoke from my lungs creeps out my nostrils as I slowly lift my head. My composure brings forth my malice, as I now stare into the eyes of the undead.

I no longer feel fear as a sudden numbness takes hold of my senses. Its control guides my actions as I casually take aim, and fade out of consciousness.

Everything then turns red.

4:32 p.m. and my eyes flicker and widen once I come to. I now find myself surrounded by the lifeless undead. Smoke courses from the barrels of my guns and caresses my arms as I notice my elevated heart rate. That which seems strange begins to make sense as I stop and look at all the monsters I've killed.

All ten of them lie on the floor around me, some twitching while the rest remain still. Their bodies covered in multiple bullet wounds begin to drip blood on the floor. Their steady streams now pool around the many bullet shells that lie near my feet.

I find it strange that I can only vaguely make out what just happened. I appear to be unharmed, yet I don't bother questioning the events that took place. It felt similar to that of the few times I would drive to work and not remember how I got there.

A somewhat effortless feeling of being on autopilot.

However the events that transpired bear little importance to me now, as I holster away my guns and grab a candy bar on my way out.

I can't help but chuckle as I eat my chocolate bar and arrive at my truck.

A small part of me begins to wonder what I've become, and if there's any shred of humanity left within me. I shove the notion aside and laugh at how farfetched it seems, seeing as how I'm the only human left alive.

Once finished, I enter my truck and continue on the freeway.

No more detours or distractions. Nothing can stop me now from heading back home; not the blood seeping from my wound or the undead, not even the shroud of darkness which has yet to come.

I reluctantly look off towards the sun which begins to descend to the west. It remains barely visible behind the overcast sky, yet still able to radiate light within the clouds.

I now light up one of the joints I rolled from Eric's house and exhale the sensation that once caused me pain. Its high relieves the strain on my wound in ways that the Vicodin couldn't, which now sets me in a blissful mood. Even though I appreciate the sensation, I can't help but wonder if the high puts me at a handicap.

My dreamlike state causes me to bask during the drive. All the pain and terror I've endured, suddenly vanish as I lean back, let the wind blow through my hair, and continue north on the freeway.

5:35 p.m. and I now enter the city of Sovereignty. Its buildings stand intact although slightly tattered in the distance. Its roads remain littered with wrecked cars, bodies, and luggage as I exit the freeway. The dark clouds above span low over the horizon, spreading sorrow and despair over the place I once called home.

Nothing has changed since I left five days ago.

The overpopulated city is exactly how I left it, a wallowing grave for yuppie middleclass inhabitants.

I find myself feeling as I did when I was a teenager, angry at having to move into a new town in the middle of my high school years. I would have given anything to see Sovereignty in despair back then. Only now I'm no longer fueled by raging hormones and rebellion, and feel more or less disappointed than pleased.

A part of me wishes that I could have witnessed the outbreak of the undead.

The brief rise and tragic fall of November.

While driving towards my old work I continue down Sanderson Avenue. For the bandage around my leg needs replacing while the wound itself could benefit from some touchups.

I take my time as I drive down the road, going out of my way to run over every undead I find until I finally arrive at work. Déjà vu hits me in waves as I exit my truck and read "Animal Care Clinic" in the distance.

The first thing that comes to mind is Presley.

It seems so long since I've dealt with the dog yet I remember him vividly. His teeth snarled with a ravenous intent, and although he now has only three legs, he still poses a threat.

I'll show the dog what for if he crosses my path, and with knowing that just one bite could be the end of me, I ready my magnum and make my way inside.

The air feels cold and smells sterile within the clinic. A vacant feeling of abandonment surrounds the lobby in ways that it didn't before. A complete opposite of what it used to be like during the hours of eight to six.

After making my way through the back office, I find myself alone in the surgery room. Its table stands in the center to which I use to prop up my leg and cut away my bandage. The bleeding from my wound is minor, such that it only seeps from the top and bottom of its ends. A little peroxide goes a long way and helps clean my laceration to reveal a torn suture; an easy fix that I tend to with a small amount of tissue glue.

Once the bleeding stops, I lightly wrap my leg with a thin layer of brown gauze and blue vet wrap. Its snug fit and slight pressure makes me feel whole again, and with my high now gone, I'm forced to take two more Vicodins.

The taste and feel of the pills is chalky as I swallow them down. No use for water as I've grown accustomed to their bitter taste, and with the effects of the drugs now on their way, I begin to put weight on my leg.

5:58 p.m. and I'm back in Dr. Kibbs' office. No trace of my former boss is found yet his cell phone lies idle on the floor. I take this moment and opportunity to rummage through his drawers to find an old bottle of Canadian whiskey. A stiff drink sounds enticing after everything I've been through, and while examining its half empty contents, I think about how it'll get me through the night.

A memory flashes before me of a time when things were simple, as I now recall partaking in a drink with the doctor after a late night surgery.

He cared for me dearly yet had an odd way of showing it, constantly pushing my limits while rewarding me with drinks and a subtle sense of bonding. He had his moments but for the most part he was a dick. Yet I still had the upmost respect for him.

After claiming the reminiscent bottle of whiskey for my own, I stop and look ahead at the vacant treatment area. Although Presley is gone I can only assume that Snowball left as well. For their bloody paw prints remain scattered about the floor while leading away from their cages.

Realistically all I have to fear is the cat's stealth, for its quiet movements could easily get the drop on me. Either way I've done what I came here to do, and now that my wound is sealed, I should be on my way.

As I step out of Dr. Kibbs' office, I halt at the sound of an alarm. It's faint chime echoes throughout the hospital and warns me that the front door has been opened, similar to that of most gas stations.

My heart begins to race as I immediately pull out my magnum and wait. Something must have come in or out of the clinic to set off the door's alarm, that or I just didn't close it all the way behind me.

I slowly pace myself back towards the lobby, scanning my surroundings with the barrel of my gun with each step I take. Eventually, I arrive at the front end of the clinic and find myself alone. I blame the wind for my paranoia, which seems logical as how it would occasionally crack open the door in the past.

Without taking any chances, I remain cautious up until I reach the front door.

Once outside, I set the bottle of whiskey in the passenger's seat of my truck while loading the medical supplies I took from work. I raided what I felt might come in handy in the long run: syringes, needles, suture, scalpel blades, tissue glue, towels, and Lidocaine.

Everything and anything I'll need for the coming days I've now acquired, but to what end? I'm not even entirely sure why I came back other than finding the undead. An estranged sense of purpose brought me here, and yet I can't help but question why.

Then I hear the screams.

Within moments of closing the passenger door, I suddenly become drawn towards the reflection of an undead. I watch it sprint quickly in the distance, its ravenous gaze now glaring at me from the window. Even while afar I can still make out its eyes, those red marble like spheres that painfully protrude from their sockets.

Unfazed by its menacing arrival, I casually turn to face the undead.

Its sprint continues at full speed, its head shaking from side to side while leaving a thick trail of blood. The short shorts it wears are also drenched in blood, revealing the many scars and scratches that run along its legs. Its brown shirt is torn at the waist above a bleeding wound, exposing the large portion of flesh missing from its torso.

With the sound of its footsteps closing in, I grab my knife and hurl it at the undead. It quickly propels forward while spinning through the air, only briefly until it bounces off my target's chest and falls to the floor.

The undead, unfazed by this, continues its advance.

My disappointment races through my mind, bringing about the rage within me as I pull out my magnum and fire.

My initial shot instantly forces its way into the undead's stomach, causing the tear on its torso to stretch to new heights. Blood along with intestines profusely escape from its gaping wound, causing entrails to spill and unravel on the floor.

With all the blood and vitals it loses it now staggers back, giving me the time I need to plug it with a few more rounds. Within two shots I put an end to the undead, each round piercing its eyes while causing its brow to cave in.

The sudden smell of gunpowder ignites my cravings as I light up another smoke. Its buzz calms my rage as I stand over my fresh kill. Soon the air feels crisp against my skin. Its cold and gentle caress pulls my hair across my face, and within its strands, I look up to see that the sun is about to set.

6:33 p.m. and the overcast sky has darkened with the exception of the sun's descent. I continue driving along the outer rim of the city, in an area known as wine country and towards a familiar place where I can rest.

My plan is to make it to an old hilltop called Dante's. A small mountain where I can watch the sunset and overlook the impressive vantage point it holds. It was the place to be when you had nowhere to go and the means to get there during high school. A place to party, a place to fight, and a place to get laid, an overall great lookout point up until the cops would show. To which they always did.

While driving, I remain alone on the road as there are no undead to be found. The path before me is all too familiar, for it's the same road that I would take to work... the same road that led me towards my fate five days ago.

Part of me is curious to see if the old man in the broken down truck remains up ahead, my second encounter with the undead. Although only days have passed, it seems like a lifetime since I escaped his grasp, an event which proved most unsavory.

Yet the stop sign where he lies is out of my way, and after zigzagging through wine country, I finally reach the trail leading up to Dante's.

My black Tacoma jumbles and scales the steep narrow road with ease, a feat that was difficult in the past with my small Elantra. Nevertheless, I finally arrive at the water towers atop the mountain called Dante's, and after some slight maneuvering, I park my truck facing west towards the sun.

7:00 p.m. and I now stare across the city of Sovereignty. Its shadows lie low beneath the crest of the sun, dawning the impenetrable night which has yet to come.

Two Amoxicillin capsules rest on my tongue, only briefly until I wash them down with a swig of Dr. Kibbs' whiskey. The taste of the Canadian booze is strong and sharp, its thickness that of maple syrup with a hint of lumber which causes me to cough.

During my past life I was never much for liquor, I usually just drank beer. Although given the circumstances, I've come to enjoy the sweet warmth that the whiskey provides, along with the sense of clarity I gain. That and the haze from the Vicodins I took an hour ago which now brings me to new heights.

I now realize that this is my new life, and I have no complaints. I never had much of a drive to accomplish anything in the past. I despised school and felt unsatisfied with my job, and my friends, although many seemed untrustworthy. The women in my life were few and far between and could never put up with me, for reasons I'll never understand. It was as if I was carrying on for the sake of living, without any real purpose.

Looking back at it all, I see that my family might have been what held me together, and now they're gone. On the bright side, I found something in life that I'm good at, and if I didn't excel in surviving this nightmare, then I would surely be dead... or perhaps worse.

Death has no hold over me and never will, for only I will be the one who decides how or when I shall die. In reality it is I who holds the lives of these monsters in my grasp, and I will never stop hunting them.

Smoke slowly escapes from my nostrils as I exhale a drag from my cigarette, its smoothness suddenly overlapped by the dryness in my throat. I attempt to relieve myself with another drink of whiskey. Its subtle burn and latching taste seem to slowly cauterize the lingering lacerations in my throat.

It feels like an eternity since I've last spoken a word, and I can't even recall what it was that I said. Was it to my parents? Was it something sweet or funny? Regardless it does not matter seeing as how I have no one left to talk to, yet it would still be nice to know.

Where one would feel loneliness I do not, for I enjoy the solitude and being left to my thoughts. I stopped wondering why the undead arrived days ago, it makes no difference. It changes nothing. My only explanation would be nature trying to rid itself of humanity, like it did the dinosaurs. Perhaps monsters ate them too.

Regardless of what's in store for me, I plan on taking this world and everything in it down with me when the time comes. The likes of which, the undead have yet to see.

For I have no intentions of showing any remorse... not anymore.

My clarity begins to get scrambled after drinking more whiskey, as I indulge in another smoke while staring out towards the city. I cannot help but admire the red and orange clouds that now shade the sunset, for their streaks are like tie-dye blotched across the sky. The vibrant color tinge makes it seem as though the heavens are on fire, which now rain its flames upon the city below.

It is then that I realize why I came back home.

The portrait of Sovereignty on fire speaks volumes to me, clarifying my purpose while guiding my will. I come to realize that I came back to bring about this city's destruction, a task which up until now, I gladly accept.

If it isn't enough that I rid this place of the undead, I'll make sure that its entire infrastructure goes down in flames. Like the ruined city of Corona, I intend on bringing death while leaving a trail of ash behind me. Though I cannot take credit for the wasteland I ventured through yesterday, I can at least set an example here.

After exiting my truck I look over the layout of the city before me. Its grid shows the four corners that I will hit tomorrow.

The one nearest lies in wine country, while the last being the suburban track homes that I once called home. One of the many wineries nearby will undoubtedly burn with ease, along with the gas station that I used to fuel up five days ago, back when it all started. I'll have to improvise with the remaining two corners of the city, which shouldn't prove a problem after burning down Zeke's Bar and Grill.

I become excited by merely thinking about tomorrow, such a drive that fuels me is unlike anything I've felt before. I try to not get carried away and reserve myself, which I chalk up to the booze and drugs, for I no longer feel the pain in my leg. With a bit of luck I can hopefully make it back to Dante's in time to watch the city burn, but for now I'll bask in the portrait before me.

Fire burns... and will eventually bring about the death of the place I once called home.

8:02 p.m. and my body sways as I urinate off the mountainside. The darkness of the night hangs above me which has now calmed the fires in the sky. It is replaced by the clear shine of stars which can be seen in their entirety from the diminished light pollution.

Soon the thousands of bright dots above begin to smear across the sky like a kaleidoscope. Their image sways with my dizziness as I stumble back to my truck.

The cigarette between my lips holds an extended tail of ash, which I put out while locking myself in the Tacoma. I glance at the empty bottle of whiskey lying on the floor, its contents now filtering through my liver.

With my mind in a state of lethargy, I sit back while carefully resting my legs on the dashboard. My vision flutters at the thought of surviving another day. Yet the more I think about it, I find the events trivial compared to what I've already endured.

Soon my eyes grow heavy at the sight of the stars smearing above. Every blink seems to last longer than the one before, and after forcing my eyes open, they finally remain shut.

Everything then goes dark.

Day 6

8:00 a.m. and the sound of my alarm rings impatiently as I awake. My head feels as though it's trapped in a vice grip. Its imaginary pressure squeezes at my temples as I suffer yet another hangover.

With my eyes sealed shut from dry tears, I let out a bear like yawn while massaging my head. Three loud snaps are heard as I arch and crack my back, my spine now aligning after sleeping in my truck. I slowly wipe the crust from my eyes and within a few blinks; I become startled by what lies before me.

My legs suddenly convulse and force my knee onto the truck's horn. Its loud sound causes my head to throb as it did three days ago, as I now tremble at the sight of an undead.

Its glare seems to penetrate the glass separating us while on its hands and knees. Its sudden appearance catches me off guard as it rest upon the hood of my truck. Like a wild animal it stares at me and growls. The sound of which vibrates through the windshield, causing an almost ripple-like effect upon the glass.

Its face slowly presses up against the windshield, causing blood to smear as it tries to bite its way through. My headache soon fades and I give the undead a stern look. Its faint reflection matches the monster before me and implies my intentions and thrust for death.

With our intimidations met, the undead cocks its head to the side and smiles. Its wide and twisted grin extends to its ears while revealing its chipped and jagged teeth. No longer able to bear its unwillingness to turn away, I feel compelled to smile back.

I then realize that this isn't just any undead… it's Dr. Kibbs.

The decaying flesh hanging off his face makes him hard to recognize, yet the white lab coat he wears is a dead giveaway. Along with his name written on his coat, I now understand the feeling of familiarity I have with the undead.

With his stethoscope around his neck and swaying before me, I watch the blood from his mouth drip from his chin and onto the windshield. He remains staring at me with his hands pressed on the glass, his smile stretching ever further as if recognizing who I am.

I lean in close and come face to face with the doctor, my hand now coursing its way towards the truck's ignition. I've come a long way since our last encounter. My fear is now replaced with rage and I'll be damned if I offer him a quick death.

With a turn of a key the truck instantly comes to life, its sounds and vibrations causing Dr. Kibbs to lean back. With his head still cocked to the side he continues to growl, all the while his chest expands with each rapid breath he takes.

I slowly move my hand towards the truck's transmission. My eyes solely focused on the undead as I'm suddenly forced to stop at the sound of his screams. I briefly stall as he jumps off the hood of my truck, his lab coat flailing in the wind as he sluggishly lands and stands in front of me.

Our eyes connect as I watch him shrug his shoulders from side to side. His movements remain jagged and abrupt, dawning seizure like symptoms as he backs away from my truck.

The son of a bitch is sizing me up as he waits patiently.

Soon an involuntary smirk works its way across my face, guiding my hands as I light up a smoke while reaching for my guns. The cold steel of the nine millimeter makes me feel complete. Its weight gives me balance while gripped firmly in my hand, drawing my gaze as I stare at the undead, and exit my truck.

The blue sky remains blotched with the gloom of overcast clouds lurking above, slowly stretching their way towards the rising sun to the east.

I begin to feel the cold and crisp air that Dante's provides, its altitude now sending its strong winds against my hair. My red scrub top continues to brush and flare against the gust as I move, all while Dr. Kibbs waits patiently for me.

I position myself directly in front of him, the cigarette resting between my lips extending its trail of smoke towards the sky. Without warning the wind suddenly stops and all remains still, and with a long drag of my smoke, I begin to admire our little showdown.

With our eyes intertwined we both refrain from blinking, and I soon grow anxious while tapping my finger against my nine millimeter. Our standoff seems to last an eternity yet I know it hasn't, and I cannot deny the itch I now feel in my right hand.

My eyes begin to water from the cigarette smoke brushing across my face, but I hold my ground, and within my brief blindness I notice the doctor lean forward.

For whatever reason, whether it be excitement, hesitation, or some strange sense of principle, I'm forced to wait. I refrain from acting as we stand alongside the water towers atop Dante's, the extended tail of ash on my cigarette now the only thing standing between us.

8:12 a.m. and with one final drag of my smoke, its ash breaks and we make our move. I watch Dr. Kibbs step forward as I raise my nine millimeter and fire, only to become distracted by another undead. Its arrival catches me off guard, jumping from the bushes nearby while latching on to me.

We both go down.

The round I fired connects with the doctor's shoulder. Its impact comes as a shock and staggers him back towards the edge of the mountainside.

My initial shot fails me as I lose sight of him while caught in the undead's grasp. Within moments I'm on the ground and struggling with the undead, the sound of Dr. Kibbs' screams now echoing in the distance.

While on my back I hold my opponent at bay, bracing it by its neck as it slowly draws near. The smell of rotting flesh brings me back again. Like a light switch being turned on, I become consumed by my sudden rage.

I close my lips tight while blood and saliva drips on my face, now desperately trying to reach for my gun which lies near me. I'm not even sure what would happen if I ingested some of their blood, or if I have already. All I know now is that most of my strength is keeping the undead at bay, and that my nine millimeter is out of reach.

Its bloodshot eyes are now dangerously close to mine, and with my strength weakening, I manage to wedge my knee against its chest. Like a rabid dog the monster continues to chew at the air, lunging its head forward with each ferocious bite.

With the leverage that my knee provides, I use my right hand to pull out the knife strapped to my leg. I now know that once I let up I'll be left vulnerable, that I must act fast before Dr. Kibbs joins in on the fun.

I use what strength I have left to push back the undead and plunge my knife sideways along its mouth. The accuracy of it all while still unscathed, fuels my rage after now rendering it muzzled.

The undead relentlessly bites down on my blade. Its sharp edge digs its way across the sides of its mouth as I push it further in. Blood spews and rains upon me as I rearrange the monster's smile. Its weight letting up on my body gives me the opportunity to dominate.

With my lips still sealed, I push and flip the undead on its back and remain straddled upon it, my weight now keeping it at by. It desperately struggles to break free, flailing about with outreached arms which I'm forced to slap away. Using what remains of its mobility it attempts to lift its head up, only to be brought down by a single punch to its head.

I put the undead in its place as I begin my relentless assault, throwing punch after punch while keeping it planted to the ground. My blows are that of a monstrous nature, forced to avoid the blade wedge within its mouth, I resort to striking its throat. The sound of its teeth chipping and grinding away against the steel of my knife is now apparent with each killing blow.

I begin to see the undead grow weak as I feel its trachea crush beneath my fist. Eventually it refrains from struggling, and I seize the opportunity to reach for my nine millimeter. I waste no time as I raise the butt of my gun and bring it down on its head, over and over until I hear the bone structure of its face begin to break.

My fatigue gradually forces me to stop, and with the barrel of my gun pointed forward, I take a moment to catch my breath.

The bleak sunlight now shines above me, providing warmth where it's needed as I turn my head away and fire. A splatter of blood paints the right side of my face and causes me to cringe, its texture remains thick and strings off the ends of my hair.

My face now trembles with disgust.

Its blood serves as fuel to heighten my rage as I look up and aim at Dr. Kibbs.

Only to find that he is now gone.

Blood, flesh, and strands of hair now stick to my nine millimeter as I lower my aim. What lies before me remains barren as the doctor is nowhere to be found.

The face of the undead below me is longer apparent, its mangled features now reduced to a broken shell of skin and bones. My chest expands with each breath I take while atop of its lifeless body, exhausted as I now wait to catch my breath.

While taking a moment to scan my surroundings, I pull myself up and begin my search for Dr. Kibbs. Although disappointed that he got away, I'm relieved that I managed to fend off the other undead. Once again I've bumped shoulders with death and came out alive, another lesson learned to never forget to mind my surroundings.

As I walk, I stop at a few drops of blood that stain the ground where the doctor stood. Its brief trail leads me towards the edge of Dante's while disappearing within the brush. Unfortunately for me the undead do not bleed as I do, for any trace of coagulated blood is few and far between. Their sporadic streaks and drops surround me at all directions, leading me every which way along the mountainside.

After a while I begin to feel the slight pain from my left leg.

Its arrival luckily did not show during my struggle with the undead, as I now give up my search and return to the truck.

8:35 a.m. as I pop two Vicodins and Amoxicillins in my mouth. Their taste, although familiar, irritates the lining in my throat while traveling down. The tar, dirt, and phlegm that lingers now spews from my mouth as I rinse my face with water. I look towards the sunrise to find it blocked again by the gray clouds that occupy the sky.

Its foreboding is that of rain.

My feet dangle as I sit on the bed of my truck and begin eating the cracker and granola bar from one of my military rations. It's provided fruit punch flavored powder spins and slowly dissolves within my bottle of water, to which I shake in between bites.

I take a deep breath through my nose as the remaining blood dries upon my face, now slightly annoyed with my pulsing hangover.

I can't help but wonder if Dr. Kibbs recognized me, and if so, could my father have as well? With little to no sympathy left in my being, I quickly assume that he caught my scent from my escape six days ago.

That or he recognized my scrub top.

The food in my stomach as well as the sugar from the juice gives me the energy I need to partake in another smoke. I give myself a few moments before I take my leave. I ensure that I'm fitted and ready to kill, tightening the knife strapped to my leg while adjusting my harness and the holster against my hip.

With my leather jacket concealing my guns, I replace the rounds in my nine millimeter with the highly anticipated hollow-points that I acquired from Gods and Ammo. Their ballistics and sloppy output will add a sense of variety to my next kill.

After starting my truck I back up over the lifeless undead, taking off while driving down the hill and leaving Dante's behind.

9:08 a.m. as I continue down wine country. The smell of grapes from the vineyards flowing through the wind blocks out the aroma of dead flesh within my nostrils. With my right hand resting lightly on the steering wheel, I remain in a state of tranquility while soaring down Citrus Road.

It isn't long before I reach my first stop, a large castle like structure to which its foundation lies to the right of the road. Upon turning into its driveway, I glance at a large circular sign identifying "McCloud's Wine and Spirits". Its large purple font is hard to miss as I pull into the winery.

I recall visiting McCloud's a few times during my past life. It wasn't much for food, although thirty dollars would get you pretty sauced during a wine tasting.

I remember taking a girl out for dinner and drinks here before. Her name was Kabrina and she was striking, her hair as black as mine along with her pale skin and matching blue eyes.

To my dismay the date did not end with sex.

However my fondest memory here was with some friends of mine, a drunken sad attempt to feel sophisticated and rub elbows with the city's higher class citizens.

Both times I've visited this establishment I was left unsatisfied, and with that in mind, I find no better place to start burning down.

As I enter the winery, I drive around a large fountain of stone fairies spewing water from their mouths. The adolescent statues stand naked with lush green grape vines wrapped around their bodies.

The fountain seems more provocative than tasteful to me now, its image drastically different as opposed to how I felt before. My perspective has taken a darker tone, a fact which I'm aware of and embrace as I turn away and arrive at the entrance to McCloud's.

While exiting my truck I use my forty-five to dispose of two undead that wander by, my hand, now accustomed to its recoil, increases my accuracy. Beyond lies the entrance to the two story winery, its path leading up towards a white ascending stairway.

I quickly reload my rounds in preparation for entering McCloud's, traveling light while the sound of spare bullets jingles within my pockets. With my forty-five at my side I continue up the stairs, carefully making my way around bloodstains and cracked marble steps.

Once atop I'm greeted by more undead that crawl along the floor. Their legs torn from their bodies lie mutilated as they drag themselves towards me. To conserve ammo I stomp on the heads of the three undead along my path. Their brittle skulls crack like eggshells and prove effortless as they break beneath my boots.

Two long rows of overgrown hedges stretch along the walls of McCloud's, both leading and ending towards its entrance. A massive set of brown double doors stands in my way along with two windows that rest on each side, their closed curtains now making it impossible to see through. The wood that makes up the doors smells of oak as I lean up against them, and I soon begin to hear the subtle sound of opera music playing from inside.

Suddenly, my body flinches at the sound of a window breaking.

The slight tingle of its shattered glass upon the back of my neck quickly subsides as I turn around. Daunted and still startled, I remain on edge at the sound of screams.

I come inches away from the undead that escaped from within.

My movements remain smooth and fluid as I plunge my knife up its jaw.

The moment it opened its mouth was when I closed it shut with my blade, and within seconds I begin to see blood drip from its nose. Although now mute, the undead continues to grab my shoulders, and with one quick motion, I pull out the knife from under its jaw and replace it with the barrel of my gun.

My instincts turn my head away as I open fire.

A spray of blood splatters across my face as I feel the tension released from the undead's grasp. My rage now builds as it collapses before me, and while sheathing away my knife, I once again become overwhelmed by the undead.

One by one they break through the windows alongside McCloud's, their screams now carried by their thrown bodies. Shattered glass falls around me while bouncing off the top of my head. The sound of its shards hitting the ground is that of a faint wind chime as I bend down and cover my face.

With my right leg I stomp on the ground and pull out my nine millimeter. Now more dangerous with both guns in hand, I shake away the glass in my hair and begin my assault.

The two undead to my right begin to pull themselves up, to which I gun down with four rounds from my forty-five. I quickly turn to find the remaining four on their feet and running towards me, their torn formal attire now stained with blood and dirt.

My feet stay planted on the ground as I take out the remaining undead, and with only my head and torso moving, I unleash four nine millimeter rounds upon them.

The first three shots I fire completely remove the heads of three of the undead, instantly causing them to pop after the hollow-point rounds enter their skulls. The last one however suffers a round to its chest, forcing a cave-in that creates a giant hole which I can see through.

While staggering back the undead continues its advance, oblivious to its wound as I fire another round to its neck. The sheer impact tears its once intact head from its body, and after a few moments of shuffling, it collapses to the ground.

9:22 a.m. and with smoke still seeping from the barrel of my guns, I now enter McCloud's Wine and Spirits. The pungent smell of death stops me in my tracks only briefly once inside. Even after so many days and so many deaths, I still haven't gotten used to the rancid smell of rotting flesh.

My eyes then widen as I walk into the massacre that was once McCloud's, its large lobby and dining area lying in shambles. Broken furniture and torn bodies remain scattered about, along with the once white marble floor which is now severely cracked and stained with blood.

A long terrace runs around the entire winery from the second floor. It lies littered with various corpses hanging off its ledge, the sight of blood tricking down from above now apparent. It doesn't take long for the undead roaming the terrace to notice me as they start to scream, their cries suddenly more vibrant while echoing from above.

I immediately open fire, and while I'm not entirely sure how many undead surround me, I only keep track of the five rounds that remain in each of my guns.

Within six rounds, I swiftly eliminate the undead that feast on corpses before me.

Their gluttonous distraction now their undoing.

Beyond them lies the entrance to the wine cellar. Its small wooden door is left ajar as it suddenly bursts open. The three undead that follow now escape while running towards me, their advance quickened by the sound of screams echoing from the depths behind them.

I make short work of them with the remaining rounds left in my guns, and by the time I replace the empty clip in my forty-five, the undead from above finally arrive.

Déjà vu hits me again as the undead rain upon me, throwing themselves over the ledge of the second floor. Their fall is reminiscent of their descent on the freeway days ago, along with their plummet within Zeke's Bar and Grill which makes me think that they never learn.

They hit the ground hard.

One by one they continue to fall, each time smashing against tables, chairs, and the marble floor.

I hastily holster my nine millimeter and ready my forty-five, picking my shots carefully as to not have to waste time reloading. The four undead that fell from above lie sprawled out on the floor, making two of them easy to eliminate with matching rounds to their heads.

My speed, although swift, proves lacking as the ones that remain rush towards me. I quicken my pace backwards while the two monsters give chase, maneuvering between tables, columns, and chairs in an attempt to gain distance. The undead, however, are not much for agility, stalling momentarily during their advance while moving around obstacles.

My wits work in my favor as I seize my opportunity and open fire.

The two undead before me lie lifeless upon dining tables, blood steadily dripping from the bullet wounds between their eyes. My attention's now drawn towards the monsters along the terrace above. The sound of their screams seems intensified with the deaths of their fallen, and now beckons me.

With six rounds left in my forty-five, I pull out my magnum and begin my ascent to the second floor.

Both sides of the terrace run parallel along the dining area, joining at the top of a stairway which stands across from entrance behind me. Its white marble steps lie chipped and stained with blood. I make my way around them as I reach the top and become greeted by the undead.

They now rush towards me from both sides of the second floor, each of them dressed in their Sunday's best and salivating strings of blood. With a single shot from my forty-five, I take out the closest one to my right and continue down its path. Although they're many, most of the undead are spaced apart throughout the long terrace, providing me with the edge I need to dispose of them in small portions.

I manage to move fast enough to evade the monsters behind me while limiting the strain on my leg, building momentum as I aim directly ahead and open fire.

One after another I slaughter the undead along my path.

Like a locomotive, I plow through the narrow terrace and shoot everything in sight, destroying the undead that approach with a vigilance and fury that's unheard of.

I find myself screaming during my rampage.

Leaving behind the remains of the undead I kill, the pain coursing up my leg causes me to press on faster until I arrive halfway around the second floor.

My fury briefly cut short as I'm now forced to reload.

After holstering my magnum I begin to replace the clips in my semi-automatics. I maintain calm and stay collected. The brief eye of the storm which I use to reload seems bleak compared to the wrath that follows.

Within seconds I rush towards the oncoming undead, my trail of carnage leading me full circle around the terrace as I approach the adjoining stairway to the first floor.

The six undead that remain now cluster together along the narrow stairway, shoving each other aside as they fight to reach me. A smug look shines across my face as I walk towards them, taking aim with both guns while pulling back their hammers.

I rapidly fire a blaze of bullets into the mob of undead, advancing my way towards them as their numbers diminish. With the final round in my nine millimeter, I tag the last one standing through its left eye. Its aftermath provides a climactic end as the hollow-point round blows half its face off.

Now lifeless, the undead falls on the small stack of corpses and remains with the rest of its kind. Its end removes the fire within me, as I take a deep breath and continue down the stairs.

While sitting on the last step of the stairway, I set my guns aside to check on my leg. I'm relieved yet I show no emotion as I see no evidence of blood within the wrap around my calf. My satisfaction now limited to the rage that still boils within me.

Suddenly, my stomach turns as I attempt to light a cigarette.

Its end loosely falls from my lips as my mouth hangs open at what lies before me. With my jaw clenched and my hands wrapped around my guns, I now stand with my eyes fixed on Dr. Kibbs.

He stands hunched over while now thirty feet away, his body swaying in front of the open entrance to McCloud's. His lab coat slightly drifts while caressed by the air, accommodating to the gust of wind which carries the strings of blood off his chin. I watch more blood arrive as it trickles down his shoulder, seeping through in clumps from where I shot him earlier.

His eyes continue to stare into mine.

The tension lasts long enough to make me lose patience as I quickly react.

With all my effort and to the point where it almost hurts, I swiftly aim my guns forward and squeeze their triggers. My anticipation however proves misleading, and forces my chest to cave in by the replacing sound of two subtle clicks.

No breakup in the world can compare to the heartache I now feel, for to my dismay I find myself out of ammo. The doctor, however, remains still, his head cocked to the side as he now grins perversely.

His confidence is the result of my negligence, forcing me to drop my guns while pulling out the knife strapped to my leg. My rage causes me to expose my teeth and snarl as I rush towards him, and within my first step, I become caught in the arms of another undead.

While panicking I turn and vigorously stab at the monster's face, gradually losing its hold on me while now caught within my grasp. Unable to control myself, I continue to plunge my blade into the undead, steadily feeling the steel sink into its flesh while tearing it apart. After awhile I grow tired and find myself atop a motionless corpse, the hilt of my knife slightly protruding from its head.

Flaps of bloody flesh now hang and fold from where its features once stood. The horrific sight is similar to that of the entrails of a pumpkin. My brief exhaustion distracts me while resting upon the undead, and after two deep breaths, I quickly look up to find Dr. Kibbs missing yet again.

9:39 a.m. as I stand facing the entrance to McCloud's. The aroma of death and vineyards from outside causes my nostrils to flare and my chest to expand with disappointment.

I keep coming back to Dr. Kibbs and how he got away, his gaze ever upon me along with his infrequent presence. Somehow I feel that he is near yet I cannot see him; a disturbing thought that now makes me feel hunted if not stalked.

My feeling of failure, although escalating, soon diminishes at the sound of screams. The cries carry up from the wine cellar in the distance, now occupying the undead that I overlooked earlier.

While racing against the sound of their footsteps I push myself to the limit, hobbling my way across the dining area until I reach the entrance to the cellar. Dozens of bloodshot eyes stare up at me from the darkness below, their cries drawing near as they ascend the narrow stairway.

With an abrasive slam I remove them from sight, closing the cellar door as the sound of their steps grows louder as I back away. The relentless undead never cease to give up, constantly banging at the small wooden door as it pulses with each strike.

While pressed for time, I position a nearby wine cart in front of the cellar's entrance and prepare to set it ablaze. Similar to that of Zeke's Bar and Grill, I begin to smash bottles of alcohol upon it, initially starting with brandy while finishing off with tequila. The smell of French Bordeaux surrounds me after breaking over fifty thousand dollars worth of wine; enough to make the strongest palate cry as I now notice the door on the verge of breaking.

With a quick flick of my lighter I set the small cart ablaze, its combustion arriving as the undead breakthrough. I waste no time as I see my opening and rush towards it, pushing the burning cart ahead while its flames lick upon my face.

I'm now unable to see the wine cellar before me.

The heat is so severe that I'm left to rely on the feel of broken glass beneath my boots, along with the call of the monsters ahead. Within a few steps I begin to brace myself for impact, no longer looking ahead but now turned away as I smash against the undead. Their resistance, although subtle, causes me to let go, forcing them back down the depths of the cellar while catching the rest on fire.

I watch my plan unfold to perfection as the undead prove no match for my battering ram. The burning cart plows through the ascending crowd, causing them to tumble back down as it reaches the bottom and strolls out of sight.

Soon the red glow of the flames begins to grow within the darkness below, stretching its way forth followed by a thick rush of smoke. Now confident that the fires will spread, I quickly muffle the sound of agonizing screams by shutting the cellar door.

I have once again bested the undead.

Such a simple act speaks volumes as I take my leave and put it all behind me, the undead, the fire, the smoke, and my wrath. All of it gone within the small frame of a wooden door.

After holstering the guns I dropped earlier I finally arrive outside, reflecting atop the stairs that lead down towards my truck.

I devote some time to look around at the undead I disposed of earlier.

Each of them lies sprawled out on the concrete floor while tattered and torn beyond measure. For a moment I start to feel more at ease, almost too sure of myself as I light up a smoke.

My smug disposition makes me think about all the alcohol in the wine cellar, a wide variety of booze now eaten up by the flames. My confidence reaches an all time high, and yet I pause as I recall the cylinders of nitrogen that might reside inside.

It all seems too late now, my ignorance and stupidity, all boiling down to my initial drag of nicotine as a thunderous bang is heard. The force of the blast sends my body soaring down the stairs as McCloud's explodes behind me, breaking my will once again as everything now turns white.

10:07 a.m. as I awake to the sound of a familiar pitch within my ears, a painful ringing which I'd soon hope to forget. The throbbing in my skull brings back memories as well. Its agonizing pulse matches that of my leg.

While lying on the ground I begin to feel small portions of gravel rain upon me, the sound of which now causes my hearing to improve. Blood splatters on the ground as I reluctantly begin to cough, spewing small amounts from my mouth which carelessly drip off my bottom lip.

I now stand but a few feet away from my truck, and with my body swaying and my head a mess, I remain appalled at the distance I covered from the blast.

The intense heat from the fires suddenly hit me as I turn in admiration to watch McCloud's burn. Bright orange and yellow flames now engulf the winery and dance around its stone structure, slowly breaking it down piece by piece. The few undead that remain run frantically within the haze of smoke, screaming in agony whilst now ablaze.

After a few moments my disorientation fades. Its jarring aftermath still lingers, yet I'm able to steady my hand enough to light up another smoke.

With my back against the truck I wait and watch the fires unfold, spreading ever so quickly beyond the winery. A mixture of blood and dirt circulates in my mouth as I puff on my cigarette, now chuckling at the thought of how many times I've almost died.

Fire burns... and it once again nearly claimed my life.

10:34 a.m. and I'm back on the road after leaving McCloud's. A trail of dirt, smoke, and ash lingers behind as I speed my way out of wine country. While driving, I arch my back and begin to feel my spine snap into place; a feeling much needed and appreciated after enduring the blast.

Black smoke now stretches out towards the sky from my rearview mirror, its density that of a tornado. Larger and larger the smog grows behind me, bellowing from the ruins that was once McCloud's Wine and Spirits.

I now rest assured that wine country will burn by nightfall.

As I finally arrive in the city, I look around at the place I once called home. Any and all remnants of my past are now long gone, soon to be buried within the ashes of Sovereignty's inevitable fate.

While driving through town I can't help but reminisce. The brief moments of my old life hit me in waves with each passing landmark. The bar I'd go to, the park Eric sold drugs at, the gym I rarely went to, the place I did my taxes, and the parking structure where I'd bang my old girlfriend at.

The good times are now killing me, slowly bringing me back to a fantasy world which no longer exists. This longing for antiquity, although limited, does not last, slowly dwindling away with the bleak sunlight above.

For a moment it felt nice to be home, but now I feel nothing.

11:27 a.m. as I pull up to Subtastic, a lonely sandwich shop which stands within a small plaza. A gas station, dentist office, and various other stores lie around its radius, spanning alongside Fragile Road while ending at a vast set of track homes. Across the road stands my old high school, South West High, home of the Sultans. Its gray infrastructure and surrounding gates are that of a prison, differing only by its football field and lack of basketball courts.

While finishing my smoke, I stand to observe my old stomping grounds, my mind finding it hard to believe that it's been four years since graduation.

The days of my youth now lost within the lonely shadows of South West High.

With my gym bag around my shoulder I enter Subtastic. Its glass doors remain smeared with blood along with an open sign which struggles to stay lit.

During my past life I would come here often after class to hang out with some friends that worked here. One of which was my friend Shannon, a very attractive tomboy whom I took out on many dates, which again did not end in sex.

The foul aroma of spoiled deli meats now fills the air as I enter the shop, a stench comparable to that of the undead. A black marble countertop full of ingredients spans along my right side, its contents rotting and swarming with flies.

I cautiously walk upon the chessboard painted floor, its black and white tiles bringing me towards a thin trickle of blood. Like breadcrumbs I follow the crimson trail, leading me around the countertop while heightened by the sound of groans.

I suddenly pause at the sight of an undead.

Its eyes glare up at me while devouring portions of its arm, sitting patiently along the blood splattered floor. With my nine millimeter aimed at its head I slowly back away, its appearance somewhat familiar as it clambers to its feet. It isn't until I notice the Subtastic visor and torn Iron Maiden T-shirt that I realize this was once my friend David.

My finger lets up on the trigger as I see it now. The mustache faintly seen through crusted blood, the above average height, and the dread locks which he took such pride in; all of which cause me to slightly lower my guard and nearly speak his name… until I open fire.

Within the blast of the hollow-point round, the left side of my old friend's face becomes blown off. His left eye and ear now replaced with a jagged tear that exposes skull and brain. Blood mists and splatters against the wall behind him as he falls down, no longer animated but now put to rest.

A small sting of sadness hits me as I stare down at David's corpse.

A feeling that quickly fades once I remember that all my friends are dead.

My insatiable appetite grows with my protesting stomach as I sit at a table near David's corpse. It didn't take long for me to raid the freezer within the store, and even though the pickings proved slim, I still managed to gather a few unspoiled items.

With the ingredients laid out before me I begin to prepare my lunch, which again consists of a sandwich made of white bread, ham, turkey, pastrami, cheese, and mustard. My diet as of late has been limited to military rations and canned foods. To actually eat something with a reasonable amount of sustenance is a luxury I should be having more often.

While ravaging through my meal, I struggle to breathe as I inhale through my nose, suddenly coming to terms with my lack of culinary skills. Even before all hell broke loose, I'm unable to recall making myself anything other than breakfast or sandwiches to eat. The thought of starvation being my undoing seems laughable, if not pathetic.

Moments pass after finishing my lunch and I'm halfway through a cigarette. Its smoke steadily escapes my lungs while putting my bloated stomach at ease.

Within my gym bag I find that my ammunition has greatly diminished, and although I have plenty to get me by, it's still not enough. Bullets and water are both necessities for me now, the fundamental element of life along with one of the many that ends them. The irony is such that it's poetic, and while I'll eventually have to restock, I'll make do with what I have.

All that is left now is to let this place burn.

11:55 a.m. as I release the gas from the oven and stove behind the black counter. Its aroma, although faint, becomes quickly overlapped by the hissing sound of its escape. While finding any and all means to bring down Subtastic, I gain satisfaction in my creative will to improvise.

During my raid of the freezer earlier I stumbled upon a storage closet. Within it held various cleaning supplies as well as two canisters of lighter fluid, which I claimed as my own. Slowly but surely the smell of gas begins to fill the air, a potent mixture which only intensifies as I douse the shop in lighter fluid.

I take a moment to say my goodbye to my old friend David, taking my leave while the canister hangs and pours lighter fluid along the floor.

Once outside the fresh air coincides with the lingering fumes in my lungs, swirling about as I now stagger with each step. For a few moments I stop at the entrance of the store, ensuring a thick layer of lighter fluid as it follows and ends near my truck.

Without taking any chances I drive away from Subtastic, backing away a good thirty yards to reach a safe distance. The extra canister of lighter fluid will come in handy during my next stop, and after setting it aside, I prepare myself for the blast.

I indulge in another cigarette during my short walk back from the truck, taking in each drag until I reach the end of the liquid trail, and ignite it with my smoke. A shot of yellow flame instantly catches and causes me to drop my smoke, quickly spreading while racing across the asphalt and vanishing beneath the doors. A flash of light blinds me as the blast now pushes me back, bringing about a heightened pitch in my ears until it all falls silent.

Soon the brightness fades and reveals the burning remains of what was once Subtastic, its structure barely standing and on the verge of crumbling. The fires quickly spread and latch on to the neighboring stores, dancing from one end to another while growing in size.

Unaware at the time I now find myself sitting upright, my arms braced behind me while in a state of bewilderment. I pull myself up and begin to regain my hearing.

The deafening silence is now replaced with the crackling of flames.

Fire burns… and gives way to all destruction, fueling my wrath while removing the remnants of my past.

12:24 p.m. as I drive back into town, my mind now at ease and rejuvenated after my hearty meal. I continue down Fragile Road for nearly ten minutes, backtracking through the empty city until I pull to a stop.

The cross street before me stretches far on either side, both ends seeming limitless as its name looms ghostly above. The green street sign hangs and sways off a single hinge below the stoplight, its image strangely inviting as I recall the library at the end of its path.

My motives are now based on instinct. Their paths lie before me in blood while ending in ash and smoke. In my mind the layout of the city is clear, its radius slowly burning in the distance while faintly calling me here. The funny thing about instinct is how it leads me towards the places I love and hate.

This however is not one of them.

Now feeling that I've trekked far enough into Sovereignty, I turn right onto Health Lane, speeding my way forth and towards the library up ahead.

12:39 p.m. and my truck mildly purrs as I coast through a business plaza, carefully scanning the area as I park.

I stop to soak in my surroundings.

Dozens of cars, busses, and trucks rest abandoned within the crowded parking lot, all vacant and unscathed. The city's local traffic court lies adjacent to a nearby recreation center, a place I'm more than familiar with given my past driving record. Beyond me lies a white two story building glossed with tinted windows, the words "Public Library" stretched across its entrance.

While approaching, I watch my reflection walk towards me through the glass doors, its hand slowly pulling the magnum from underneath its leather jacket. The man in front of me carries a stern smirk, darkness surrounding his eyes with blending soot upon his face. His red scrub top hides beneath his jacket, now seeming darker with patches of blood and ash streaked across his chest. I fear not my reflection but the shadow it bears, my dwindling sanity now hanging at my heels.

Within moments I reach for my reflection's hand, acknowledging its presence at the door's handle yet startled as it abruptly bursts open.

The cold steel of the door's frame hits me square in the face, causing me to stagger back from the undead that follows. While dazed and blinded, I fire three rounds ahead, my luck bearing with me as I hit the undead once in the pelvis and twice in the throat.

I slowly regain focus to find the undead fidgeting on the ground, its neck partially blown off by the .357 rounds. I quickly reload my magnum and shake the pain from my head. The blood lingering in my mouth drips loosely as I spit it out and enter the library.

The sound of the gunshots draws the undead's attention once I arrive. Their eyes fixed upon me to the point where their sheer gaze seems to burn through what's left of my soul.

Six of them now roam before me on the first floor, as well as what I believe to be five more that scurry above. They do not hesitate as they rush towards me, constantly stumbling over chairs and desks while drawing near.

With all six rounds of my magnum, I drop four of the undead, forcing me to back away as the remaining two arrive. Their wrath and speed proves too much for me, causing me to drop my gun and begin fleeing. With death at my heels I keep on running, the pain from my leg now constricting as I'm forced to turn and fight.

The undead closest to me stalls after hurling a nearby stool at its face, giving me the moments I need to introduce it to the barrel of my gun. I squeeze my index finger and open fire, summoning a flash while sending a hollow-point round in-between its eyes. I take a step back as its body collapses, revealing the undead that follows at its now close proximity.

Unable to fire another round, I maneuver myself around a large copying machine that stands between us. The sound of my boots shuffling is heard as I dance back and forth, steadily evading the rabid undead while keeping it at arms reach. Our eyes remain intertwined as we rock from side to side, slowly sizing each other up as though we're boxing.

Within moments, my patience grows thin as I move around and fire at the undead. Both shots instantly make short work of its knees, causing them to immediately pop and spray blood on me. With its new found lameness it lies face down and amidst struggle, screaming in anger as I arrive to finish it off.

I open the cover of the copier while lifting the undead up. Its thin greasy hair slips through my hands and feels that of dampened silk, proving difficult to handle as it constantly struggles. I manage to brace its arms behind its back while pulling it up. Its unwillingness to cooperate forces me to kick at the back of its knees, each time tearing flesh and spouting blood.

The sound of its torn ligaments and bones grinding is now faint compared to that of its head slammed against the scanner. Still unfazed after gaining the upper hand, I hold up the lid of the copier and watch the undead.

The right side of its face remains exposed while pressed up against the glass, desperately struggling while gargling blood. If it wasn't for the lingering fear that I live with, I wouldn't relish moments like these. A slight sense of amusement that masks the terror I feel, giving me the will to carry on.

While bracing my body against the undead, I bring the lid down upon its face. Again and again I crush the monster's skull with the cover of the machine. For I have no intent on stopping, even as I now hear the glass steadily break beneath its face.

Slowly the scanner cracks and fills with blood after each slam, forcing my hand faster as the copier suddenly turns on. A barrage of photocopies spit out from a nearby tray, displaying the mangled images of the undead's face until its body remains still.

My anger quickly subsides as I calm my storm, no longer finding fulfillment in my excessive onslaught.

To which I finally stop.

12:58 p.m. as I recover from my brief exhaustion. My fits of rage now seeming more frequent, tend to leave their mark. Whether it be bodily harm or fatigue, there is always a price to pay.

The undead above, although scattered, remain frantic as they scurry about, snarling and glaring down at me as I now take aim. With six rounds left in my nine millimeter and plenty to spare, I observe my five targets. Easy pickings as they have yet to find a way down.

With a barrage of bullets I rain lead upon the undead, stopping only briefly to reload as I continue my spree.

One after another they begin to fall, their bodies contorting, over the railing above followed closely by their screams. It isn't until I hear the sound of desks breaking and the imminent thud of five bodies, that everything goes silent.

I stand surrounded by the lifeless undead. The aroma of rotting flesh emitting from their bodies now decaying the very air I breathe.

It is the one thing that I'll never get used to, yet I try to mask the scent by lighting another smoke.

The eleven disfigured corpses lay broken and still, blood slowly excreting from the many wounds I inflicted. They never stood a chance, for their odds of survival came limited with my arrival.

After holstering my nine millimeter, I make sure to grab the magnum I dropped earlier before I begin my search. With all the spare time I have I find it wise to browse for some literature. The library is vast and full of choices. Two stories worth of reading material, yet all I can think about is how easily they will burn.

I take my time while exploring my surroundings, checking any and all crevasses for any lingering undead. My pace remains slow and carefree, scanning aisle after aisle of books in hopes of finding something of interest. The majority of the library's emphasis consists of elementary level reading: Dr. Seuss, Bernstein Bears, Goosebumps, and that stupid big red dog that I use to love so much, all of their material laid out in display.

Further deep into my search I acquire a book called "Island of the Blue Dolphins", a children's book, although one I thoroughly enjoyed. Its depicting tale of a young girl's survival and revenge while isolated on an island now seems all too familiar. It does however have a happy ending, in a matter of perspective.

Yet happiness is only seen through the eyes of its beholder.

Most of the books I acquire are of a survival genre which seems fitting, although I do make it apparent to grab some educational material. A book on medicine as well as plant life seems appropriate, as well as a few wildlife survival guides which makes my search nearly complete. Though I can't help but feel that something's missing. An abundance of books I have, yet for whatever reason I was expecting more.

While nearing the end of my search, my attention becomes drawn towards a corpse resting its head on a desk. The puddle of blood spreading beneath it now surrounds and hugs my boots as I approach and move its body.

With a small thud the corpse drops to the floor, revealing the Bible it rested on as well as the space where its face was torn. The thin layer of skin surrounding its features slowly begins to fold inwards and deflate, filling the gap as I find no skull present within its head. A crimson hollowed out surface is all that is seen within the dark void of its identity, soon to be tainted by strands of hair which now course into its depths.

While trying to avoid the possibilities of what might have happened, I turn away and pry open the Bible. The writing within is illegible as the book itself is saturated in blood, each page stuck together while nearly sealed shut. I'm not even sure as to which section of the good book I've opened to, which to be honest seems irrelevant. I care not for the words of implied wisdom, for my faith now relies on the cold steel holstered against me.

3:43 p.m. as I place my bag of literature within my truck and grab the canister of lighter fluid. A strong gust of wind blows through my hair as I stare up at the gray sky, no longer searching for the sun, but for the off chance of rain.

The thought of all my hard work today being extinguished is troublesome. Although part of me realizes that if fate wanted this city to survive, then it wouldn't have brought me here.

I quickly walk back towards the library with the canister in hand, but am suddenly stopped by what lies below me.

My anger now mixes with fear, forcing my eyes to close as my blood boils at the sight of a stethoscope near my feet. All the distractions from McCloud's to the library have made me almost forget about Dr. Kibbs. Almost forget that he's out there.

I can once again feel his presence, it feels so close yet he's nowhere to be found. He's fucking with me now, playing with my emotions unlike any undead I've encountered. Either that or it's all in my head, a sheer coincidence that this undead so happens to arrive and escape rather frequently.

I try to recall if I overlooked the stethoscope when I arrived or stepped out of the library, but it's no use. My gut instinct and feeling of being watched tells me all that I need to know. The trend of encounters so far has been the same, and I don't expect to face Dr. Kibbs anytime soon.

However if I do, I'll make sure to count my rounds and be ready.

Once back inside, I stand at library's entrance and observe its interior. Feeling relieved that there's nothing explosive here, my subconscious tells me that it's time for an old fashioned book burning.

I make my rounds throughout the inside of library, dousing shelf after shelf with lighter fluid until I eventually run out. The smell is such that it almost stings my nostrils, slowly building as the fumes gradually fill the air. In an attempt to block the aroma I light up one of my smokes, no longer fearing death as its embers draw near my dampened hand. For a while I take my chances and enjoy myself, relishing each drag until I flick the cigarette towards a bookshelf to my right.

Within seconds the shelf catches on fire, instantly combusting while causing me to step back. Its heat and smoke builds so quickly that it's difficult to bear, and soon all I can hear is the crackle and snap of paper burning.

With my body frozen I'm now stuck admiring the flames, its trail racing throughout the library while destroying everything in its path. My hesitation and immobility brings me back six days, bewildered by my first encounter with the undead. My fascination with the flames keeps me in trance until the heat tells me otherwise. Eventually the library begins to cave in, its walls and frame slowly breaking as I'm forced to leave.

Once outside I take a deep breath of what should be fresh air, now substituted with the stagnant and stale taste of death. It's as if the world's ozone layer has died and become replaced with the exhales of billions of undead. Even the once blue sky is tainted red, which seems to decay with the dying sun.

Fire burns…. and takes with it all traces of humanity.

Its creations and ideals now reduced to a smoldering pile of ash.

4:24 p.m. as I drive down Fragile Road, a long stretch of asphalt which heads north through town; towards the outskirts where my old neighborhood lies, back to where it all began.

This town hasn't changed since I've left it six days ago, but I have. A somewhat different outlook as I find myself scanning my surroundings in a different light. Where I was once looking for shelter, I now search for more monsters to kill. A selfish need that never seems satisfied yet is held at bay by the fires that build in the distance.

To the east rises a mountain of black smoke bellowing above the glow of orange flames, overcoming what was once wine country. Its trail of fire and ash continues to spread throughout the city, bringing about chaos and death beyond the library behind me.

The final corner of the inferno lies ahead as I drive through town, back towards Subtastic. Although it's only been hours, the explosion seemed to have no difficulty making its way around. The shopping plaza where Subtastic stood has now burnt down. Its fires stretch far and wide while still ablaze at the nearby track homes.

Numerous large bonfires remain scattered throughout road, each patch burning idly while a few devour cars. From the looks of things it seems as though the flames have gradually spread across the street, jumping from one end to another and eventually reaching my old high school.

To which I now get to witness the beginning of its fall.

The once bold green letters that spelt out "South West High" have burnt to a black and blotched font, along with our mascot which was once an Arabian knight. The portrait of its steed and clothing after the constant licks of flames have turned it dark, removing all color while resembling the very image of death. The only difference being the curved sword it holds as opposed to a scythe.

I was never much for school which seems cliché of most students, and although I'm a different person now, it takes a special type of alumni to watch their city burn. Yet I care not for how this may appear and press on, racing by the flaming wreckage as I continue back home.

4:32 p.m. and I finally arrive at the gas station near my house. Stricken by a sudden sense of Déjà vu, I pull up to pump number seven and exit my truck.

It's hard to believe that it's only been six days since it all began, since I was last here. Frightened as I once was, the lingering fear of death is still there, yet I find myself feeling more alive than ever.

The higher elevation gives me a clear view of the city below. Its smoke and fire seems limitless while reaching out towards the sky.

Like before, I slide my credit card through the automated cashier to fill my truck with now premium gas. The thought of this causes me to smile and chuckle at my own amusement, pretending to be some asshole while getting fancy fuel.

Everything I do now seems vaguely familiar.

It brings about a new sense of routine as I walk towards the gas station yet again. But even I know that nothing is the same, everything has changed... especially me.

I pause at the sight of blood covering the sliding glass doors.

Its image is different than before as I pull out my nine millimeter and approach them. Their lack of functioning is a bad omen, constantly jerking back and forth while only halfway open. I keep my gun held down and prepare to squeeze through, anticipating the worst with each subtle step.

Within my approach I'm suddenly greeted by the undead. Both of them appear out of nowhere while trying to press through. They scream and fight as they constantly struggle, desperately pushing the doors to no avail with outreached arms.

Their lack of coordination is now my gain.

Their abruptness has little effect on me, my anticipation saw to that, and as my heart remains calm and my hand steady, I take aim.

Eventually the undead catch on and squeeze though one at a time, each one taking a step forward while getting gunned down with matching rounds. Their bodies remain still while lodged in-between the doors, both of them stacked upon each other while keeping the entrance ajar.

With my aim ready I gently creep inside, taking caution as I'm suddenly forced to fire yet again.

I make short work of the lingering undead with my remaining rounds, expelling my entire clip while restricted on space to move. Blood and flesh smears across racks of newspapers and countertops as they now lie dormant. Their pathetic attempt to flank me proved their undoing.

Now removed of all possible threats, I replace the clip in my nine millimeter and begin searching the store. Curiously enough I find nothing of interest. The sight of food is unsatisfying and the smell of booze uninviting, yet I can't help but take a swig of whiskey as I break bottles throughout the store.

I once again prepare to bring the burn, pouring bottle after bottle of alcohol throughout the gas station while making my way towards checkout. I pause for a moment and stare at the cartons of cigarettes behind the counter. A must for my travels, yet I'm hesitant to face what lies below.

The tattered and naked image of the undead's lust.

My hands curl tightly around my gun as I aim low and slowly move around the counter, prolonging the inescapable feeling of disgust.

To my surprise I come to find an empty puddle of blood.

Its remains thickened with clots and flesh, showing no signs of disturbance while surrounding a single red high heel. The shoe itself rests sideways within the small crimson pool. Its skinny heel is chewed off with strands of hair wrapped around it, now much darker after being stained with specks of blood.

For all I know the naked limbs could still be out there, walking aimlessly in search of its next rape victim.

I sigh with relief as I holster my gun and begin grabbing cartons of smokes, using my feet to kick the shoe and broken glass aside. After acquiring what I need, I take in the aroma of alcohol filling the store. Strong as it may be, it begs a warning for me to wrap things up and take my leave.

The warmth from the whiskey now stirs in my belly as I arrive outside. Its sensation reminiscent of the numbness I feel, which instantly fades once I spot the rack of propane tanks to my right.

I now have the means to bring this place down, and with it I feel complete.

I quickly place one of the propane tanks behind the sliding glass doors while loading the remaining two in my truck. The explosives, although not ideal, will prove ample in my burning of the shopping plaza.

While removing the gas pump from my truck, I stop to stare at the large convenience store in the distance. I would've never thought that I'd end up back here, in front of John's Club, where I once feared to tread. Its large structure remains intimidating, yet seen as nothing compared to the sea of wreckage before it.

The labyrinth as I initially saw it still consists of demolished and abandoned cars, so vast that it covers the entire parking lot. Any and all pathways leading through are too narrow for my truck to squeeze through, which leaves me with no option but to proceed on foot. However the propane I found should be enough to ignite John's Club, and if I'm lucky, the parking lot as well.

With the nozzle of the gas pump held down by its lock, I gently set it down and let fuel flow onto the asphalt. A steady stream of gas now spreads along the ground and marks its path, slowly stretching towards the gas station and hopefully John's Club as well.

As I enter my truck I catch myself almost lighting a smoke, but restrain myself from making a foolish mistake. If I live long enough I know that cigarettes will eventually bring about my end, and I'd rather it not be out of sheer negligence or getting blown up.

I now drive back onto the street leading towards my old neighborhood and park in the middle of the road, far from the expected blast radius, yet close enough to walk to. I take a moment to reload my clips as I intend on traveling light, the weight of the propane tanks now making me regret my plan. One by one I remove them from my truck and continue on foot. Feeling slightly exhausted with the subtle pinch from my left leg, I stop to swallow two Vicodins and Amoxicillins, and press on.

5:05 p.m. and the red sky now grows dark as I stand in front of the labyrinth. The parking lot itself is not extremely large, however the clutter of vehicles smashed against each other will make navigating difficult. I stop to think how I could easily climb the cars and run across the parking lot, yet my leg will not allow it. For its strain is now more pronounced after carrying the propane.

In my eyes the vehicles resemble tall grass hedges that form a maze ahead of its castle, which in reality is John's Club. After readjusting my grip around the two tanks, I continue through an opening within the wreckage, and begin to make haste.

Darkness shrouds over me along my path as the car's shadows limit the daylight above. Its grip and enclosure at certain points is unsettling and cold. I cannot begin to imagine what happened here, how all these cars could be crushed together in such a way. Each one of them holds the bodies of the deceased: men, women, and children, all of which remain torn apart while very few stay intact.

I now find myself deep within the labyrinth, my enthusiasm and pace swiftly diminished by the tightening pull on my leg. The smell of metal and blood is constant throughout my path, a chalky iron-like taste that lingers on the tip of my tongue. Each flavor of death I come across proves worse than before, a genuine reminder of what once was and things to come.

Within minutes I see John's club towering over the cars ahead, its protruding rooftop resting thirty yards away. Now excited and anxious at nearing the maze's end, I push myself further, treading along while forced to sway the propane tanks to build momentum.

Then I hear the screams.

It was too good to be true, my lonely path through the parking lot. Its narrow halls and many dead ends would not be complete without the company of the undead.

I quickly drop one of my propane tanks and turn to face my assailant, its approach distant yet closing in fast. The very image of the monster sprinting down the wreckage forces my hand as I pull out my nine millimeter. My aim, although ready, hesitates on the trigger, now stopped at the sight of the cars awakening.

Suddenly, the doors from the surrounding vehicles burst open and spew out the undead residing within. Every corpse I passed by was just waiting to attack, their bodies still and their presence unknown.

Within seconds my target is lost and replaced with the flooding undead. Their arrival is swift while crowding the maze, revealing my fear as I'm now cornered.

I quickly step back and open fire, desperately holding on to the remaining propane tank in my right hand. I expel five rounds towards the hoard of undead but am suddenly caught in the grasps of one behind me.

Panic hits me in more ways than one.

Its shock overwhelms me and heightens my fear, the likes of it similar to my escape in Corona. Yet the darkness within me prevails, forcing my hand as I turn and repeatedly pistol whip the undead to the ground.

I finally break free.

The crowd now approaching is relentless, pushing me forward as I limp through the maze and come to a dead end. My irritation and fear is nothing compared to that of the hunger and rage behind me.

A rusted blue van now blocks my path. It stands roughly ten feet tall while its edge cuts off the entrance to John's Club. With what remains in my nine millimeter I fire at the undead, each shot providing me with the seconds I need to scale the van.

After hoisting the propane tank over I begin my climb. The sound of it hitting the ground is nonexistent to the constant screams.

One after another I frantically kick away at the undead, their outreached arms grasping for straws which prove to be my legs. Once atop, I slowly stand while overlooking the labyrinth below, my chest now receding as I breathe heavily through my nose.

Behind me lies the gray entrance to John's Club, its exterior free of potential threats while tucked away from the wall of cars. Eventually the undead begin to scale the van but fall short of success, their mass in numbers quickly filling every path within the darkened maze.

It won't be long until they figure a way out of the wreckage. Their wrath, although limited, always seems to find a way, and with them now trapped together, I look for the propane tank I dropped earlier.

With my forty-five in hand I continue to search through the undead, scanning the floor until I spot the small white tank within the crowd thirty yards away. I lick my lips and steady my aim, blocking out all distractions as I calm myself and lock on.

Regardless of how still I try to maintain, my body fidgets at the impact that I will soon endure. The moment I felt hesitation is the moment I open fire, and with one shot I accurately hit my mark.

Everything then turns white.

6:02 p.m. as I lie on my back before John's Club. All I can hear now as I come to is the crackling of flames and sound of cars exploding. The last thing I remember from the blast was glass spraying from shattered windows and the combustion of the undead.

Their screams ever distant, yet beckon me from my fading deafness.

Multiple explosions are now caused by the abandoned vehicles that make up the maze. Each of them rapidly creates a chain reaction throughout the parking lot, all the while tearing apart the monsters within.

Darkness creeps along the sky above and rains ash and blood down upon me, the remnants of the once undead now becoming one with the air. With a twist of my neck, I clench my teeth and arch my back while lying on the ground, faintly feeling and hearing the shattered glass roll off my leather jacket as I pull myself up.

Blood begins to seep from a small cut on the back of my head, its small volume dampening my hair as I run my hand across it. An insignificant injury which I brush aside, one that is nothing compared to the pain from my leg.

Heat rises from the fire's rage and overwhelms me as I notice the blue van ahead. The obstacle which I stood upon that has yet to explode. I desperately back away from the flames and nearly trip over the propane tank that I threw over earlier. My mind still scrambled from the explosion, makes the heat intolerable as I quickly grab the tank from the ground.

John's Club now lies only a few feet away, its entrance holds two large glass doors that vaguely reflect the flames behind me. While facing the fires again I continue backwards, narrowly escaping its raging heat that builds before me. The explosions within the maze become more frequent and visible, each time causing vehicles to flip and peer over the wreckage ahead.

Eventually, and not a moment too soon, I back up against the entrance to John's Club as the blue van explodes. A thick wave of heat radiates from the blast and takes my breath away, its force knocking the wind out of me as I drop the tank of propane. Feeling fortunate that the heat alone has not yet caused the tank to explode, I begin to catch my breath and embrace the cold glass that rests behind me.

Soon vibrations are felt from the glass doors as a few more cars explode, each time forming new paths within the wreckage. With the van flipped to its side I'm able to see more of the fires spread, along with the many undead that have now caught ablaze. Each of them continues to run frantically through the flames, vigorously smashing into vehicles while screaming wildly. Their elongated cries carry on and inevitably fall short as they collapse to the ground.

With the heat now tolerable I turn towards the entrance to John's Club. My anticipation suddenly cut short as I stare at the face of death yet again.

Five undead press up against the doors and attempt to claw through. Their torn flesh smears and spreads across the glass along with the blood that follows. Soon nails and fingers begin to chip and break away from the impending undead, their means of penetrating now limited to their gaze.

The dumbfounded monsters are unaware of the complexity and illusion of glass, such that I take this opportunity to look around. To my right I find my truck still waiting on the road and far from the inferno. Before it stands a fifteen foot high chain link fence which runs along the shopping plaza and street. An obstacle I tried to avoid by cutting through the maze, for the sake of my leg as well as the propane I carried.

The cold chill from the glass gets absorbed through the palm of my hand as I slowly run it down the door. Its trail followed closely by the eyes and jaws of the undead.

After making sure that the doors are locked, I casually step back with my propane and forty-five in hand. I've now grown accustomed to the heat brewing behind me as I take aim, gradually bringing the barrel of my gun upon the unfortunate undead. Although still bleeding, my head has finally leveled; my deafness and disorientation regressed as I squeeze the trigger.

Blood instantly splatters as the bullet pierces the door and lodges itself into an undead's skull, followed closely by a rapid web that cracks and spreads throughout the glass. With a deep breath I put all my strength to my left arm, pulling back on the propane tank while hurling it at the door.

The remaining four undead become caught in its path.

Its broad and steel structure effortlessly breaks through the glass, knocking over one of the undead as it carelessly rolls out of sight.

I quickly brace myself and steady my aim, patiently waiting as the monsters begin their escape. One at a time they willingly rush towards their demise, each one dropped with a single round in perfect succession.

Each one funneled towards their unavoidable end.

I then focus on the undead peering out at the end of the hallway up ahead. Its long blue corridor leads the entrance to the store, where from its corners they begin to arrive. Eventually the hallway fills with another herd of my next victims, their approach slow yet growing faster as they multiply.

While expecting as much, I calmly bend down and take aim, scanning the area until I find the propane tank at the end of the hall. Its distance, along with my obscured vision from the undead surrounding makes my mark difficult to hit. Yet I remain calm. My will keeps my focus and intent clear, guiding my hand as I lock onto the small white tank and fire.

I've once again underestimated the blast.

6:29 p.m. and I sit on the ground facing the broken entrance to John's Club. The shockwave and flash of the explosion proved too close and caused me to stagger back and fall. After getting blown away so many times today, one would think I could avoid such pain. Yet I'm pleasantly surprised… surprised to be alive.

The white blast that rumbled through the store caused the approaching undead to scatter into pieces. The remnants of their fallen bodies now decorate the hallway ahead. A barrage of glass sprayed from the once intact doors that faced me, causing a thick shard to fly forward and lance the tip of my left ear.

My eyes squint and my head flinches as I remain seated and apply pressure to my ear. The pain from the cut, although minimal, stings like hell, which I imagine could be worse if I wasn't on drugs.

Blood leaks from my hand and runs down the shoulder of my jacket as I pull myself up. Staggering at first, I take a moment to get my bearings and slowly make my way inside.

The interior of John's Club reeks of propane and decay as I walk down the tattered hallway. Its once light blue walls are now splattered with blood along with the torn cadavers on display.

Small fires begin to bloom throughout the vast store as I reach the end of the hall. Their progression remains slow as they eat away at the charred portions of the blast. Although not visible, I can sense the undead that linger inside. Their presence is strong as I feel them running throughout the aisles.

Blood saturates my hands from my leaking wounds. Their dampness causes me to fumble with my nine and forty-five millimeter. Short of the stinging pain from my leg and multiple cuts, I slowly feel my heart rate drop as I ready my pistols with both hands. My beats per minute, although faint, inadvertently skip at the cries of the approaching undead.

Screams of what seems like laughter now draw near and surround me within the store; their echoing pulse constantly follows my path. The sound of footsteps causes me to lessen my pace as I arrive at the first aisle, the anticipation of my pursuers now getting the best of me.

I quickly turn to face my enemy as they approach, pinpointing my shots while keeping a close eye on my surroundings. The two undead employees before me run wildly in their navy blue aprons. Their eyes bear the same crazed look of terror that would once paralyze me.

I let them run until they reach the third aisle and open fire, sending two rounds from my forty-five into both of their skulls. The constant screams grab my attention as I turn into the first aisle to find another undead.

Without thinking I begin walking towards it, my right arm instinctively lifting and pointing my gun ahead. Our proximity, although limited, becomes compromised as another crazed employee rushes down the aisle.

They both advance quickly.

Blood sprays across the shelf of beers to my right as the initial undead arrives, now put to rest by the last round left in my forty-five.

Yet one still lives.

Within seconds my nine millimeter guides my hand upwards.

Its automated thirst satisfies my intentions, bringing about a will of its own which connects with my next kill, and opens fire.

I feel impressed at how my aim has improved substantially within the past few days. A sense of hubris much deserved, as I watch the remaining undead drop to its knees and collapse to the floor.

A decent start to the rage that now builds within me.

As I reach the end of the aisle I replace the empty clip in my forty-five, suddenly noticed yet again by the undead. All seven of them become interrupted while eating a corpse to my left, their chews and moans now turned to screams as they sprint towards me.

I fire a round from each gun and manage to bring two of them down. Their progression still at hand causes me to retreat back down the first aisle. The five that remain follow me closely as I sprint, pushing myself further until I find two more waiting for me up ahead.

I'm now surrounded.

I'm closed off at both ends while frightened and basked in fear. The sensation is reminiscent of how I felt when it all began, such that I continue towards the two undead waiting before me.

With my aim held high I arrive inches away from the undead, a distance so close that I nearly feel the barrel of my guns press upon their heads.

I no longer hesitate and pull the trigger.

The blast from my nine millimeter sends the undead to my right flying back, whose recoil I use to push aside the one to my left. Once outside the aisle I begin to cringe at the pressure of my sutures getting pulled. The pain is enough that it causes me to stop as I now turn to face my fate.

The undead chasing me have finally joined the one I brushed aside as all six draw near. I've lost complete track of how many shots I've spent. The decreased weight in my guns is all I can go by, as I relentlessly unleash round after round upon the undead. My malice has now replaced my fear, forcing my resolve as I look the devil in the eye and open fire.

7:14 p.m. and the bodies of six undead lie before me, four of which remain lifeless while the rest struggle below. The two on the ground desperately strive to get up; their lameness caused after getting tagged by God knows how many rounds.

The clicking sound of empty clips is all I now hear.

It brings a sense of accomplishment as I stand admiring the strands of smoke seeping from my guns. Steady my heartbeat becomes as I breathe through my nose and proceed towards the undead. I approach the nearest one which lies face down on the ground. Its strength barely able to lift itself up as it bleeds out through its legs.

My mind remains empty while I holster away my guns.

I don't think or question my intentions, as I pull out the knife strapped to my right leg and plunge it into the undead.

I watch its body fidget and turn with each twist of my knife, slowly sinking the blade deeper into its skull. Within moments it stops convulsing and goes limp. My onslaught however is far from over, and with fresh blood trickling off the tip of my knife, I walk over to the remaining undead.

While on its back my kill now jerks from side to side. Its left leg remains intact yet only by a few strands of muscle and tendons below its knee. With my boot upon its neck, I gently apply pressure as I kneel down and slap its arms away. The grinding sound of its teeth cracking sends a chill up my spine as it desperately tries to bite.

Blood seeps from the flesh torn between its lips and the side of its mouth from its pathetic aggression, each bite causing its rotting teeth to chip and break away.

The sight of which, although relieving, bears little satisfaction.

With my knife dangling over its head I stare into the undead's eyes, its enlarged red spheres now protruding from its sockets. Soon its irises cross and meet the tip of my knife as it rests on its head, no longer delaying as I slowly push its way through.

After a few moments and shots of pressure, the blade breaks its way past the bone and impales the monster's brain, instantly putting it to rest.

Lifeless the undead now lie as I pull myself up and clean my knife.

My actions, however cruel, hold no bounds, and still cease to amaze me.

Heat and smoke begin to course around me from the fires spreading within the store. My distractions blind me from their progression while now forcing me to move.

Through aisle after aisle I run and follow the sound of screams, replacing the clips in my guns until I collapse to the floor.

I instantly feel the sutures stretch and pull on my leg.

Its hold is strong yet tight around my calf, forcing my fall while planting me on my knees. The pain is sharp and that of a razorblade, slowly dragging its edge up from my ankle to my thigh.

My body feels weak again, perhaps more so than it did before. However my will remains strong. An ongoing drive that fuels me to press on from hearing the monster's screams.

As I pull myself up I take notice to the undead that approach. Their advance is quick as they rush across the store, the distance from which lies within the produce section. While now staggering, I limp my way to greet them, my nine millimeter stretched out before me as I open fire. Four painful rounds later I put an end to the three undead, my pace never ceasing as I press on.

The fires now spread and continue to dance throughout the store, growing larger by the minute as they leap from one counter to another. Part me wonders if I should just leave John's Club, for I have nothing to prove, yet I'm compelled to finish what I've started.

An orange glow soon surrounds me as I continue down my warpath, gimping across the store while chasing the faint sounds of screams. In an attempt to wrap things up, I quicken my pace as the flames eat away at the ceiling above. It's chipping and crackling sound chases my steps as I finally arrive at the produce section.

The screams have now intensified as I find myself amidst a dozen undead, eight of which continue to feast on two corpses while the remaining four catch my glance. The very image of their crooked posture and surrounding fire is that of hell itself. Their silhouettes are that of demons most children fear whilst swaying with the flame's embrace.

Within moments one of them approaches with its jaw torn off. Its chipped and broken layer of teeth stick out as its bloody tongue hangs and flickers a gargling sound. Although its initial shout is unthreatening, it soon becomes followed by the stares and ravenous cries of the remaining undead.

All of which now begin to rush towards me.

Multiple explosions erupt around me as I open fire, the sight of the flames now reflecting off the monster's eyes. While strafing to my right, I blindly expel the rounds that remain in my nine millimeter.

Their fury, although quick, manages to take out two of the undead that approach.

Now desperate, I separate myself behind a counter of stacked apples and replace my nine with my forty-five. My delay proves untimely and fatal as two more undead suddenly arrive.

They flank me on both sides while left vulnerable.

Despite their surprise it does not come without repercussions, and in my panic I stand while firing at the undead to my right. My swiftness however is not enough, and in my rage I suddenly feel the one behind me grab a hold of my shoulders.

Its mouth and rancid breath draws near.

The heat it expels with each pant overpowers the flames around me, bringing about terror as I endure the familiar press of its tongue upon my neck.

I twist and bend away from the undead.

Unable to free myself from its grasp, I reluctantly pull my gun over my left shoulder. Its barrel is instantly felt against the monster's face, providing the resistance and confirmation I need to open fire.

The deafening sound of the blast consumes me as I send my assailant back, causing gunpowder to spray on my ear and within my wound. My concentration becomes challenged by the muffled ringing in my ears. I abandon all hope of eliminating the undead, forcing my retreat as the remaining eight now approach.

7:38 p.m. and my legs carry me forward while followed closely by the undead. I now push myself to the limit, passing numerous aisles to my right and the meat and seafood department to my left. I use my surroundings to my advantage, gaining distance by pushing over carts and racks of food to block their advance. The fires within the store have also become a problem, their rage blocking paths while chipping away at the ceiling above.

As I turn, I make my way down the pastries section and run backwards, preparing myself to unleash hell on my pursuers. Their end if not from me will be met by the flames spreading above, and as the eight undead arrive, I open fire.

I forget to count my rounds again as I spray lead upon them. The surrounding gray smoke and orange haze makes it difficult to see, and before I know it, I'm out of ammo.

The immediate sound of the hammer hitting the empty chamber causes me to react and pull out my magnum, just in time to meet an undead arriving five feet away, which I put down with a single round.

Within seconds I look up at the ceiling towards a crackling sound, disorientated by my environment, yet able to see something large falling down. While unable to make out what falls above me, I throw myself backwards and narrowly escape the debris that crashes upon where I stood.

I've once again escaped death, yet it is far from over.

Scorching red flames now rise from the pieces of ceiling and ventilation that lay before me, creating a wall of fire that separates the undead and I. One of them seems to have been crushed beneath the rubble. Its torn and broken arm reaches out for me until eventually falling limp.

I can see the monsters halt and stare at me from the other side, pacing back and forth as I pull myself up. Unaware of how many lie before me, I now take aim at those blocked by the flames. Their silhouettes are vaguely seen through the smoke and fire.

Hard as it is, I manage to lock onto what rests between their shoulders.

With a deep breath I retain focus and pull the trigger, taking down what I believe to be three undead with matching rounds. Although relieved, I take a moment to collect myself, exhausted and in pain, yet once again forced to run.

The heat radiating within John's Club is now unbearable.

Its flames continue to spread and devour the entire store, leading me towards the blood splattered hallway which I entered earlier. Once inside I can't help but slow down, for each step feels heavy and takes longer than the last. My body sways as I desperately stumble towards the exit, causing me to pause and cringe at the sharp pain coursing up my leg.

Its occurrence is untimely and a constant annoyance.

I'm so close to the exit that I can almost taste it, and as I find the strength to move on, I suddenly stop at the sound of screams.

Two of the undead that I presumed gone suddenly appear. Their bodies burst through the flames and remain ablaze as they sprint towards me. Their speed almost seems heightened while on fire, their legs quickly moving as if they're about to melt off.

I turn to face them and remain appalled as they rush down the hall. Their burning bodies stumble over the charred cadavers on the floor, granting me seconds as I take aim. While still feeling dazed and slightly nauseous, I struggle to maintain, putting the pieces together until I see the flames before me and fire.

The .357 round makes short work of the approaching undead, forcing its head to snap back as it collapses to the floor.

Yet I am too late as the one that remains swiftly follows.

The flames it wears shed heat upon me as I stand inches from its grasp. Its wrath is such that I'm left with no options, but to shut my eyes, turn away, and pull the trigger.

Fate it seems has more in stored for me as the final round in my magnum pierces the undead, but to my dismay causes it to fall upon me.

I find the irony in such things less than amusing.

My back now slams on the ground as I become pinned down by the dead weight of the burning corpse. Its blood slowly seeps from the wound on its head while trickling down my collarbone. The dampness I endure, however moist, is quickly overcome by the flames eating away at my clothes.

I slowly begin to feel the fire burn a layer of flesh along my neck, a pain which causes me to grab onto the undead. The sizzling sound of my palms melting forces me to scream as I now withstand excruciating pain.

An agony which I never thought existed.

My adrenaline overwhelms me and fills my arms with the strength needed to push the corpse away. However my screams do not cease as I break free and find myself still ablaze.

Fire burns... and I feel it first hand as it begins to spread across my arm and leg. Stop, drop, and roll, comes to mind as I vigorously twist from side to side. It brings about flashbacks from what I learned in elementary school in-between cries.

Despite my distress I cannot stop as I roll around, over and over until the pain recedes along with my screams. Eventually the flames diminish and my exhaustion takes hold, leaving me bound to the floor while now charred and out of breath.

7:57 p.m. and I slowly pull myself from the ground, my body now aching from my many endeavors. The strings of smoke seeping off my burnt leather jacket coincide with the crackling sound it makes, subtle at first, yet growing louder with my every move.

Behind me burns the interior of John's Club.

Its fires spread while its structure begins to collapse.

The hot air from outside now brushes across my face as I wedge through the shattered doors that I entered earlier. John's Club would have undoubtedly been my grave if I was to linger, and to my disappointment, I escape one fire only to embrace another.

The labyrinth of cars has now been reduced to a metallic bone yard that continues to be eaten away by flames. As expected, the path through remains blocked by the vast inferno. Its reach stretches far and forces me to trek towards the chain link fence to my left. My truck, ever distant, lies beyond, beckoning my name while forcing my body to press on.

Darkness now overcomes the night sky, its shroud kept at bay by the illumination of the fires.

As I arrive at the fence, I rest my head on its chain links and holster away my magnum, aggravated and annoyed at my final obstacle. I take a few moments before I endure the pain of my burnt hands curling around the fence. Adjusting my grip accordingly as I reluctantly begin to climb.

The smooth and waxy feeling on my palms makes it difficult to grab onto the chain links, slippery now with my fingerprints fused together. Once atop I stay seated with my leg hanging off its edge, taking a moment to catch my breath and observe my wrath. The exterior of John's Club is now ablaze along with the parking lot below, its waves of heat resembling shifting sands of orange flames.

Within seconds of resting, my eyes suddenly catch the sea of fire quickly swirl and branch out to my left. I completely forgot about the gas I let flow from the station earlier. Such a good idea at the time now proves unnecessary as I desperately climb over the fence.

Before my eyes I witness a large snake of orange flame quickly branch out from the parking lot. Its path is swift and relentless, zigzagging its way across the asphalt and to the gas station. Its lightening speed is unmatched and unlike anything I've ever seen.

I am once again too late.

The entire gas station now erupts in a massive explosion. Its shockwave along with its tremors briefly extinguish the fires while causing cars to flip over. My distance, although safe, has its repercussions, causing the fence to shake as I now lose my grip and fall to the ground.

Upon impact I begin to cough profusely, trying to put together what went wrong and what will come next. My body feels broken as I remain lying on the grass, breathing heavily while gazing towards the night sky. I don't bother moving as I light up a smoke, sighing with relief while inhaling my inevitable death.

My mind slowly settles as the rich trail of nicotine exits my lungs, gradually working its way through while seeping out through my lips. With one long drag I muscle up the strength to stand. The crimpling sound of my jacket now apparent as I spot my truck waiting before me.

My cigarette dangles from my lips as I endure the pain from each step I take. Unable to gain the will needed to pull it from my mouth; I allow its tail of ash to fall upon my chest.

I finally arrive at my truck.

A feeling of satisfaction overwhelms me once I'm inside, the warmth of my truck now fitting as I mold into its driver's seat. While staring out towards the fires, I bask in the light that it provides, giving me comfort in knowing that I've rid most of the undead.

But to what end I wonder? What will tomorrow bring? I was fortunate enough to make it out alive today, given made the same mistakes twice. I got in over my head again, narrowly escaping death as I've done so many times before.

Although I can't help but feel that I did so purposely.

My will to live now rests on the tip of a knife, swaying from one end to another with little regard as to where I'll fall. All I care to feel is the constant brush of death that makes me feel alive.

For in reality, I'm already dead.

8:33 p.m. as I drive through my old neighborhood and pull up to my house. My Hyundai Elantra, although dusty, remains where I left it days ago. Its ghostly image is now alien to me as I park behind it; a strange sensation given how much I relied on the car during my past life.

Soon darkness surrounds me as the streetlights no longer seem to function, yet offer me comfort in my solitude. The silence of it all subdues me as I shut off the truck's engine, bringing about the vacancy that the world provides.

An eerie setting suddenly lies before me, as a thin layer fog rises above the street and moves slowly ahead. Regardless of what hell awaits for me, I find solace within my truck. For whatever reason I'm unable move, and even if I could… I probably wouldn't. I'm now content with where I'm at, slowly melting into the driver's seat while within the fog's embrace.

9:03 p.m. and I'm still enclosed within the comfort of my truck. I'm neither asleep nor fully awake, but floating silently between realms of consciousness. This is what I believe being in limbo would be like, stuck with only the company of your mind while surrounded by a bleak setting. I can't say I mind it though, most people would be driven insane by the loneliness, but not I. For the first time within the past week I feel content. I did what needed to be done here. I sought out the undead that plagued this city and brought fire upon them.

I can now rest easy knowing that I've done one thing right.

In my mind I know that I should rest in my house which lies only a few feet away. My body however will not allow it, as I now begin to feel my limbs gradually fall asleep.

Without running the risk of losing comfort, I quickly swallow two Amoxicillin's and Vicodin's while quenching my insatiable thirst. I can't even remember the last time I took my pills, or let alone how long I've been on them. Not long enough I figure, for the pain in my head and back now overpower the strain on my leg.

Soon after cracking open a window, the cool breeze from outside begins to widen my heavyset eyes. My craving for another cigarette feels right at the moment. Its rich and smooth flavor is something I long for, as I pull out the smashed pack of smokes that rest in my leather jacket.

While taking caution to not drain my truck's battery, I unplug my MP3 player and rummage through my bags for a pair of headphones. The intact and bent cigarette rests firmly between my lips and drops flakes of tobacco on my tongue. However I do not care. I swallow them down and brush them aside while lighting up my smoke.

"A Warm Place" by Nine Inch Nails now courses through my ears and fills my mind with tranquility. Its sound puts me at ease as I suddenly achieve clarity.

I think to myself that this is it. This moment right here is worth dying for.

Eric had it right all along by killing himself, he knew that down the road these things would be the death of him. I can picture him lying there on his bed, feeling the bliss that I feel now. With his music playing and the drugs coursing through his veins, I can see him slip through his downward spiral.

The smoke from my cigarette drifts past my eyes as they now focus on the gun on my lap. The forty-five millimeter feels heavy in my right hand, its cold steel exterior bringing out its allure.

I now feel nothing. No fear, no pain, or pleasure... just stillness.

My only regret is that once I die that there will be no one left to bury me. My corpse will become the undead's next meal as I've vividly seen in my nightmares.

While yawning, I put out my smoke to find my limbs still asleep. Its sensation makes it difficult to lift up my forty-five, and with my mind adrift and fading from consciousness, I slowly bring its barrel underneath my jaw.

My suicide gun.

Seems fitting that I use this piece to kill myself after how I acquired it.

The gray fog from outside now grows thick and surrounds me, creating a dark sheet that obscures my already hindered vision.

I smile and tell myself that it's going to be okay. My head's so heavy that it's now held up by the barrel of my gun, to which I slowly pull back its hammer.

Death has become the fog around me as she arrives to share her embrace. Her cloak is the mist while her sickle is the forty-five, and in turn her voice is the music whispering in my ears.

She now carries me towards my impending fate.

My eyes grow heavy as I finally drift, all the pain soon to be gone as I now close them shut. My mind remains empty and at peace, bringing about my stagnant clarity and willingness to die.

I lightly press on the trigger.

Then everything goes dark.

Day 7

6:02 a.m. as I awake within the confinement of my truck. My eyes now burn as I slowly pry them open, perplexed as to my familiar surroundings.

I could have sworn that I died last night.

I begin to wonder if I am in fact truly dead, only briefly until I glance down at my boots. To my disappointment I find my suicide gun resting idly below, its hammer still cocked and ready to fire. With a deep sigh I think of how I must have passed out before I had a chance to pull the trigger.

It was the perfect moment from what I can remember, one worth dying for.

A new day arrives with the blue sky above as the sun raises, its brightness pushing the lingering storm clouds away. Its natural warmth melts away the frost covering the windshield, slowly bringing about the lonely streets that were once my neighborhood.

This would be glimmer of hope has no affect on me.

Regardless of the beauty looming above, I care not as I remain seated and stare at the gun on my lap.

I suppose I could kill myself now but it wouldn't be the same. It wouldn't feel right. That opportunity has long passed and I can now only hope for another, and when it arrives... I will not hesitate.

My body however has seemed to recover, as the aching pain from my head and limbs has greatly subsided. I remedy what lingering strain I have by swallowing two Vicodin's and Amoxicillin's, using what remains of my water to wash away the rancid taste in my mouth.

With a crack of my neck, I liberate the tension that chokes over my body. Its sensation is almost painful, yet provides incentive to move as I find that I'm still alone.

6:20 a.m. and I stand against my truck while indulging in a cigarette. The sunshine to the east provides me warmth as I bask in its rays before unloading my bags.

I feel tired and filthy, drained of my very essence and in need of a hot shower. My hunger catches up with me as my stomach growls while approaching my house. For I demand sustenance and can only hope that the food left within has yet to spoil.

The unlocked door now squeals as I slowly push it open, revealing the emptiness that was once my home. Déjà vu hits me for all the wrong reasons, as I fail to remember the good times I once had here. All that is left for me to recall is the day when it all began, the day I killed my father.

While making my way around the kitchen, I take notice to the dry bloody footprints that scurry down the hall.

It all seems like a distant memory now, my life before this week.

After setting my bags and guns aside I proceed towards my bathroom. My muscles and joints throb with each step I take as I eventually make my way inside. Broken glass crushes beneath my boots as I observe the tattered remains around me. The shattered sliding glass door to my old shower stands stained with blood, showing scattered evidence of my past struggle.

Just thinking about my naked assault and the damage inflicted sends a chill up my spine. Unable to use my old bathroom, I now backtrack down the hall to use the shower in my parent's room.

I slowly follow the barrage of bloody handprints that remain imprinted along the walls. Their presence marks the trail of my first kill, all the while leading me towards the doors of my parent's bedroom.

I don't know how I'll feel when I see my father's corpse on the other side. Part of me doesn't want to find out, questioning if the fragments of my past will resurface at the sight of his body.

With a deep breath, I abruptly open the doors to reveal the corpse lying before me. Its smell, although rank, does not bother me, as I now step towards the dry blood that surrounds it. While slowly making my way around, I casually sit along the foot of my parents' bed.

My poor old man... such a sight for sore eyes now that he's not trying to kill me. For a while I stop and stare at his corpse, waiting for something to happen. Yet nothing occurs, I feel nothing, only the raw emptiness that should occupy my soul.

6:44 a.m. and after taking the time expected to soak in my lack of sympathy, I begin to undress. My white skin is blotched with smears of blood, once again entangling itself with the hair on my arms, legs, and chest. The blue bandage around my calf seems dry while spotted with blood, an expected result from all the tension endured as I slowly begin unraveling it.

While removing the third layer of Vet Wrap, I feel the cold air breathe upon my wound. Its sutures on both ends have come undone yet the skin remains closed. Its hold feels strong from the tissue glue I once applied, as well as the remaining stitches which seem intact.

The laceration appears clean and free of any infection, and from my experience seems to be healing. Its mend however could be better if I would stop putting strain on my leg. Despite my discomfort, the Vicodin's do help to numb the pain that it now gives off.

I once again stand naked in my parent's room, although this time smeared with blood, dirt, and ash. With the shower head running hot water, I stop to stare at myself in the mirror. After so much death and blood, I no longer hesitate to watch the stranger grin at me from the other side of the glass.

Where I once denied him, I've now come to embrace us as one.

The darkness around my eyes has increased while the cut portion of my left ear adds to my choppy disposition. Strands of black hair hang low over my forehead and bring about cruel intentions, their uneven and fringed lengths undoubtedly caused by the fires.

The palms of my hands still feel waxy and slick, now similar to the shiny tinge of burnt skin along my neck. As the days go by I resemble the undead even more, the only difference being my blue eyes and lighter skin tone.

For a moment I lose myself within my own gaze, caught by a strange sense of allure until the steam filling the room slowly hides my reflection.

7:45 a.m. and my skin begins to prune during my long shower. The blood and dirt escaping my body now covers the floor while spiraling down its drain. After shutting off the water I stop to collect myself, blood trickling from my many wounds as I step out of the hot shower.

I feel nothing against my damp and naked body. No cold, no chattering teeth, or shivers, only the lingering ache that remains in my throat. As I dry myself off, I set the bloody towel aside and light up one of my smokes, suddenly appeased at my new found rejuvenation.

Now anxious, I wipe away the fog on the mirror to reveal the newer, healthier looking me. Although my pale complexion has darkened, my overall appearance has strayed from the undead.

I take in one long drag of my cigarette as my reflection smiles, guiding my hands towards my dad's pomade. It's as if I have no control over what I'm doing. Like my nightmare, I can see and feel what is happening, yet I have no say in doing so.

The man before me now stands with his hair slicked back... my hair slicked back. Not my typical style considering my face no longer hides behind short strands of hair.

Though I can't say I mind it.

I now recognize and no longer fear the man that is my reflection.

8:00 a.m. and I'm still nude and in the comfort of my old room, now sitting on my bed while tending to my leg. The band aids covering the cut on my ear barely stick and frequently pull every time I swallow. Yet I don't mind the pain. I carelessly brush it aside as I replace the two sutures on my leg. In fact it seems to be the only thing that makes me feel alive, that and killing the undead.

I find myself having difficulty suturing my wound with burnt fingers, wishing I had thumb forceps, yet still able to make do. Once finished, I rewrap my leg and put on a fresh pair of navy blue boxers. Its fabric is soft and deserving against my skin. A much needed appreciation over the tattered clothing that I've worn, and burnt.

While leaving my room, my stomach growls all the way to the kitchen as I scavenge for food. Unfortunately for me all the meats within the fridge have spoiled along with the milk. All the fruits have gone bad while the cereal remains stale and the eggs now rotten.

My frustration builds along with my hunger, settling for a box of croutons as I continue my search. Eventually I'll have to resort to what I can find for food, but at the moment I feel that I deserve more.

After falling short of disappointment, I come across a box of Macaroni and Cheese which seems to never expire. The lack of milk will make this batch somewhat interesting. I remember eating such foods when I was a kid, my cravings for it in particularly came after I went swimming. Nostalgic as it is, I'm merely glad to eat anything other than military rations or soup for a change.

9:14 a.m. as I sit with an empty bowl before me. I feel much better after eating the entire box of Macaroni and Cheese, amazed at how satisfying it turned out after supplementing milk with more cheese and butter.

While finishing my glass of fruit punch, I let my food settle as I partake in another smoke. For whatever reason I feel tired, and although my stomach's full and my body's clean, I still feel fatigued.

I must rest.

I now lie on my old bed and wait for the welcoming feel of comfort, but end up disappointed. This bed is not mine anymore, I have no claim to it, for I'm no longer that person. Regardless it's a hell of a lot more comfortable than sleeping in my truck, and within moments I get over feeling like an outsider.

My eyes then grow heavy and sink into my skull, now closing as I drift into darkness and every goes black.

10:37 a.m. as I casually awake from my nap. While still in bed I stretch and pull the tension that resides in my joints, each snap creating a sense of elongated bliss.

I'm now ready to leave.

My time here is done, and with that I forsake this house and city. I care not for the ties that brought me here, for they are now severed.

While preparing my leave, I light up a smoke and begin to grab some of my old clothing. The crisp pair of black Dickies I put on feels nice around my legs. Their looseness and fabric causes little to no friction to the bandage around my calf. With the weather seeming warm, I throw on a red A-Shirt underneath my now tattered and burnt leather jacket, which I refuse to leave behind. My gun harness feels snug against my chest and brings closure to my preparation, along with the knife strapped tightly to my right leg.

A thick trail of smoke follows me out to the garage and back to my room after grabbing a suitcase. Having to carry around two bags of supplies has been troublesome. Their inconvenience makes traveling difficult as I plan to combine their contents.

While scrounging through my effects, I come to recall that I'm dangerously low on ammo. All I need is the will and an objective to carry on, and at the moment it relies on more bullets.

After all I've been through it seems that fate has paved me a new path.

With much force I manage to cram my supplies within the large suitcase, yet dread the thought of having to grab anything from inside. I feel much more relieved that I have everything I need in one bag. Its weight however is something I'm not grateful for, which seems to have doubled in mass.

Before I depart, I make one last attempt to connect to the internet via my laptop with no success. I expected as much and don't feel the least bit disappointed, as I am now truly ready to leave.

11:05 a.m. as I exit my house and set down my supplies. The bright sun rests its rays on the back of my neck while closing the front door. Its warmth, although calming, is suddenly interrupted by my killer instinct.

I can't help but feel it, my blood boiling at the presence of death behind me.

It begins to smell. A stench of rotting flesh now carried in the breeze. Its taste is that of a sour blend of blood, sex, and decay.

I don't bother turning around though, not yet. For the image of the undead behind me is seen from the window ahead. My intuition tells me all that I need to know, as I now stare at the tattered reflection of Dr. Kibbs.

All the pieces are to be falling together now, my anguish and revenge.

He's been stalking me endlessly, each time narrowly escaping, but no longer. I feel neither hesitation nor fear. Only the subtle rage that slowly guides my right hand over the knife strapped to my leg.

The doctor's white lab coat appears torn and burnt from the fires, its ends swaying with the wind along with his sluggish movements. My eyes remain fixed on his reflection, slowly sizing him up as I grab a hold of my hunting knife.

While still facing away, the image of Dr. Kibbs suddenly rushes towards me, his jaw hanging low as he lets out a high pitched scream. For a moment time stalls with the doctor's advance, my seconds now drawn out to minutes. I no longer feel rushed while pulling out my knife, and in one swift motion I turn and hurl it at the undead.

My blade fails to spin after being thrown.

It quickly soars through the air with its killing end pointed directly ahead. My aim is sharp and true as it stops the doctor in his tracks, its sheer impact causing him to now stagger.

As expected, everything is falling into place.

With his head held back my knife lays embedded in his throat. A mixture of gargles, coughs, and screams is now heard as the hilt of my blade rests under his chin.

With a sinister smirk I walk towards Dr. Kibbs, watching his movements as he forcefully brings his head down upon the knife. We immediately lock eyes, only briefly as he rushes towards me yet again.

My movements remain automated as I tag both of his knees with my magnum. Within seconds he collapses to the ground, immobilized and maimed, no longer a threat with both his knees now shattered. Yet he still screams. Blood pours from the knife wedged in his throat while on his hands and knees, and still he screams.

Satisfaction, efficiency, along with a hint of arousal overwhelms me as I stroll towards my prey.

Nothing can stop me now as I stand behind him.

He struggles, and struggles pathetically to reach me. All the while his screams are replaced with the gargling of blood that continuously drips from his mouth.

My smirk grows wider as I grab onto the doctor's head and pull it back, effortlessly bringing my hand around his neck while taking a hold of the knife in his throat. In a sad attempt he vigorously drops his jaw up and down to nip my hand. I have no fear of getting bitten though, I won't allow it.

Nothing is going to happen to me, for that I am sure.

The doctor's moist screams intensify as I now twist the blade within his neck.

Everything so far is going so well, my intentions, my reflection, my purpose, my wrath. The depths of my mind now flooded with ecstasy as I begin sawing away at his neck.

The sharp knife easily eats away at his muscle and flesh, clipping veins and arteries along its path. As blood escapes his screams become less muffled and more define. My smirk has now developed into a full on grin, my amusement unsound as I begin to feel pressure against the blade.

Faster and faster I continue saw away at his flesh, my rhythm increasing with its resistance. As I reach the halfway point around Dr. Kibbs's neck, I'm suddenly forced to pull out the blade.

He screams.

They all scream, up until I'm done with them.

His head now hangs loosely off his body as I hold onto his hair, still trying to bite me while only able to jerk to his left. I can't help but laugh, and as I switch hands to keep a grip on his head, it becomes hysterical.

His screams are now inferior to my echoing laugher.

I grow tired of the sound, yet I can't help myself as I repeatedly plunge the knife into his face. The blade gracefully sinks into his left cheek and jaw, over and over until I finally bring it around his neck once again.

The screaming continues as I begin to vigorously cut away. Only this time, I realize that the cries aren't from Dr. Kibbs, but from me.

Unable to restrain myself, I continue to scream and hack away at his neck.

Unaware at the time, I now notice that the doctor has been silent, yet I keep cutting. For however long his suffering has ended is irrelevant. I care not for I continue to tear away at his flesh, until all that is left is his spine.

My laughter slowly subsides as I brace my foot on his back, and with one final scream, I push forward and snap his head off.

All the blood... seems unimaginable that so much could possibly reside in a person or in this case an undead. The corpse of Dr. Kibbs now lies fidgeting on the ground, the torn tip of his spine protruding from the jagged stub that once was his neck.

My chest rises with each breath I take as my smile begins to diminish. The bright sun and beautiful blue sky remains opposite to the horrific sight before me. Yet its warmth offers me comfort, to which I carelessly toss aside the decapitated head.

Strings of clotted blood steadily drip from my hands along with the undone hair around the edge of my knife. My entire demeanor, a reflection of the massacre I just induced.

I calm my rage with the cigarette between my lips.

The storm within me swirls and recedes with each victorious drag, and as I exhale through my nose, I admire my fresh kill.

I am now truly ready to leave.

Nothing left for me here but ash and regret from my past life, for the smoke bellowing in the distance is proof of that.

I glance once more at the doctor's head.

Moments like last night are worth dying for, and I can only hope that the next opportunity won't slip through my fingers.

But not now though... not just yet. Moments like these are worth living for.

12:09 p.m. as I now speed through the freeway. Most the fires I started yesterday have died down while a few remain ablaze. Its fury engulfed the city and reduced it to a smoldering pile of ash.

Smoke rises and begins to blotch the bright blue sky as it slowly fades in the distance. My memories now disappear almost as fast as Sovereignty does through my rearview mirror.

I find myself speeding.

I push my truck for all its worth while quickly evading the wreckage on the road. The naked freeway stretches endlessly before me as I head north, towards whatever hell now awaits me.

I make it a point to look for a store that could potentially hold ammunition, somewhere new to clear out and take shelter. After bringing death upon the city I once called home, I figure I should let myself heal, if just for a few days. The idea of it all sounds nice, yet I wonder if I could rest a single day without exploiting my rage.

Soon mountains turn to trees and trees to mountains until the freeway branches out of the valley, spouting a single crow in the distance. The black bird carelessly sways from side to side, my envy only due to its ability to fly. I can't help but wonder if it's even aware of what's happening around it. Its calm and carefree glide makes it oblivious towards all the death and chaos surrounding it.

Eventually the crow drifts away in the distance, now begging the question if it was undead? Turned by whatever infection or plague that has killed everything except for myself?

I've come to terms that there is no logical reason for what's happened. The dead could have very well just risen from the ground. I could be wrong though, and if I wanted the easy way out, I'd blame God.

12:37 p.m. and the sun shines high above me. The clear blue sky along with my beautiful setting puts me in a better place. Its atmosphere remains calm, spouting endless plains of green pastures along both sides of the freeway as I continue north.

I have yet to even come across any towns which doesn't surprise me, as the occasional wandering undead has been few and far between. Yet they still suffered the impact of my truck's grill.

My surroundings are serene and tranquil, bringing about a feeling of peace which causes my speed to decrease. The lush green hillsides mound up and down like waves as I drive by, their smoothness not to be trifled with.

Now appalled I can't help but slow down, unaware as to why until I come to a screeching halt. My eyes deceive me yet bare truth as I now see it, a murder of crows circling to my right. Dozens of them soar meekly through the air, all revolving atop a large grassy hill. Their black bodies stand out and bring about despair while compared to their surroundings.

All of them remain silent, yet distant nonetheless.

"Your Skull is Red" by Team Sleep now calmly plays as I sit with the engine running. I observe in awe at the sight before me, only briefly as I catch what lies below the crows.

Through the rays of sunshine and the shadows above, a dark figure rises from the hillside. It stumbles with its arms held high while waving back and forth, distant yet animated to a different degree.

My eyes squint to focus on what lies ahead.

The dark figure now just a blur stands up high, and collapses to the ground.

12:49 p.m. and I stand in the middle of the desolate freeway. Its roads on either side expand far beyond where I can see. A part of me already knows what I will soon find, the thought of which compels me to press on.

I slowly pace myself as I limp towards the grassy hill.

Its fine and level blades of grass now disturbed with each imprinting step I take.

While halfway across the field, I stop to light a smoke and ready my forty-five, preparing myself for the worst to happen. My regret for approaching the site soon fades as I begin to scale the hillside. The crows above remain silent and have been the entire time, for only the fluttering of their wings is carried in the wind.

With the cherry of my cigarette at its halfway point, I calmly ready my aim. The murder of crows swirling ahead, although quiet, show no signs of fear as I now approach.

Smoke slowly creeps from the side of my mouth as I suddenly stop at a familiar sound, the sound of coughing. My mind now indecisive begins running and lowers my guard. Yet it doesn't stop. The cough, although subtle continues, and as I follow its trail I reveal the man before me.

My eyes now focus on what lies before me. A man lying on his back upon the grass, his clothing tattered and his body broken.

He slowly attempts to pull himself up.

Blood stains the grass around him as he desperately presses on a wound near his stomach. It leaks and seeps through his hand as I carefully scan him for any other injuries.

His short brown hair is messy and crusted with blood. The darkness around his eyes and pale complexion make me wonder how long he's been wounded. His youth would put him in his mid twenties, although difficult to tell given his shoddy condition.

I take notice to the shotgun he uses to brace himself with as he sits before me. Its barrel aims towards the sky as he curls his right hand around it, trembling to keep himself up.

For a few moments I'm unwillingly forced stare, appalled by his existence while the crows soar above. With my eyes fixed to his wound, I take a long drag of my smoke which causes him to speak.

"Help me... please."

I can't help but stare as he desperately tries to stand.

"I'm not... *them*... please."

I slowly glance at his trembling hands, both of which are saturated in blood.

He speaks again.

"Please... help."

My cigarette has neared its end as the man reaches out for me with his left hand. His fingers are stained with dirt and crusted blood, now shivering in the air as they stretch out towards me.

"Who... are you?" he asks, his breath now shallow and struggling with each word.

Who am I, I wonder? The thought has been running through my mind for the past few days. The birth name from my past life is all I can think of.

With one long drag I finish and put out my smoke, licking my lips while clearing my throat from not speaking in days.

I extend my right hand to grab a hold of him, his weight giving way as he instantly lets up. He relies on my strength to hold him up as we draw close. His forest green eyes gaze upon me with desperation, and soon a subtle smile creases the left side of his lips.

I slowly pull him forward, only slightly before I finally answer.

"My name is Issac." I reply, and with my voice now shallow and full of disdain, I bring the gun upon his face and fire.

1:36 p.m. as I continue north on the freeway. My right hand rests idly on the steering wheel, exposing my apathy as I lean back and embrace the wind in my hair. A twelve gauge shotgun lies sideways along the passenger's seat of my truck. Its black steel barrel and wooden fore-end and stock, bring no sense of remorse as I'm left to my thoughts.

I keep coming back to the man I just killed. His hopeful gaze instantly wiped by the barrel of my gun. It all happened so quickly... my voice, his eyes, and the gunshot.

He had no time to react or say anything.

I remember the crows scattering with the echoing blast, my hand still gripped around his while supporting his body. I recall the blood and smoke slowly escape his hanging jaw, and eventually letting him fall to reveal the bullet wound near his stomach.

Killing him doesn't bother me though, however knowing he's been alive does.

He thought I feared that he was wounded by the undead, yet I can't help but wonder what he meant by *them*.

Either way I was going to kill him.

The bullet wound near his gut also told me that there are others out there, other survivors. Knowing that I'm not the only one alive now changes things. My perspective remains the same, and that those alive or dead will eventually bleed for me.

I thought that killing a man would feel different from the undead I put down, yet I feel nothing; no lingering sense of guilt or hint of satisfaction. Killing him was more of a nuisance than anything, a means to an end which lead me to the existence of potential survivors, as well as a shotgun.

I take in all that I've done and reflect upon it with the smoke that exits my lungs, and with one final drag, I glance at myself through the rearview mirror.

My name is Issac and I'm a monster. Neither the living nor dead will escape my wrath. The human race had already expired before the dead rose, and while those that survived have only escaped their inevitable fate, a fate which I will gladly oblige them to. This is the way it was meant to be. Only I am meant to survive. I feel nothing for myself or others, and all I know is that I will be left standing.

Nothing can stop me now.

It all started a week ago... it began in November.